MORE FROM TONY DEL DEGAN

NOVELS and NOVELLAS

Sacrosanct
Rusthook
In River Cardinal
Ceres
The Recognition
The Plight of Steel

SHORT STORIES

The Chrysalis
Depthcrusher
Moist Gossamer
The Becoming
Eden Sank to Grief
Do Not Stand By My Grave, I Am Not There
The Bus from the Inner City
My Front Door, a Finchhole
Bǫlverkr

Visit tony.deldegan.ca to explore the Red Runnel universe.

s: me in my mother's tomb, So I knew the Word of God.

Exalted King who walks for tw

Exalted King who walk

RUSTHOOK

BY TONY DEL DEGAN

tony.deldegan.ca

Second paperback edition 2026

Book designed by Tony Del Degan
Edited by Celina Berrade
Front cover by Jane Gurney

Visit tony.deldegan.ca for updates, content, and more

ISBN: 978-1-7782331-1-1
(Ebook) ISBN: 978-1-7782331-4-2

For Tito and Tita
You would not have liked this book...

A Night in 2000

He'd never noticed the intricacies of the crocheted hood. Little golden buttons ran from the puppet's neck to its knees, where the hood cut off. Its head was a flesh-colored thing–plastic. Chipping painted eyes. A beak. Long, thin legs and arms hung out from the bottom mouth of the hood, like tentacles. It was sitting in a little recess by the laundry room door. Jesus was crucified to its left–cross cradled by a little metal folding stand. Wax had dried long ago as it ran down Christ's chest, down his legs. Ancient wax–from a candle, perhaps. There were candles everywhere. None lit–ever. Some had Mother Mary in printed ink on the sides, others had Flamenco dancers or Toreadors whipping capes over the heads of angry bulls.

He looked away from the doll and the crucifixion. Looked for his mother. Steam wafted up from the kitchen around the corner, taking flight into the high cathedral ceilings of the house. Conversation. He couldn't understand the words.

"What are you doing?"

He spun in place.

"What are you doing, little mousie?" She grabbed him, snickering and cackling.

Now he laughed, and tried to break free.

She let him go, then fixed his collar, brushed his hair with her hands. "You like grandma's little doll?" Aged hands plucked the puppet out from the recess. "My *mami* made this. Did you know that?"

He shook his head, scratched his nose.

"Yes. She made it for your mama when she was a little baby. And when she gave it to her, mama didn't want it, okay? So I kept it instead."

The puppet stared–beady, black eyes.

"Why didn't mama want it?"

"I don't know. She started crying when she saw it." Another snicker. She straightened the puppet's hood, arranged its dangling limbs. "But my *mami* crocheted it and sewed the legs and arms here."

"What is it?"

"It's a mousie. Like this mousie." She grabbed him again and rubbed his hair. "You can look at him, but you have to put him back."

It was handed over. He took it and examined the face.

Not a mouse, he saw, but he didn't say that. Thin scratches on the beak revealed streaks of unpainted plastic. On its fabric feet were little crochet boots.

Grandma was gone. Raised voices came from the kitchen. *"¿Qué es esto? No seas estúpida, mamá."* A pause. *"¡Mamá! ¡Vete a la mierda!"* A dark shape stormed around the corner, carrying a platter of something–vegetables. Not grandma. Her face was twisted in anger beneath a sheet of makeup. For a moment, she glanced at him, and her eyes were burning.

He clutched the doll, fled to the basement stairs. They were at the center of the house–plunged into a dark pit below. Wooden railings on all sides. He sat on the top step and cradled the puppet in his lap. "Hello, *Mousie*."

Silence.

"Why are you so chipped?"

Silence.

"What's in the basement? Can you see?" He turned it around, made it face down into the dark. Waited. "Maybe your eyes are better–like a cat." He positioned the dangling boots to stand on his knee, then turned the body back and forth–allowing it to search for him. "Maybe we should go down and you can guide me."

Silence.

"But I might trip on something." A pause. "I think

grandma has a flashlight."

Silence.

"But it's out of batteries. Maybe grandpa has batteries." He spun the puppet back around. "Where's grandpa, Mousie?"

Silence.

"*Hey...*" A whisper.

He froze, looked down into the dark–where the stairs were swallowed. His heart started thumping behind his ears. Nothing. No movement. The soft flesh in his throat was constricted–inflating. His face was cold. He stood up, squinted. His mind conjured images of something crawling up from beyond the edge of light–or running up. "Mousie, can you see?" He held the puppet up. "Maybe it was Mama's voice from the kitchen. Or maybe *Tia.*" One step back down, then another–he sat back in place.

The puppet slipped, fell down a few steps.

A pause.

"Don't go down there, Mousie." He got up, went fast–snatched up the puppet. A warning sounded in the back of his head as he sprinted back up into the light. He glanced behind. Nothing. He sat down again.

"*Polloico.*" Grandpa–standing by the railing. His features were brushed with ambient light. "What are you doing?"

Martin held out the puppet. “It fell down the stairs.”

Behind grandpa was a taxidermy bull head, bolted to the wall. It was watching, quietly. “Don’t go down there when it’s night.”

“Why?”

“That’s where the bad man lives.”

A pause. “Who’s the bad man?”

“He waits in the basement, at the bottom of the stairs. You don’t want him to get you, do you?”

“No.”

“Good. Come, *polloico*. Put that back.” He held out his hand, took the puppet. It went back to its recess, resumed its seated stasis. “Martin. Come. Dinner is done.”

One last glance into the dark. There was no face, no voice. But he could feel it there, staring back at him. He tried to imagine its face–what it looked like. But he couldn’t.

1

A television was bolted to the wooden patio framing. Its glow caressed the empty tables. Martin sat at the closest one to the door, just beneath the television. It felt like the glowing news anchor was watching him. "*Queen Elizabeth the Second celebrated her Diamond Jubilee on Tuesday. The event marks a sixty year milestone for the English monarch. She was coronated in Nineteen Fifty Two, and is so far the longest ruling monarch in the country's history.*"

Steam was licking the cold night air–rising from a half empty cup. He sipped, put it back down. A flaking paperback was pinched in his one hand. Occasional wind tried to rip it away.

"What are those tattoos?"

He looked up. "Sorry?"

She was turned red under the light of the coffee shop sign. Her eyes were big and dark. "On your arms… sorry."

"Oh." He rolled his sleeve up farther. Both arms were

fully inked. "This one is a cardinal–like the bird. Um… this is my mother's name. That one was my girlfriend's name, but she cheated on me, so now it's a–it's the Virgin Mary."

"This?" She pointed. When he gave her a confused look, she took his arm and touched the image.

"That's a mouse."

"Oh. Why?"

An involuntary chuckle–half broken. "My grandma used to call me '*mousie*,' so I… well, yeah."

"My grandma called me '*pollito,*'" she said. "That's 'little bird.' I don't know why, but I think it's cute." The wind whipped her hair. She reached up to pull her fluffy bangs back down. "So… what are you doing here alone? Just…"-she did a little shrug-"Reading? Drinking coffee?"

"Uh… getting out of work, I guess." He checked behind–in front, "Do you wanna sit?"

"Oh, I have to get home, but… I just saw your tattoos and…"

"Yeah."

"Yeah, so…"

"What's your name, sorry?"

"Bonnie Alo." She shook his hand.

"Martin Navarro," he responded. "I like your hair."

She went red. "Thanks. Um… I'll see you."

He watched her get into her car–waved. Then she was

gone. He attempted to read his book, but he couldn't see the words anymore.

—

The glass of the shopfront sign was shattered. *ROADRUNNER*. The television was torn off its bolts–lay in the dirt. Its screen was in a million little reflective pieces. A cloud of dust came in from over the rooftops; old rainwater stains were tracked down the windows.

There was a cup on the table. Time had withered the paper, soaked it through with brown and black splotches. Half an inch of coffee remained stagnant at the bottom of it. A million things floated on the surface.

Martin stood there, looking around. He remembered her–standing where he was now. How she touched his arm. The air had smelled of ground coffee then. Now it was wet and pallid.

Graffiti grew like mold across the brick walls.

Kill yourself now!

I fucked her, and I'll fuck you!

I shot a kike!

I dismembered a Transcensionist!

Skulls and something phallic. Rainwater wept over all of it.

He stepped through the torn-down doors, into the stench of moist wood and rotting drywall. Movement. He turned, saw it blinking. A cat, orange and thin. It was sat squat on the old shop counter. It yawned. He said, “Hi, baby.” It blinked.

A tinny voice. Like someone was speaking through a can.

It came from a yawning doorway behind the counter. He made quiet steps, pulled out his pistol. An *S.P.S. Pantera*. Uncertain glow emanated from out of the doorway–flashed in the polished metal of the gun. He reached up to brush his dark locks away from his eyes–they fell back again. Every breath out made them lift a little. Every breath was heavy. His heart was a drumbeat.

The image of the lit television crept around the splintered door frame. A dark figure sat on the floor, captivated by the glow. On the screen was a corpse on an operating table. Nothing else. *LIVE* stuck out in the top left corner, blinking.

“Don’t move.”

The dark figure spun around, stared in fear. A man, mid-thirties. Unshaven. Ungroomed. He looked down the barrel of the pistol. “Who the fuck are you?”

Martin slid his finger onto the trigger. “What’s your name?”

“What?”

"Answer, asshole."

Silence.

"Answer the fucking question or I'll smoke you." He chambered a round. "I'm not kidding. I'm not gonna stick around here while you think it over."

"Ed." The man was side-lit by the flickering screen. He was pallid–like a skeleton.

"I'm gonna look around here, alright? Just sit there." The pistol stayed locked as he carved a wide berth. Occasional glances at Ed punctuated his searching–through drawers, under tables, under chairs. Shelves held picked-through and rotten coffee bean bags and stacks of flaking paper filters. A dirty grinder, a pack of green and fluffy strawberry jam packets.

"What are you looking for, mister?" The skeleton man had a languid Virginia drawl.

"Quit."

A pause. "No one's come through here in a brick–they all pass it by on their way."

A drawer slammed open. Metal rattling. Cutlery jostled about before going still. He slammed it shut again. "How's that t.v. running? You have a generator?"

"Yes sir."

Nothing had changed on the screen. The corpse was still. It looked months old.

"Where?"

"Well I ain't gonna tell you that. Steal my fuckin' gasoline."

Some chairs were stacked against the back wall. He checked under them. Hardened gum and flaking upholstery. "Tell me now: did you see a little gold ring around here anywhere? Had a bird on it."

A pause, then, "No sir. Can't say I have."

"I know it was in here."

A shrug. "I've been here near on one year now. Never saw no ring."

Martin's gaze passed between the man and the television. Out of the corner of his eye, he saw a vent near the floor. A small one, for air conditioning. He walked over to it and knelt down.

—

"Oh shit!"

A golden flicker. It skittered off somewhere and vanished.

"Where'd it go?" She scanned a circle, peered around the legs of passing customers. "Martin?"

"I didn't see it." He bent down, threw his gaze around under a table–under the front counter. Nothing. There was an air vent blowing quietly. The slats were big enough to fit the ring, but the odds of it having slipped through were slim. "Sorry, Bonnie."

"It's okay. It wasn't you."

He stood back up and fixed his hair. "It was a pretty ring."

"My mom gave it to me when I was sixteen." She smiled after a moment. "Doesn't matter anymore, though." Her dark eyes were made darker. She bit her lip, looked off out the cafe window. Cars were humming by behind the glass–the painted words: *ROADRUNNER.*

"I'll buy your coffee."

"No," she folded her arms, "No, it's okay."

"Please?"

She considered, locked eyes with him. The overhead fluorescents danced there in those eyes, like he could see her soul. "Are you sure?"

"Yes."

"Okay, then I'll buy yours."

"No. Absolutely not."

Her sweater sleeves were pulled up over her palms. She scratched her nose. "Such a gentleman." Her cheeks were red again. "Thank you."

—

The screws were loose. He used his fingertips to work them the rest of the way out. Then the vent cover tipped over. Inside was a shiny trinket covered in dust and dirt.

A ring, with a bird on it.

He plucked it out into the light.

"What's that there shining?"

It went into his pocket. "Just stay by that t.v., alright?"

"I'm poor, sir. If that's gold, then I need it. Gotta buy food."

He looked hard at the man, zipped up his jacket. A wind was blowing outside, making the building hum. "I can't do that."

"This is my fucking house, you hear? I live here. Anything inside is mine."

Martin checked over his shoulder. "Sorry."

"Don't you step out that door!" His eyes were wild now–face twisted. "You're stealing!"

The pistol clicked. "Don't get up."

Silence.

The skeleton man lunged into the dust, arm outstretched, reaching for something behind the television set.

Two snaps. Smoke leaked from the pistol's mouth.

Ed's blood grew in a puddle. The television screen was reflected in the crimson surface. *LIVE.* On and off under the static.

2

Groaning. Metal snapping and wrenching.

A little light blinked behind a black mirror. *1... 2... 3... 4... 5...*

Martin held the ring inside his pocket. His fingertips traced the grooves and features.

Ding!

The doors slid open and he stepped out into the apartment hall. It was a long stretch of faded, psychedelically-patterned carpet and yellowed, peeling wallpaper. Numbered doors marched along on either side, both directions. He went right, passed under a flickering wall sconce. He stopped at a gray door–struck it with his knuckles.

Silence.

He bent down and pulled the ring from his pocket–stuck it under the door and gave it a flick. It skated on the wood, was swallowed up. Now he went to the neighboring door, pulled his key, unlocked it.

His apartment was plain and comfortable. He shut the door, idly scanned the laminated fire escape document taped to the back. A two-pronged hook impaled the loop on his jacket collar and held it. His footsteps thumped the floor. The scent of smoke had managed to slip in through an open window. It was cut off as he shut it–locked the latch. A car was on fire outside. Dark figures fled the scene into an alleyway. He didn't care to watch for more than a few seconds.

A hollow sound.

He went to the wall, pressed his ear up against it. There was movement there, through the drywall and the insulation. His knees hit the hardwood too quick, made him suck in breath through his teeth. A moment of positioning–trying to get as low as possible.

A vent in the wall.

The cover was already on the floor, set aside with its screws.

His breath spoke back to him as it pulled dust up out of the cavity. A shred of light leaked through as the neighbor's kitchen fluorescents sparked to life. There were footsteps, thumping from left to right. He watched a shadow flit past. The neighboring vent cover was like a blinded window.

RING A LING A LING A LING A LING!

"God…" He rolled over, got to his feet. The phone was rattling on its receiver. Its rubber buttons were chipping–the numbers faded away. He touched one. "Hello?"

Her voice on the other end was shallow and sparkly–fed through an ancient wire. "*It's mama.*"

"How are you?"

"*Am I interrupting you?*"

"No, mama. What is it?" He scratched his arm, leaned on the counter. Dust had gotten into his hair. Idle fingers pulled, flicked it away.

"*That bitch called me again.*"

He put a pen back into a pen holder on the kitchen counter.

"*She demanded I come and help clean up grandma's house–her clothes and garbage. I told her I couldn't, 'cause I'm not well, and she knows that, and then she started screaming at me and saying I killed grandma and grandpa and telling me if I didn't come over, then she would tell the whole family how much of a bitch I am and how evil and… I don't know.*"

"She can go fuck herself, mama."

A cough through static. "*Then she started yapping about that little doll that grandma gave you–you remember that one? The little bird?*"

"Yeah."

"She said if you don't bring it back to grandma's house, then she'll take both me and you to court for noncompliance with her power of attorney–whatever the hell. Her lawyer is on standby, she says."

"She won't do anything, mama, okay? She never did anything last time, and she won't do anything now. She's an angry bitch that likes to threaten people who don't do what she says, alright? Just don't even answer the phone if she calls." He glanced over, saw the puppet sat on a side table, propped against a picture frame. Mousie the bird. "You need to stop using a landline, 'cause it won't tell you who's calling."

"*I don't want a smartphone, hijo.*"

"Yes, but it'll make your life a lot easier."

"*Your father has one, doesn't he?*"

"Yeah, he works at a store that sells them."

"*Oh, I didn't know that.*"

"Yeah, well… whatever."

A laugh. "*Whatever.*" A pause. "*What are you doing today?*"

"Just the same, mama."

"*How is work?*"

"I'm not working anymore."

"*Right. Okay, well... are you finding any work?*"

Tapping on the window. It was starting to rain. Streaks

ran through the dust and soot painted across the glass. Martin rounded the counter into the kitchen and searched the fridge. It was almost empty again. Three eggs, and a cloudy mason jar of milk. The fridge light bulb socket was hollow. "No, not really. I'm okay–I'm looking."

"*Alright, well you need money.*"

"Quit, mama." He shut the fridge, unclipped his pistol holster. It clicked heavy on the counter. "I have to go, alright? Don't answer her calls."

"*Okay, hijo. I love you.*"

"Love you. Bye." The cheap, plastic phone was seated back in its place. He looked at it for a moment, then snatched it back up. Its buttons snapped under his fingertips, beeped numbers into the LCD screen on the receiver. He put the phone up to his ear, then hurried back to the vent–got down on the floor.

"*Hello?*"

Her voice came from two places at once.

"Hi, it's Martin."

"*Oh, hi! How are you?*"

"Good. I slipped something under your door. I might've found it while I was out today." He waited, listening to his own breathing.

"*Oh my God... where did you find it?*"

"At Roadrunner. It was stuck in a vent."

"*Thank you so much, Martin... I thought it was gone forever.*"

He could see her through the slats, sitting on her bed. She had the ring in her hand, turning it over with her fingers. "Just thought it would cheer you up," he said. She slipped it on as he watched, and it caught the light of her bedside lamp. Glowing gold.

—

"What is she doing now?"

A car rumbled past–rusty and thumping like a drum.

The payphone spat. "*She calls over and over, hijo. It won't stop ringing, even at night. I answer and she screams into the phone. No words–just screaming.*"

"Mama, don't answer. Pull the line if she does that." Martin leaned against the phonebooth glass. Through the thin, cloudy veil on all sides, the rotten world went about its business.

"*She wants the doll. If you just give it to her, she'll stop.*"

He groaned. "I'm not giving her shit."

"*It's just a doll.*"

"I don't care. She's abusing you and she's trying to abuse me. I'm not gonna give her fucking satisfaction. Don't answer the phone, mama. Quit."

A pause. Then: "*It's getting hard, hijo.*"

"Mama, it's so easy to make it stop. Just do what I say."

"*Okay. I love you.*"

The phone snapped into its receiver. He pulled back the booth door and stepped out into the morning chill. The air reeked of gasoline and smoke. Steam rose from chimneys and vendor stalls lining the sidewalks and alleyways. Over it all stood the Red Abbey–on a tall hill. When the sun hit a certain angle in the sky, its light was reflected from the church tower in crimson. Like a bloodshot eye overwatching.

A tune played over the air, spit out from a cacophony of metal speakers–bolted to buildings or atop tall wooden poles. Three notes ascending, made by a whistley mellotron. Like a broken *Strawberry Fields Forever*. Immediately following, a voice rang out. Inescapable, and everywhere at once. "*A nineteen year old woman has gone missing.*" The voice was emptiness and decay. Sonorous, yet piercing. "*Slender build. Blonde hair. Freckles. Blue eyes. Five feet, four inches. An index finger was found and matched to the missing girl. It was bent backward. If you find her, or you see Mr. Crooked, find the nearest phone and alert the police.*"

A sparkle, a pop, then silence.

Martin stepped into an alleyway. Deep-set into the wall of the left building was a thick, steel door. He pounded it with his fist. Waited.

Shifting.

Up against a dumpster, a bum sat amongst his filth. His overgrown face was grim–eyes hard. He didn't say a word, or move. Just stared.

"Mister Martin?"

Martin turned, saw the door was open a crack. An old woman was framed there, between the metal and the brick. Candlesmoke and the scent of lavender trickled out in a hot stream. "Hi, Ayla."

"Come on in, darling. Heat your bones up." She held open the door, let him through. Her hair was a mess of black curls. The door shut tight–her rings clicked against the lock as she fumbled. "How are you doing?"

"I'm alright." He stepped over one carpet, onto another. Each was decorated with occult symbols, matted and stamped in with dirt. Chimes and chains of beads hung from the ceiling rafters in every available space. Hundreds and thousands and maybe more. A low, purple couch embraced him as he lowered himself.

The woman came over. She was large, wrapped in patterned drapes and scarves. "Fucking speaker's right outside my door. Get a racket in here every time it starts yappin'." Her chair groaned. She scratched her brow. "What can I do ya for, darling? Tell me about your mama."

“I called her just two minutes ago.” A pause. “My bitch aunt won’t stop calling.”

“That’s tough. That woman’s a damn witch.” She pulled out a cigarette. Her lighter was covered in purple rhinestones and emblazoned with a sunface. It sparked and spit. “I tell ya, I can put a curse on her if you ask me. Simple as baking cookies, darling.”

“No thanks.”

A cloud of smoke wafted up into the canopy of hanging beads. “Back in New Orleans, my baby cousin got shot dead in the street. I cursed the cocksucker that did it, and next thing, they find him lying face down in a ditch somewhere. *Merry fucking Christmas*. It works now, darling.”

“Do what you want, then. I won’t stop you.”

Another puff. “We’ll see what’s in the cards. I might do.” Firelight cast warmth across her dark features. “But you wanted to meet me, mister. Tell me what’s got your knickers all tied.”

“Well, uh…” He brushed dirt off the couch arm. Went quiet.

“Where’d you get that shirt? That’s nice.”

He looked down. It was mustard yellow with thin, vertical stripes. “I had this forever.”

Ayla smiled. Her teeth were off-white. “Yellow’s the color of happiness and success.”

"I thought it was mental illness and cowardice."

The cigarette sparked. "Depends who you ask, darling. Depends who you believe."

Silence.

"You were saying something?"

He shifted, spun his leather bracelets.

"I remember you talking about some kinda feelings you had about certain people. Jog my memory, if you would." Puff of embers. She coughed into her arm.

A pause. "I wanted to shoot a cricker in the back of the head."

Smoke passed across her dark eyes. "But you didn't do it."

"Course not."

"If the man's still holed up and fishing by the crick from his cardboard box, then there's no problem, is there?"

A frown. "What kinda answer is that?"

"You've gotta ignore those thoughts when they come knockin'. Intrusive thoughts, darling. We all get 'em sometimes. Some days I walk down the street and wonder what it would feel like to step in front of a truck. Doesn't mean I'm gonna."

He rubbed his arms. "Felt like something was telling me to do it. It didn't feel like a thought. Felt like an instruction."

The woman groaned, adjusted herself in her chair.

"Sometimes they do. You want some pills, or something?"

"What pills?"

She got up, crossed over to a glass-faced cabinet. Hundreds of white bottles were stacked messily on every shelf. It took a minute for her to find what she was looking for. "Take this. Instructions are on the label."

It sailed across the room. He caught it, spun it around. *Clozapine*. "This is a schizo drug."

"You're welcome. Do what your doctor tells you, darling." Her cigarette shed ash onto the carpet. "Any other issues?"

"No."

"Then get on home, darling. You come back if you figure all this shit out. If you don't, I'll smoke a pack for you and hang some beads. Mustard yellow."

Now he was standing in the alley. The door shut and locked. He turned, saw the dumpster–no bum. He was gone, having left his ratty blankets and empty tin cans.

He slipped out of the alley, started down the sidewalk.

3

A dusting of snow had fallen–continued to fall. Flakes sparkled under street lamps in the half-lit evening. The apartment building rose into the bone white sky–some windows smashed, others boarded. *THE TOWNSHEND.* The sign was faded–painted above the front door. There was no one around, except for a single black silhouette waiting beneath the crystalline glow of the entrance sconces.

Martin saw her–wanted to turn back. But his feet moved him forward.

She hadn't aged nearly at all. *Botox*, maybe, and heavy tanning. When she heard his footsteps, she turned. There was nothing at all behind her eyes. Once he stopped in front of her, she said: "It's cold."

"Yes. It is."

A pause. "You've grown."

"What do you want?"

Her hair was almost Egyptian style. Midnight Cleopatra.

Heavy curtains hung down over each side of her face. "You know."

He looked up into the swirling evening. "The fucking doll?"

Silence.

"Why does it matter so much?"

"That was your grandma's doll. It's part of her estate. So it's up to me what happens to it."

"She gave it to me before she died."

The empty eyes widened. "That's a lie. Don't lie to me. Your mother gave it to you after she stole it from grandma's house."

He tilted his head, cracked his neck. "You have proof?"

Silence. She stared–didn't blink.

"Since you decided to grace me with your presence, I'll tell you something myself. If you keep calling my mother and harassing her, I'll help her get a restraining order. So you're gonna quit, or I swear to God… I'm not fucking around."

Silence.

"No one ever tells you '*no*,' do they? Huh?" He scratched his beard. "You've been bitching and acting like a brat since I was too young to understand it. I used to wonder why my dad hated you. You're seriously damaged, woman. I feel bad for you. Now if you don't mind, I'm gonna go upstairs and have a drink, and you can take your pampered ass back on home. That clear enough for you?"

She blinked. "You used to be such a nice boy." Her darkness seemed to suck at the street lamp's glow as she passed under it. Off she went, growing gradually smaller as the distance consumed her.

Martin pulled open the front door–stung his hand on the cold metal.

The elevator rumbled around him, ascending.

He found his keys, stuck one into the doorknob.

His grandpa's golf clubs toppled loudly–struck by the opening door. He shut it, then bent down to collect them. One was missing. The seven iron. He never golfed in his life.

Car headlights flashed through his window. He went to the kitchen counter–fumbled for the pill bottle rammed into his coat pocket. It clicked against the countertop. He put his head in his hands, rubbed his face.

Three ascending tones–muffled through the concrete walls. Then the omnipotent voice: "*Tomorrow is the day of Blessed Sabbath. Our doors are open. God shall visit the Red Abbey to observe our worship and abstinence. All are welcome.*" There was a pause. "*The corpse of a whore was found in a ditch. Decapitated. All fingers were bent backward. If you see Mister Crooked, find the nearest phone and alert the police.*"

Silence.

Martin pulled open the pill bottle. A puff of acrid powder escaped from inside. He shook it until a single round, white pellet was lying centered on his palm. It tasted of metal. He swallowed. His throat touched it curiously as it went down. Now his head was back in his hands. "Fuck…" His eyelids began to shut unconsciously.

Tick... tap...

A quick glance. The window. It was hard to see through–it was a black mirror. Behind his reflection, there was movement.

A leg. A boot. Then a hand pressed against the glass. Pushed off. Up, and out of sight.

He stepped back from the counter, pulled his pistol.

Silence.

It took half a second to reach the window. He pulled on it–forced it open. The gun went out first, followed close by his head. He scanned up, down, both sides. Nothing. Back inside. The window had a lock. He levered it into place.

The medication kept him up all night, seeing dark shapes in every corner. He thought he saw her face through his bedroom window–made up and overly tanned. Dark curtains of hair. Smiling.

Morning sunlight saw him wake, cold with sweat.

—

Mousie had hardly aged.

The crocheted hood was slightly yellowed by time, and there were more scratches on the black eye beads–but a layer of dust had kept it safe and neglected. Martin picked it up–turned it around in his hands. He'd sat it up against a picture of his grandparents. Stoic and hard-faced. *American Gothic.*

Light from a passing car filtered through the translucent curtains–washed over the dresser upon which the puppet sat amongst a collection of other trinkets. A doll of a Flamenco dancer. Her dress was fiery red–skin monotone plastic. A bull, flocked plastic. Plastic Jesus stapled to a plastic cross.

He put Mousie down.

A sound from next door.

Cool air was blowing up through the vent hole. He got down on the ground, wedged his face into the opening. Hot breath. She was walking around her bedroom in her underwear, trying to find something to wear. Unkempt hair. Streetlamp light side-lit her body in orange.

He watched until she left the room.

Then someone knocked on the door.

And he turned over–cold and still. Silence. He went over and looked through the peephole, and saw a face on the other side. It was wrinkled and nearly cro-magnon. Bright blue eyes sat deep in shadowed sockets. A blink. Two blinks. Then he spoke. "*Can you see me, mister Navarro?*"

His breath stopped in his throat.

"*You don't know me, but you will.*" A pause. The ventilation started to hum. "*I'm from the Church of the Holy Transcension. Something's required of you.*"

Martin's hand drifted down to his belt, felt the hard metal. The pistol's mouth was forced up flush against the door.

Silence.

"*When you were a boy, you witnessed God.*"

Silence.

"*I looked into your past myself, in fact. I'm what we call a Blessed Eye.*" He cleared his throat. "*I can see you even now, son. Behind this thick wooden door.*"

His finger fell gradually to rest against the trigger.

"*So let's get on with it. You earn your scant sums of cash picking over dead bums and street rats. We have hot food, son. When was the last time you ate well?*" A pause, and no answer. "*You are a direct line to the fourth dimension, and to God. We have been trying so long to even see it. But you spoke to it. And at so young an age.*"

"How did you find me?" Martin felt as if he'd thrown his words into a vacuous nothing, and regretted it.

The man's expression never changed. "*I was guided,*

son. I asked a question to the ethereal and was given an answer."

"Bullshit."

Silence.

"Get the fuck away from my apartment or I'll blow a hole in your skull!"

Through the fisheye glass of the peephole, the man was still. His stare was piercing. "*Check on your neighbor.*" A shuffling of robes. The man faded out to the left, warped by the glass.

Martin rushed across the apartment, leapt over a coffee table. The vent was now breathing heat. His shoulder slapped the hardwood and he sucked in through his teeth. Through the slats of the neighboring vent cover, he saw Bonnie–seated on the edge of her bed. She was painting her nails.

He could feel his heart drumming behind his ears. He spent the next hour there, watching with his gun by his chin. And saw nothing at all.

4

She struggled to line up the sights. The wind was tugging at the barrel.

CRACK!

Whizzing, then a thud. Nowhere close.

“Here, it’s like this.” Martin stood behind–gently grabbed her arms. He saw the sight from over her shoulder, through the windy trails of hair. “You see that?”

“Yeah.”

“Okay. Sho-”

CRACK!

The empty pop can splintered into metal tongues–flew off into the tallgrass.

She yelped, then started laughing.

Her smile was like a warm flame against the cold morning air. It took him away from where they were–standing on a grassy bluff, the town below in its enclosed little valley. A bell tolled deeply. Church tower. Some meters away. It was an abbey–castle-like. Hulking walls of ornate stone and gargoyles leering over the crenelations. It was like something had plucked the thing out of some European metropolis and accidentally dropped it on the way to somewhere else.

"What's this?" She got close to him, touched shoulders.

His chest seized. "What's what?"

"This here. *S.P.S.*"

He watched her run her pointer over the letters. "That's the company name."

"What does it mean?"

"Like…"

"Super Powerful… Shit." A snort. There was mint and coffee on her breath.

Martin chuckled, took the pistol from her. "I don't remember, actually." A pause. "But that's probably better than whatever it really is." He felt her head against his shoulder–the brush of dark hair on his neck.

"Where'd you get it?"

"Uh… my grandpa." It turned over in his hands. Ornate hammer. Ornate trigger. His ghost stared back at him through the polished reflection. "It's a Spanish gun, so he bought it there. Brought it over, I think… No… Maybe one of my mom's cousins bought it for him… Doesn't matter."

Her breathing brushed him gently. "You don't seem like

a gun guy."

"No?"

"You look like it on the outside, but I know you."

He searched for words. "You're sweet."

The church bell went quiet.

"You're pretty sweet too."

Wind came rushing in from heaven. Her lips touched his cheek. Warm, and wet.

Silence.

She put her head on his shoulder again, and his mind went blank.

—

The hardwood had flattened his ear against his head. He felt every muscle from head to toe flex. Cramping. A pendulum cracking against the insides of his skull. "Fucking…"

She wasn't in her room. Loose strands of micro hair and particles of dust floated across the vent grate. There was a rumbling from down below, then the building started to breathe. Hot air in his face.

Thirty minutes. One hour. Sunlight caressed his back like a warm mother.

No Bonnie.

Then the silence was broken by the muffled sizzling of

water. He got to his feet with a groan, felt the stiffness crack out of his chest. His pistol was in his hand–he couldn't remember pulling it. Careful footfalls carried him to the bathroom door–now ajar, puking light into the half-lit hallway. He looked in.

Murky water in the tub. The shower pelted its surface. Something dark swam around inside, but he couldn't see clearly. The door moaned, almost erotically. His boot smacked the linoleum tiling.

The dark thing was a catfish. It wriggled, pushing fins. From one end of the tub to the other, over and over.

Martin sat on the porcelain edge, reached up to pull the shower head off its hook. The water was spurting miserably out of calcium-crusted holes. He held it over the murk–over the fish. It cleansed the shining scales for microseconds, then the clean water joined the shit. It was all shit, and the catfish pushed it through its gills and let it between its lips–searched through it with frantic whiskers.

His vision was blurring.

Clean fish.

Clean fish.

CLEANFISHCLEANFISHCLEANFISHC
LEANFISHCLEANFISHCLEANFISHCLE
ANFISHCLEANFISHCLEANFISHCLEA
NFISHCLEANFISHCLEANFISHCLEAN
FISHCLEANFISHCLEANFISHCLEANFI
SHCLEANFISHCLEANFISHCLEANFISH
CLEANFISHCLEANFISHCLEANFISHC
LEANFISHCLEANFISHCLEANFISHCLE
ANFISHCLEANFISHCLEANFISHCLEA
NFISHCLEANFISHCLEANFISHCLEAN
FISHCLEANFISHCLEANFISHCLEANFI
SHCLEANFISHCLEANFISHCLEANFISH
CLEANFISHCLEANFISHCLEANFISHC
LEANFISHCLEANFISHCLEANFISHCLE
ANFISHCLEANFISHCLEANFISHCLEA
NFISHCLEANFISHCLEANFISHCLEAN
FISHCLEANFISHCLEANFISHCLEANFI
SHCLEANFISHCLEANFISHCLEANFISH
CLEANFISHCLEANFISHCLEANFISHC
LEANFISHCLEANFISHCLEANFISHCLE
ANFISHCLEANFISHCLEANFISHCLEA
NFISHCLEANFISHCLEANFISHCLEAN
FISHCLEANFISHCLEANFISHCLEANFI
SHCLEANFISHCLEANFISHCLEANFISH
CLEANFISHCLEANFISHCLEANFISHC

LEANFISHCLEANFISHCLEANFISHCLE
ANFISHCLEANFISHCLEANFISHCLEA
NFISHCLEANFISHCLEANFISHCLEAN
FISHCLEANFISHCLEANFISHCLEANFI
SHCLEANFISHCLEANFISHCLEANFISH
CLEANFISHCLEANFISHCLEANFISHC
LEANFISHCLEANFISHCLEANFISHCLE
ANFISHCLEANFISHCLEANFISHCLEA
NFISHCLEANFISHCLEANFISHCLEAN
FISHCLEANFISHCLEANFISHCLEANFI
SHCLEANFISHCLEANFISHCLEANFISH
CLEANFISHCLEANFISHCLEANFISHC
LEANFISHCLEANFISHCLEANFISHCLE
ANFISHCLEANFISHCLEANFISHCLEA
NFISHCLEANFISHCLEANFISHCLEAN
FISHCLEANFISHCLEANFISHCLEANFI
SHCLEANFISHCLEANFISHCLEANFISH
CLEANFISHCLEANFISHCLEANFISHC
LEANFISHCLEANFISHCLEANFISHCLE
ANFISHCLEANFISHCLEANFISHCLEA
NFISHCLEANFISHCLEANFISHCLEAN
FISHCLEANFISHCLEANFISHCLEANFI
SHCLEANFISHCLEANFISHCLEANFISH
CLEANFISHCLEANFISHCLEANFISHC
LEANFISHCLEANFISHCLEANFISHCLE

He screamed.

There was no more water in the tub.

The fish's stomach was cut clean open. Entrails seeped translucent pink. Water and blood. Something clogged the showerhead. He felt vibration. Thick, chunky whiteness came in pulsing bursts. It mixed with the water and the blood. He dropped the showerhead. It shot discharge across the floor–sprayed across the walls.

Now he spun around, reached for the doorknob.

But the door was gone. Red, pulsing flesh filled the crooked frame. At its center was a bestial sphincter. At the resting of each pulse, the flesh would pull back to reveal rows of teeth.

"Let me out! LET ME OUT!"

A rumble, like a stomach without food.

The door-mouth opened–shot something at him. It struck him in the neck.

He lost consciousness and fell against the bathtub, cracking his head on the porcelain edge.

—

Ringing. The phone.

The hardwood had flattened his ear against his head. He felt every muscle from head to toe flex. Cramping. A pendulum cracking against the insides of his skull. He got to his feet, went over to the cheap plastic noisemaker–snapped it off the receiver. "Yeah?"

"*Have you made a decision?*"

He sucked in a breath. "What?"

"*It's Roman Ward. Do you remember me?*" Crackling. Static.

"Yes I do."

A pause. "*Did you hear the announcement yesterday?*"

"I did."

"*Our abbey is open to the public–for anyone who wishes to seek a place of clarity.*"

He blinked, looked down at the vent, at the hallway to the bathroom. "What do you mean about my neighbor? Why should I check on her?"

"*Come to the abbey, son. Will you? Just come.*"

"But she's still here. I can see he-... I heard her through the wall."

"*Just come.*"

Crick. A pulsing hum behind static.

The phone was seated in its place, then Martin went back to the vent. He got down–peered through. Bonnie was pulling clothes out of a plastic bag. Store tags dangling. She held each one up to her body–checking herself in her standing mirror.

—

They hadn't torn down the fence. Its wooden posts were crooked and split by the rain. He saw something glimmer through the overgrown grass–bent down to grab it. A soda can–bullet hole. From his gun.

The abbey had grown. It was still a castle, but the gargoyles had been snapped off at the legs–replaced with effigies made of rusted metal. There was no bell in the tower anymore; they'd put a mirror up there and caged it behind red stained glass. The beacon–*eye of God*. Bloodshot.

More rusted metal was nailed into the white stone, like dirty braces on teeth.

Shuffling figures emerged from out of the town, all along the road. Up to the large wooden doors. Two symbols cut from sheet metal were bolted there, one on each door. The symbol. Seal of Golgotha.

He shuffled too, through the doors. The air reeked of blood and sage.

"*Maybe they'll give us food.*"

He didn't see the speaker. It could have been any of them. Filthy and beleaguered. Wind penetrated carved archways near the ceiling–played the building like an instrument. A sonorous hum. *The voice of God*.

"Come now. Please follow." The man was clad in robes–colored like dried blood. Golgotha's seal was sewn a hundred times over his shoulders, collar, and down the trailing redness that enveloped him waist-down. "We are beginning the morning with prayer. Watch, or participate as you like."

The far back wall was a brutalist concrete grid. Skylights painted angled shadows. A chancel, and a podium. A hundred black pews. Some cradled penitent ghosts bent over themselves in prayer. Silence hung hot and weighted.

Martin picked his way through the wandering mass, up to the chancel. The Blessed Eye stood there, bolt straight–his eyes were already on him. Blue as crystalline Heaven. "Welcome to the Red Abbey, Mister Navarro."

"I'm here. I came."

A smile broke the corpse-like mask. "Use those stairs."

Martin looked, then looked back. Waited. Then he went over and ascended onto the chancel. The Blessed Eye watched, hands folded in his sleeves. His body didn't seem to radiate any heat. He spoke from the shadows beneath a wide, red hood: "You are welcome here, Mister Navarro." A pause. "Would you like some coffee?"

Martin stuck his hands into the pockets of his sandy overcoat. "No."

The holy man had eyes like a basset hound–downturned,

sagging. “Food?”

“No, thank you.” He felt the butt of his pistol wedged in his belt. “What am I doing here?”

“It’s time for you to be useful, Mister Navarro.”

Martin frowned hard. “What did you just say? Useful? Tell me something, you old fuck: why are you threatening my neighbor?”

“Golgotha tells me things that I need to know. Don’t think me a voyeur. I don’t look where I’m not supposed to.” His head tilted under the hood. A knowing glance.

Martin clenched his jaw. “Fuck you.”

“We are flawed animals, Mister Navarro. Do not hate yourself.”

Martin scanned the sea of heads–saw across to the doors where more were trickling in. “I don’t hate myself.”

“Of course not. Not in any way you would readily admit. But we all hate ourselves somehow.”

“Quit. I’ve already got a shrink.”

The saggy eyes never left Martin’s face–never blinked. “Can I begin, Mister Navarro? There’s lots to explain, and not much time.”

Something somewhere in the vastness of the abbey struck and echoed. Martin’s eyes drifted away from the priest–onto the numerous stained glass windows depicting scenes of bestial horror. “Yeah. Please do.”

"You know Mr. Crooked?"

"Heard of him."

"What would you think if I told you he was not a man?"

Martin scratched his beard. "Is he a woman?"

"No. Not at all. He is a lesser deity from Heaven. Do you know our faith?"

The room was crowded now. "Can your Golgotha read my mind and let you know?"

A pause. "Golgotha is King of Heaven. Beneath him are his Seraphs. Then there are lower things that inhabit Heaven. Cherubs and sprites. Some are good and others are wicked."

"And?"

"Mr. Crooked is a Cherub. An evil one, crossed over. Do you understand?"

Martin stifled a yawn. "That sounds like a load of shit to me."

"Bold to speak like that while you stand in the mouth of the lion."

Silence.

The priest moved slowly, like he was floating in water. A burgundy satin glove reached out to lift the cover of a tome sitting heavy on the chancel lectern. Flipping pages. Grotesque illustrations mingled with ones of beauty and elegance. "But this Cherub is especially cruel. A threat to Golgotha and the kingdom of Heaven. So we have to snuff him out." The tower light fizzled to life far above–threw red glow through the skylights and onto the chancel. "Your life is unremarkable, is it not? When you steal petty coins from dead homeless rats, what satisfaction do you get? It's enough to last one more day–buy one more can of beans or a shriveled vegetable at the market."

"Nothing wrong with that."

"Popping pills in a destitute apartment. Calling mother on the phone. Have you ever considered taking the whole bottle?"

Martin stepped forward–a half lunge. Reaching for his pistol.

The priest didn't move, or even flinch.

"And what of it?... Huh? You're fucking spying on me. You have cameras in my apartment? Microphones?"

Silence.

"Talk to me, old coot."

"You have a unique connection to Golgotha. He shows things to you."

A frown. "Is that right?"

"The catfish. Swimming in your tub."

His head started to swim. "That's… I've seen shit forever. I think it's the meds I'm taking. How the fuck did you know that?"

"Tell me about the man in the basement."

Martin's eyes peeled back–wide. "What did you say?"

Silence. The wrinkled mask was nothingness. Cold and without feeling. "What did grandpa say about the man in the basement? The bad man at the bottom of the stairs." The satin glove slipped out again from its red sleeve. It touched Martin's shoulder.

He was crying. Tears reflected the red overhead light.

"You saw him." Crystal blue eyes. Breath of sage. "He whispered to you in the dark. So long ago. King of Heaven."

"*King of Heaven...*" The room echoed. A hundred voices from the gathered worshipers. Like they were all under a spell. "*King of Heaven...*"

The Blessed Eye smiled. There were a million times and places behind his eyes, and a million voices spoke out in unison.

You
are
special,
Martin.
Find
Mr.
Crooked.
Bring
the
Cherub.

k i n g o f h e a v e n

"*King of Heaven...*" The voices shook the walls. "*King of heaven... KING OF HEAVEN... KING OF HEAVEN!*"

5

Slobber fell in hot strings from the mouth. The snout was flaring. Slow motion–like a dream. Hooves kicked up dirt; a cloud floated with the wind. Its horns were sharpened roughly. Muscle under night black fur contorted and pulsated.

"*El toro está enfadado, seguro.*"

Television light changed the color of the walls–an uncertain painter, with too many colors.

"*Mira mira. El torero. Mira... AY! Casi fue empalado!*"

Martin was sitting bolt upright. The sofa enveloped him. His eyes followed the bull. He could feel the rage in its black marble eyes, cutting through the fish-eye static. The Toreador pulled a thin sword–it hadn't been shown where from. Red fabric fluttered, spinning up and around. Unseen crowds wailed and shrieked. Hooves cut a wide, round trail, then the horns were lowered. A snap, and the Toreador was wrenched sideways. Blood welled from a hole in his sparkling, colorful silhouette. Pulsating.

Phone. Ringing.

Martin turned slowly and watched it skitter on the receiver. Got up, plucked it free. He waited in silence to hear a voice through the white noise.

"*Martin?*"

"Yeah?"

"*It's mama.*"

A pause. "Hi, mama."

"*How are you?*"

"I'm alright. How are you?"

Sputtering. "*Well, your aunt called again.*"

Silence.

"*But I hung up.*"

"Good. So you listened to me."

"*But then she came to my house and was pounding on the door for two hours–and screaming. My God. She said you were yelling at her and threatening her. Why did you do that?*"

His grip tightened. "What do you mean?"

"*When I opened the door, she'd beaten her fist bloody. It was all over the door.*"

"Why didn't you call the police?"

She coughed. "*Why would I call the police?*"

"Mama…"

"*It's that doll, hijo. Just give her back the doll, please?*"

"Please don't fucking ask me that anymore. Alright? Quit. I'm not giving her the doll, and if I have to shoot her in the fucking head to make her leave you alone, then that's what I'll do."

"*Martin. No you will not.*"

"Yes I will. Bitch deserves it. If you won't call the police, then I'll do it."

"*No, please. Don't get them involved.*"

"Then I'll blow her head off."

"*Stop! Stop saying that! You will not!*"

Silence.

"*If this is about your pride, hijo, ask yourself if it's worth it. Give the doll to her and she'll leave both of us alone.*"

"You know she won't."

"*She will.*"

"Like she did last time? With grandma's necklace?"

"*That was a different t-*"

"No it wasn't! Mama, for fuck sake! Stop it! Stop it! Stop it! STOP IT!"

CRACK!

Plastic shattered on the wall. Wiring spilled like guts. The force had plucked the power cable out of the wall, dragged the receiver off the counter. It all lay in a pile. Messily.

He stood looking down at it. Warmth. On his hand. There was blood seeping out of three thin cuts where the plastic shards had bit back.

—

Three tones ascending. Whistling spirits locked inside the rusting metal speakers. A pause, a snap of static, then a voice: "*To those who joined us yesterday at our abbey, we extend our thoughts of gratitude, and will pray for all of your souls. Police discovered the corpse of a young woman bent backward over an alley fence. Her spine was torn out. If you find Mr. Crooked, find the nearest phone and alert the police.*"

Martin could still smell the blood spilled there during the night. The air was hot, and hung low around him like a wet gossamer. They'd removed the body, but the fence was still covered in its seepage. It would be cleaned by rain and animal tongues. A spurt of wind threw dead leaves at his feet as he continued walking. Across the empty street was a black dog–thin and wiry. It looked like a jackal and its eyes were glowing. He stopped, met its stare.

It turned in place, then padded onto the dead grass of the park behind. An overpass loomed over the swingsets and dented metal slide. There was a hole in the concrete–

maintenance door, busted off its hinges. The dog went in.

And Martin followed.

Playground gravel crunched under his heels. A concrete slope lifted him to the space under the overpass. Unintelligible graffiti in hundreds of colors was splattered everywhere. Anarchy ejaculate. Through the maintenance doorway was a thick, black darkness. He pulled out his keys, found the little flashlight dangling from a chain. It spit into the shadow just helpfully enough.

There was no rumble of cars passing over his head. Dust was thick in the air. The graffiti spilled in from outside–coated every wall and every space on the floor and ceiling. Something smelled like fish.

No sign of the dog.

Pipes ran along the ceiling. He followed them.

A wall emerged from out of the dark. Dead end. But there was something taped to it. He squinted, aimed the flashlight.

SEXY SAMANTHA! Trendiest lingerie making 1998 sizzle.

Time had washed some of the color out of the glossy page. A half-nude woman was reclined on a couch, covered only by her bra and the bolded headline. Something dull had cut her paper eyes out of her paper head.

"The fuck…"

The light flicked away. It found a camping chair stuck into the corner. A rolled up paper was wedged into the drink pocket. He slid it free; it shed dirt. The handwriting was fast and sloppy: *Tourist Center Past the Fence. Art installation.*

He rolled it back up, replaced it. Something stuck against his boot. The light moved quick. Latex rubber, filled with mucus. And blood.

"Jesus." He headed for the doorway, shining the light into every corner–looking for the dog. But it wasn't there.

—

The road had once led out of town. Asphalt–poured straight and wide, until it curved to the left behind the soft edge of a hill. At the top of a short wall of dirt and rocks, the grass lifted to a treeline. Through the trunks was only darkness.

He kicked the steel fence pole. Vibration waves–left and right. On and on. It was rammed into the asphalt, reinforced on the outside by an angled girder. A sticker was flaking at eye-level, curved against the pole. *Radius Chain Link Fencing.*

The chain links were wrapped with sharp dagger points and barbs. A metal rosebush. In place of flowers, there were severed heads from dogs and cats and birds and squirrels. It all reeked. They were skewered on purpose, staring down any who approached them. Gods of the forest–or sacrifices to them.

Martin peered through again, searching for an opening between the mess. Light leaked through, into his eyes. Bright and warm.

Thunderheads snapped in the distant sky.

"It's not much better out there."

He pulled away, found the source of the voice. He recognized the uniform–just in time. His hand came away from his beltline, went back into his jacket pocket. "Morning."

"I could stamp, boy, you had some ill-advised intentions." The officer wore a gray shirt and trousers–tall black boots. He watched Martin from under the brim of a black campaign hat. "Or were you admiring the scenery?"

Martin looked up at the fence. A bloody rottweiler face looked back–crow-pecked and eyeless. "You were up at the abbey yesterday?"

The officer sniffed. "No, boy. On duty."

"Well… Roman Ward gave me a special task."

A pause. "That right?"

"I'm supposed to hunt down Mr. Crooked."

A smile. "That so?"

Silence.

"We've got boys in our force doing the same thing,

matter of fact."

Birds crossed over the fence, high over the treeline. He watched them for a moment. "Uh… I'm sure you do, sir. I just got special instructions."

"Well, I'll let you in on a secret, son. What mister Roman Ward says and does is none of my business." He spun his lanyard idly. There were keys on it, chittering in flight.

"Alright then."

"So you can go on back into town and look if you're so inclined." The lanyard caught, wound itself up around his hand, starting spinning the opposite direction.

"I'm thinking Mr. Crooked lives out past the fence."

Eyebrows lifted. "Yeah?"

Silence.

"What makes you say that, son?"

He smiled. "You wouldn't really believe me if I said."

"No, come on now."

The wind was getting colder. Martin sighed, shifted on his feet. "Would you let me through if I got permission from Roman?"

"If he came here and said it to my face."

Silence.

"If I had a dollar for every person who came up here saying old Santa Claus needed help at the North Pole filling a shift, I'd be Rockefeller. Mister Roman Ward doesn't even leave. There's no gate. What do you want me to do, son? Help you find a ladder?"

Martin smiled, scratched his beard. "No one tries running a truck through?"

The officer tilted his head.

"Thanks for the chat." He turned, started back down the road into town. Once he was far enough, he broke off–plunged into the trees. The underbrush was thick; it grabbed at his jacket and jeans. Fading sunlight sparkled through the canopies. Eventually he came to the fenceline–nearly blended with the colorless trunks and branches. A footpath was cleared alongside it for the patrolmen. He stayed off–hidden by the brush.

Endless metal chain. rusty spikes. Blood of desperate idiots, staining the rust. The officer stamped past, eyes down sometimes–searching sometimes. Martin kept going, paying attention to the fence.

Now he was by the park and the overpass–he saw it through the trees. He slowed down, paid more attention. The fence looked the same–a rotting, wiry spiderweb.

But there were trampled bushes.

And blood on the leaves.

He looked back up at the overpass. The maintenance doorway under the bridge was a dark portal. There might have been a pair of glowing eyes there, low to the ground, but it was too far away to tell.

The trampled bushes led to a section of the fence. It didn't seem peculiar. He checked left and right, then emerged onto the footpath. He could smell the rust. At least there were no more animal heads.

He touched the fence with his boot–gingerly. It seemed to give. Harder. It gave. When he let off, it eased back into place. "Oh… shit." He considered it. Ran his eyes along the snips in the chain links–now obvious when he knew they were there.

Clenched his fists.

Looked behind, into the trees. Wind was whipping the leaves and creating strange shapes in the darkness. Hesitation. Too much.

The lantern was approaching from around the corner, sparkling through the trunks.

Martin ducked back under cover–lay flat. The bushes and undergrowth swallowed him. Footsteps from the officer passed by, far too slowly. Then stopped.

Hot breath left Martin's lips, swirled against the dirt and back up into his face. He didn't dare shift, or a twig might snap. His ears perked up, hoping to pick out what the officer was doing by pure sound. It felt as though he had his back to a bear–was playing dead in the woods.

Swinging lantern. Footsteps. The light faded into

twilight, and the unsure shapes of the trees resumed their dancing.

Martin stood. Started moving. The walk back to his apartment was cold. He thought he saw dark shapes in every alleyway. A passing car with one headlight. It honked at him–he didn't know why. It made him jump. A distant scream–it could have been a coyote, or maybe a human. Outside his building, a hunched mass stood near perfectly still. In its rigor mortis fingers was an empty needle, dripping clear liquid from its sticker. The air reeked of body odor and burnt narcotics.

He grabbed the handle of the building's cage screen door, pulled it open, then tapped a code into faded rubber buttons beneath a lock. A beep. He slipped in, shut the door behind and heard the deadbolt slam into place.

The lobby was lit only by a sconce on the wall. The air smelled like unwashed carpet.

A deep breath. His hands were shaking. Out came the white plastic bottle. One pill sat in his palm. Then it was gone–swallowed. Back went the bottle, into his coat pocket.

There was peace and warmth in the lobby. Nothing could get in. The darkness here was different than the darkness outside. He passed under the sconce; there were moths fluttering circles around the bulb. Two halls dissolved into shadow left and right behind barricades of furniture. His finger woke the elevator button–made it glow orange. A hum. *Ding!* Metal doors parted. Behind them was a woman in a sundress and heavy parka. She stepped out, offered Martin a blank glance, conveying nothing. Before she could get to the front door, he was inside the rusting elevator, and the doors were beginning to close.

A hum.

He watched the buttons light up to indicate his upward movement, and thought about the border fence–wondered why he'd gone there at all.

He couldn't remember.

"Now we've just recently had some new neighbors move in. I'm sure y'all have been chatty about it by now–heard some rumors. The man himself is here to answer any questions y'all might have, so get 'em ready now. He's come up to our beautiful little town from Roanoke, and he's brought a group of his associates and colleagues. He's bought the big church up there on the hill, which was all run down and ready to cave in, and his colleagues and him are gonna be fixing it up. Today he's gonna be talking to you all about a movement he's started up... uh, called Transcensionism. It's all about living the best life you can live, and being kind to your fellow man–and as I see it, it's a sect of Christianity not dissimilar to that of our Lutheran or Baptist brothers and sisters. But I'll let him do the explaining himself–so here's Doctor Roman Ward."

Philip Masterson, Mayor of Snowy Oaks. Press conference 2011/08/02

His teeth snapped off a length from a meat stick clenched roughly in his hand. "Yeah, alright. Uh… give me a can of beans then. The spicy one with the bacon. Yeah." A string of white Christmas lights vomited fractalized light onto the man from above.

The vendor rifled through her stock.

"You hear about Chris?"

"No." A can of beans appeared in her calloused hands. The vendor was heavyset and scraggly. A butch wearing sparkling crystal earrings and gold bracelets. She scratched her collar bone between the splayed collars of a plaid shirt–set the beans down on the weathered counter.

"Pigs found his wife bent backward over a fence with her spine ripped out. After they told him, he went off to suck-start his shotgun." Another bite of the meat stick. "Mr. Crooked got her."

"That's the one got played over the speakers the other day."

"Yeah, right. Exactly the one." He roughly pocketed the bean can, replaced it on the counter with a handfull of coins. "Wonder what that freak's doing with the parts he takes."

"Huh?"

"Well he's taking parts from every body. That's what I'm getting from the reports. What's he doing with 'em?"

"Maybe he's feeding 'em to his pigs. Who gives a shit?"

She snatched up the coins and opened the zipper on her fanny pack. They twinkled as they fell in.

Martin sat down at one of the bar stools. The vinyl covering was stained and flaked nearly all the way to the stitching. He put his elbows on the counter.

"You look like a wet dog." A dim neon sign hovered above the vendor's head. *ROADRUNNER.* Glowing red. Deja vu. Her figure was washed out against the glow, and he thought he might blink and be back on that patio–that she would ask about his tattoos and he would offer to buy her a coffee. But when he blinked, he saw an old, stocky woman in a plaid shirt. "Yeah, Ethel. Thanks."

"What can I get for you?"

"Um… a coffee, please." His eyes walked along the back wall of the kiosk. Hung there were pitted metal road signs filled with bullet holes, water damaged pin-up posters and firefighter calendars, framed pictures of half-lit faces, and messy crayon drawings on crumpled papers. A coffee machine choked and squealed, then squirted dark liquid from its crusted nib. "I went into your old place this week."

Ethel turned. "Oh yeah?" A pause. "And?"

"There was, uh… there were lots of animals living in there."

She took the coffee cup out from the machine and set it down in front of him. "Animals, huh?"

"Yeah."

Her brow narrowed. "I haven't made a pastry in years. Last thing I baked was rock-hard bread. I fuckin' miss that shitty truckstop. Fuckin' Transcensionist cunts."

The man with the meat stick: "Why'd you sell it to 'em?"

"They hung a couple million in front of my face, mister. That's why. Now that's more than I ever made running that place. But where is that now, huh? I've got more god-damn money than the two 'a y'all put together, and all I can buy is cans 'a beans and meat sticks and shrunken little vegetables Yamato's garden shits out now and again."

Martin's coffee was a black mirror. Bubbles spun in circles.

"How do you get this food anyway, Ethel?" The meat stick was nearly half gone.

Thin, flaxy hair fell over her sopping brow. Violent motions ran a cloth around the inside of a coffee mug plucked out from the sink. "Guess it." She paused, then answered herself: "Fuckin' cultists give it to me. They've got me by my nuts. I've gotta pay 'em tax every month–what the hell for?"

"How… do they get the food?" Martin's nose twitched.

"Eh?"

He shifted. "I was talking to a patrolman by the fence–said the Transcensionists don't even leave town." Wind.

Coffee steam was pulled away from his cup.

"Bullshit. Them pigs don't know their pinky from their pecker. I drove up to get my goods one time and while I was loading the crates, I saw a box truck parked outside the fence behind the trees–least I swear to Jesus it looked like one. White sides, big wheels. Fence goes up there on the hill, you know–goes back behind their big ugly church. I'd bet you there's an exit way up behind it."

"Naw, it was probably just some truck left there and eaten up by vines and shit." What remained of the meat stick vanished into the man's mouth.

"Might be. But they get the food from someplace. And unless they've got some Mexicans growing the beans, it's from outside of town."

A sip of coffee. Martin heard a vehicle engine. He looked over his shoulder and saw a patchwork station wagon parting the small clusters of bodies in its path. It moved lethargically while irate figures came at it like dogs, bending over and pounding on the windows. Shrugs from the driver, flipping off, and a blaring horn. Someone shouted, "no vehicles, shithead! Foot traffic only!" Before long, a gray-clad man in a campaign hat tapped the windshield with his baton, and stuck his head in through the rolling-down window.

Ethel stacked her coffee cups. "Guy does that every

week. Says he's paralyzed from the waist down. Must be pushing the gas pedal with his dick."

"That's below the waist." The meat stick man pulled out a cigarette.

Searching fingers pulled a pill bottle onto the counter. Martin shook one out, swallowed it with some coffee. He looked back up–Ethel was watching. She didn't say anything. "You ever been outside the fence?" He waited for the man to realize he was speaking to him.

"I'm not dead, am I?" A puff of smoke.

"What's that mean?"

"Means I never tried it. Never got shot by a patrolman or skewered myself on the barbed wire."

"But Mr. Crooked gets in somehow. How does he do that?"

A snort from behind the counter.

The man leaned in, serious. His eyes were hard. "Now you're talkin' to the expert on Mr. Crooked, mister. I've been following everything–every little god-damn thing. I have theories on how this freak works. The church ain't telling much–just what they say on the morning announcements."

"Alright."

"What makes you think Mr. Crooked lives outside 'a town?"

A pause. "Uh… I guess they haven't found him yet.

Must mean he lives outside."

"Sewer system. Woods. Underground bunker, maybe. Left over from the fifties. That's where he'll be. There's patrolmen every fifty feet around the fence. Not one's come up dead or reported anything." Ash fell onto the counter, glowing.

A wet, filthy coffee filter came out of the machine–thumped heavily into a trash bin. "I'd bet Mr. Crooked doesn't exist at all. Church is probably killing these girls and using their parts for sacrifice." Ethel found a clean filter, fitted it back into the machine.

"Naw, he's a real man. But he's either real fuckin' good at hiding, or the pigs are working with him. Could be a pig himself, maybe. That'd be wack, alright. And I wouldn't even put it past 'em. Who knows what he looks like? Ain't been no sketches or descriptions or nothin'. Could be you, could be me. But there ain't no god-damn way he lives outside the fence. Every night'd be a risk coming in and sneaking past the pigs. You tell me he never once slipped up?"

Martin finished his coffee–slid the mug away. "Yeah, fine. Guess you're right."

Behind him, the station wagon was leaving, escorted by the cop. He turned to watch, and thought he saw something through the car's back window. A face, watching right back–

pale as death. Maybe a reflection, caught at the right angle.

—

She shut off the engine. A *Chevrolet SSR*, black like the rest of everything she owned. Her little, pale face was just visible through the driver's side window. It was smiling at him. The door opened–out came a chunky black boot and fish net stocking. "Do you like it?"

He scanned the car front to back. "Yeah, it's cool. Like a pick-up truck for girls."

Flying fists, pounding lightly on his chest. She was enveloped by his arms and squeezed tight, giggling and trying to kiss his neck. "I'm gonna eat you. Okay? Eat you up until you're all gone." Pointer and thumb came together–she held the gesture up to his face. "'Til you're that big. Just a little crumb."

Lips peeled into a smile. He kissed her forehead, then made a cartoony chewing sound as he buried his face into her hair. Through her manic laughter, he said: "Alright, open up your girly truck and we'll start."

Keys came out from her jacket pocket. Once he let her go, she walked to the trunk, stabbed it with a selected key. The flatbed top ascended like the upper jaw of a yawn, revealing cardboard boxes.

He frowned. "Are there more?"

"Nope." She idly fingered his sleeve. "I'll probably spend most of my time in your place, so this is just the minimum I need to convince my parents I'm not if they ever come over."

A smile. "They could've saved a lot of money if you just moved in with me."

Her eyes widened and she feigned sudden concern. "But sweetheart, what if you break up with him!" She grabbed his shoulders and shook him back and forth. "What if you break up with him!"

Long arms wrapped around her again and held her close. "Okay then. Let's move all your fake shit."

"It's not fake. It's minimal."

"Ah, right. Minimal. For the minimalist." He unwound himself from her and reached into the trunk to grab a box.

7

He used a dustpan to collect the shards of his shattered phone. The main body sat amongst them like picked-over carrion in some desert savanna–electronics exposed and wiring intestines spilling out onto the kitchen tiles. It hung from a reluctant grip as if he'd plucked it out of a dumpster. His boot stomped the lever on the kitchen garbage bin–lid flung open, hungry. He fed it the corpse phone, then it slammed shut loud and rattling.

Now he stood there, hand on the peeling faux-wood countertop.

Searching fingers ran through every pocket until they found his flip phone. The little plastic keys snapped like insects under his fingertips. A dial tone… waiting. He softly kicked the base of the counter; dark streaks were left across the white paint.

"*The number you have dialed is currently unavailable. Please leave a message at the tone.*" *BEEP!*

A breath. "Uh… Hi, mama. I'm just… I'm really sorry. I haven't snapped in months, but something really… uh… … …" He trailed off. "It just hurts me when you don't take my advice seriously. I'm trying to help you. I got mad 'cause I know that bitch is really upsetting you–and she's hurting you–so I'm giving you advice on this and you're not listening. Call me, okay? On my cell–I uh… my landline isn't working right now. I love you… Bye." The plastic clam shut and fled back into his pocket.

Wind–a strong gust–started to rap on the window.

He traversed his sickly lit living space, going from the kitchen to the living room to the bedroom to the bathroom to the vent in the wall. Got down. Looked through into her world. She was there this time, sitting on a shag carpet with her back against the bed. Facing him. If she knew where to look, their eyes would meet. In her hands was a book. Though the cover was faded, he could read faint titling. *I Have No Mouth, and I Must Scream.*

Flip... Flip... Flip....

"Ouch… shit." Her brow furrowed. Paper cut, maybe. She looked down at her thumb for a moment, pulled the skin. It must have been superficial; she went back to reading.

—

"What is this?"

"It's a short story about a computer that kills everyone except for… like, four or five people. 'Cause it wants to keep them alive and torture them forever."

"Why?"

"'Cause it hates humans."

"Why?"

"'Cause they created it."

She was straddling him on the couch, forehead planted against his. The book was between them in the little cavern created by their bodies. They both looked down at it–watched as her fingers pulled the pages. Her nails were painted sparkling black. Light flickered there. "That's kinda sick." A pause. "If you were a computer, would you kill me or keep me around?"

A smile. "Keep you around forever."

"Would you torture me?"

"No. Probably not."

"What if I asked you to?"

He slipped his hand up under her arm and tickled. She squirmed and giggled, then kissed him. Her breath tasted like coffee. Her hair smelled like charcoal as it fell around his face. When her lips came away, she looked into his eyes, and he looked into hers. They were dark pools of warm water, caressed gently by moonlight.

"I love you."

He felt himself smiling. "Never leave me, Bonnie."

She kissed him again.

—

A tear came down, rolled across his cheek. It collected, then fell onto the hardwood. Somewhere deep beneath him, the apartment began to breathe. Hot air was exhausted into his face. The noise drew her attention. For a second–or two–their eyes met. Breath froze in his chest and his heart skipped. Like it had when he'd seen her face for the first time.

But she didn't notice him behind the vent cover. The book soon had her attention once more.

Flip... Flip... Flip...

And his phone rang.

It made him strike his elbow against the floorboards. With gritted teeth, he got up to a sitting position–pulled the flimsy vibrating clam out of his pocket. "Mama?"

Silence. Then: "*No.*"

"Sorry… uh… yes?" He suddenly had a headache.

"*This is Roman.*"

"Oh."

"*How are you, Mister Navarro?*" Background noise.

Thuds and muffled speech.

Martin got to his feet and went back to the kitchen counter. “I’m fine.”

“*How is it going?*”

“How is what?”

Silence.

He gathered up something to say from amongst his cluttered thoughts. “I found a cut part of the border fence. There was a dog.”

“*Yes.*”

“Yes?”

“*The dog is friendly, I’m sure.*” A deep, static-y breath. “*Did you go through the hole in the fence?*”

“No. I didn’t.”

“*Please do.*”

Martin shifted on his feet. Pushed hair out of his eyes. “Why should I do that? I’m not looking to get shot.”

“*But you won’t. Golgotha won’t allow it. You are very close, Mister Navarro, to making something of yourself. Think of how you will be treated as the man who found Mr. Crooked.... Your mother would be proud of her boy. The hero of Snowy Oaks. No longer the man you once were–no way to deny it then. Do you understand what I mean?*”

He gripped the phone hard. “How do you know about that shit?”

"*I believe I've already explained it to you.*"

His words stuck in his throat.

"*Will you do it tonight, please? Before another young woman is raped and dissected?*" A pause. "*Oh, Mister Navarro: young women love a hero.*"

Click.

Flustered hands pulled down along his face–ran through his mess of hair. He put away his phone and glanced at the open vent hole. It had his gaze held tight–stirred contemplation. He felt for his gun, pulled his coat off the wall and opened the front door.

—

Under nightfall, the shadows cast by the impaled animal heads made it look like they were moving–turning to follow him as he crept through the bushes. The crest of the fence, studded in barbed wire, was the only part of it clearly seen against the backdrop of the dusky sky. The rest of it blended with the natural overgrowth of the Virginia countryside. A tall post stuck up above the fenceline. Atop it perched another metal speaker, as well as an industrial light–now dead. Maybe burnt out, maybe turned off.

Martin stopped behind a tree–watched one of the border patrolmen with his lamp, making his way along against the fence. Once he was out of sight, Martin moved up. He got as close to the patrolmen's dirt pathway as he dared, then followed it as he had before. All the way until he could spot the concrete overpass through a gap in the trees–and the portal into darkness where he'd followed the dog.

A lamp. He waited, flat on his stomach.

Faint chatter getting loud: "*F..king... as...ole... To...ledo. Some...one's* gotta smoke that son-of-a-bitch one day. God… Now I'm in a god-damn mess of shit." The officer was talking to the ground, lazily swinging his rifle. He stopped to peer through the chainlinks, lifting his lamp as if it might brighten the expanse of woods on the other side. "Jesus… makes ya wonder. Ha! Throw Toledo out there at night and listen to him screaming. Eaten by wolves, yes sir." He started moving again. Before long, the light of his lamp was gone, and Martin approached the fence.

Careful exploring. His fingertips searched for the cut links. When he felt sharpness, he pulled away, then launched his hands back forward again. The cutout was done cleanly, allowing for minimal shaking of the fence when the section was pulled open. But he still managed to send tremors up and down into the darkness. A boot wedged in to get leverage. He found a handhold that wouldn't give him tetanus, then assisted his foot. He pressed himself through, careful of his exposed neck. Awkwardly. He let go, pulling his hand away.

It shook the whole fence violently. He sprinted for cover–dove into the tallgrass.

Silence.

Now a crawl–up the bluff and into the treeline. He waited, listening to his breathing. Once or twice, he heard a passing patrolman on the other side of the fence–saw the vestiges of lamplight twinkle through the gaps. Still, he waited. The night was paralyzing–the expanse of forest stretching off into oblivion. There was no more fence. He was outside. It occurred to him that he could run away now, but that thought was gone as fast as it had spawned. Like something had killed it. Something that wasn't him.

Then he heard footsteps. On his side.

His throat shut, eyes widened. He'd already put his hand by his pistol; now he gripped it tight and clicked the safety.

The steps grew louder–heavier.

He smelled blood and sweat.

Felt radiant warmth.

Then a lumbering giant passed by only a few feet away. The dusk had gone completely now, making it impossible to tell any details. But it was massive. It was carrying something bladed. A tool with a long shaft. One large hand pulled the section of fence aside. Something grabbed its attention about it. The night hid its face, but it turned–

scanned the treeline.

Martin didn't let out his breath until it was long gone–through the fence and into the town.

The darkness was a weighted blanket. After a while, the light of the patrolling officer twinkled again. If it had only been two minutes early…

A gust of wind. Caresses on his chin–gently. The fingers of God, pulling his attention to the side, where a dog stood erect in the swaying switchgrass. Its eyes were white, just like before–glowing pinpoints beneath pointed jackal ears. The eyes made him stand up out of the bushes. The eyes made him follow.

—

Snowy Oaks Tourist and Historical Center

The air smelled of pine. Woods leered on every side, venturing curious branches into the clearing. Grabbing for nothing. There was no porchlight by the door–no light in the windows. The building was a quiet goliath just off the winding road.

Martin stepped off the asphalt and onto gravel. This was once a parking lot, but there were no cars anymore. Foliage grew over the welcome sign; rainwater had dragged the paint of a cartoony cardinal mascot. Below it read: *Hi! I'm*

Cardel! I'm a Northern Cardinal, the state bird of Virginia! Welcome to Snowy Oaks, and enjoy your visit!"

Paws scratched on wood. Then the dog was gone through a swinging doggie door.

Martin climbed the wood plank steps, gun in hand. His breath fogged the dirty windows; there were curtains shut behind them. Wind made the trees talk and dance–rustling madly.

He pulled open the door–no lock.

A smell barreled into him on its way out. Sour and sweet. Enough to close his throat and force a gag. "What the fuck…" Then came the sounds–mechanical and rhythmic, like a hundred clocks all keeping different times. It was too dark to see them.

He entered, shut the door. His sleeve sealed poorly over his nose, but it kept some of the smell out. After some fumbling, he had his flashlight, and he cast its glow around.

A face, to the left of the door.

His heart rattled, and he aimed his pistol. "Hey!"

Silence.

"Are you fucking deaf?" He waited. "Do you live here?"

Silence.

The head turned, stopped. Turned, stopped. Turned, stopped. He moved the light onto the woman's body. She was fully naked–fingers rigid and outstretched, arms locked at a ninety-degree. They pivoted at the shoulders–up and down. Up and down. He moved the light again–down to the legs, and noticed the steel pole bolted to the floor.

His vision started to blur.

BANG!

The front door flung open and some hundred pounds of weight knocked him to the ground. The hulking thing grunted; every breath was raw and angry.

Pain, then darkness.

8

"Ya know, kid… I smelled ya from the off."

He opened his eyes and saw he was standing on the ceiling–or else the grotesque was hanging from the floor. A kerosene lamp burned quietly on a crooked desk. The odor it gave off mingled with the sourness of the air. The hulking thing sat in a too-small chair, hunched over–long greasy hair. It continued: "I put my sneakhole right. Every time. Pigs don't notice it that way."

There was something off in its deep, Virginia drawl. Martin squinted and saw a face–one that shouldn't belong to a living thing. Everything from nose to brow was crunched upward, pulling back the upper lip to expose gray toothrot. He couldn't see eyes if there were any–just swollen pits.

"You talk, kid?"

A cough. "*Hah…. fuck…*"

"You're a geeker, kid. Moan like a two dollar whore."

Martin looked up–or maybe it was down. Thick rope

bound his legs together–and to a steel crossbeam bolted to the walls. He swung a bit, bent his knees with a hard effort. It lifted him slightly, but his blood had all gone to his head. He went limp.

Wet laughter. "You're a fun little fucker, ain't ya? Most lively one in the room."

His struggling made him spin. As he did, the rest of the room came into view, and he saw he wasn't the only thing hanging. Rusty hooks clipped to chains were pushed through soft, dead flesh. Naked human corpses bisected from head to crotch, like pigs in an abattoir. "Fuck!"

"You like my girls? Don't touch 'em now. Keep that little cock in ya pants or I'll make ya sing castrato in the school choir."

"What the fuck!"

The brutalized mouth peeled into a grin. "Watcha doing runnin' around outside the fence? Eh? Y'all are cattle in y'alls pen. Can't have runaways now." Beside him was a mattock, leaned up against the desk. The flat end was sharpened and the wooden handle was stained red. "Gonna come and disturb farmer Forsyth, eh? I'm a butcher, kid, and you wandered under my cleaver. I only work with heifers, ya understand. Bulls ain't loose enough. They ain't sweet."

"Cut me down!"

Mucus was pulled into the hulking thing's throat, then

spat out. "Nah. Can't let any a' y'all just enter my living space. This here's a private residence." Up came the mattock; metal dragged heavy across the floorboards. "Got work to do now." A heavy hand pushed open the door. Tinny slide guitar was playing on a radio somewhere. Fluorescent light shone across a lumpy, black garbage bag–the shadows had been hiding it. "Caught one last night. Needed a spine." A pause. "I'll come back around before long. There's work needs doin' and you're a capable bull."

The door shut tight. A lock snapped into place on the other side.

It wasn't long before the lantern sputtered out, leaving Martin in the dark–under the watch of a dozen cold, pale faces.

Time passed.

Maybe an hour, or two or three.

Wind hammered the walls–shook the room and made the hanging meat sway. The smell was awful. Overwhelming–coating the soft interior flesh of his nostrils like grease. Blood was pooling in his brain, blurring his vision.

"What's a nice boy like you doing in a place like this?"

His neck muscles pushed hard to move his bowling ball head. "That's a good god-damn question."

"You're in a mess 'a trouble, honey."

He blinked. "Looks like y'all are in worse."

He could see the bisected mouth and throat constricting and loosening with the effort of speech. Half a set of lips went to flapping: "Tell me about it. I'm hanging up here with my tits and guts out. Ain't no blood in me anymore. I bet I look like a snowman."

"You're damn pale, that's for sure." His eyes wandered over the woman. Most of the organs had been pulled, leaving empty cavities. "How'd he get you?"

"Eh?"

"Catch you. Where'd he catch you from?"

She used her one attached arm to gesticulate. "I danced down at Country Hoes. You ever been there?"

"Uh, no. Can't say so."

"Shithole. It's under Leland's–that little pleasure house by uh… the bridge there on-"

"-Yeah, I know it."

"Just fine. So anyway I was coming out the back one night and walking home. There was this group of crickers or something near the water. I didn't want nothing to do with 'em, so I went wide on that path by the treeline. You know that one?"

"Ya."

"Right, so shitstack jumps out of the woods and snatches me up–pulls me through to the fence and out. Then he buries that metal pick or whatever he's got into my neck to keep me from yappin' too loud. Next thing I know, I'm dangling here." Her arm came around to itch the soggy, gray flesh inside her torso.

"That's tough."

"Damn right. The other girls here had it worse, though–some of 'em."

"That right?"

"See that dark girl over behind me? That's Nellie." A dead finger pointed. "Mister-fucked-nosejob decided to get his rocks off with her corpse after he pulled her head off–with his bare hands, by the way. Did it right in this room, so I saw the whole show."

Martin felt the nerves in his hands start to fizzle. The numbness crept slowly up his arms. "Well, so happens I'm supposed to bring the fucker to the abbey on the hill. Mister Roman Ward wants to have his way with him."

Martin got to see how the human throat constricts around laughter. "Ha! Great job, honey. You're doing fine."

He didn't have the energy to respond.

"Tell you what… I might be able to help you out."

"How's that?"

"Turn around for a second."

He obeyed, forcing his muscles to comply. Nothing happened. There was only the rattling of the wooden walls–the odor.

Crack!

Luck somehow kept him from snapping his neck on the floorboards. He lay in a heap, clothing sticky against the coating of blood on the ground. His throat blew air like a rusty flute. It took a minute for feeling to come back to his limbs, then he got to his feet–a swimmer through reality. The monstrosity had left his pistol on the crooked table. He retrieved it–stuck it back through his belt. A glance over his shoulder at the corpses–silent now. Clouded eyes, like dead fish–mouths hanging.

He gripped the door handle. Locked.

All his force and energy was transferred through his boot into the latch. The hinges screamed and the door struck the outer wall. His pistol came out, preceded him into the hallway.

Nothing.

The main room reeked just as awfully. Motors turned gears, which lifted metal bones. There could have been sixty automatons, each involved in a unique imitation of life. All were women, some nude–exposing Frankenstein stitching–others clothed in dirty garments.

He crossed the room–a foyer. Sunlight poured in through the building's front doors.

Scratching… pencils on paper. Dead hands scribbled lines of gibberish while floating heads tracked back and forth. Beside them, a lifeless face mashed itself into a stack of bricks. By the doors, a woman held her hands over her breasts and flapped her elbows up and down like a chicken. Her eyes were glass–her eyelids had been cut off.

Martin pulled open the doors and slipped out. He sprinted for the treeline and dove under cover. Then he lay, looking up at the shifting leaves. The clouds made shapes while they drifted.

He ran back home through the woods, seeing shadows following behind. Once he had reached the fence, he waited for the patrolmen. The fear made his eyes water. His neck was a swivel and his head a wind vane, never keeping still. Left, right, back, then left again. Over and over. Once the lantern had gone behind the fence, he tore the cut section back and leapt through, not caring how he left it. Then he walked home, and didn't feel safe until he was behind the codelock and metal screen door of his apartment building.

—

A chicken beat its wings, throwing feathers.

Three ascending mellotron keys. The thin metal speakers trembled at what they spit into the air: Gregorian choral beneath the announcer's inhuman drone. "*Friday is the Splitting of the Curtain. This week shall be one of preparation and jubilation. Please join in the prayer: 'Exalted King who walks for two; Center of our worldly form; Grace above all other things; Guide in what I'm wont to do, Guide of hand and fire rod; Sword of Heaven 'gaist the storm; Touched me in my mother's tow; So I knew the Word of God.*'"

A truck with a welded sheet metal shell rumbled along with the road all to itself. Foot traffic jumped clear of the hot breath from the front grill. *GMC Syclone.* The badge was rimmed in rust.

Martin hammered on a metal door. "Hey! Ayla!"

Silence.

"Open up! I'm not fucking around!"

Gray figures passed across the mouth of the alley. The chicken stood by a dumpster, pecking at something. It clucked.

He pulled his hand out of his pocket and tried the handle. It gave. The door swung inward. Instead of incense and warmth, there was nothing rushing out to meet him. He stood in the doorway, looking around–at looted shelving units and empty boxes. Concrete basement walls were canvasses for angled sunrays.

His one wary footstep snapped around the room, then cut off. Shattered mason jars littered the floor with their sharp entrails. He didn't go in further. Faded, ink-labeled cardboard boxes were strewn amongst the mess. *Pfizer. Siemens. Cardinal. 3M.*

"What… the…"

No hanging beads. No rugs and cushions. No Ayla.

He shut the door.

—

The abbey's doors were never closed, except at night. Under the morning sunlight, a robed man knelt by a crop of flowers. Beside him on the grass was a trowel and a pair of rusty shears.

Martin felt his bottle of pills in his pocket. He took two, then approached the grand doorway. Stopped. Stood. He turned to watch the robed man trickle water into the dirt from out of a wooden cup. If he'd noticed Martin's presence, he was ignoring it.

The wind was playing the building's high ceiling at a discordant tone. He looked up and noticed for the first time a hundred or more statues up near the windows: angelic creatures with uncertain forms and the wings of birds. They hung against the walls amidst marble clouds. Beneath this stone conflagration, sparsely populated pews cradled penitent figures.

He walked up the center.

The Blessed Eye stood off to the side of the pulpit–watching already with his crystalline vision. His robe enveloped him, like the wrapped wings of a dragon. He waited for Martin to stop at the foot of the chancel, then he sucked in a long breath. “I’ve seen what you’ve seen.”

Martin fell to his knees–rested his forehead against the chancel. Tears were tugging at the back of his throat.

“Such a vile creature.” Another breath. “The extent of his cruelty was humbling… But you had no reason to fear for yourself. Golgotha walks where you walk.”

Silence.

“Mr. Crooked can’t hurt you with earthly things.”

Martin sank back to sit on the black carpet. He couldn’t find anything to say.

Fluttering. A bird sailed in through the open door and found a perch. It was a cardinal–feathers blood red.

The Blessed Eye kept his eyes on Martin. “Birds are special things, can I tell you?”

Silence.

“They’re spirits from Heaven coming back for a visit. Most are those who have transcended checking in on what they left behind.” His hands shifted under his robes. “We see many Cardinals in our abbey. All the time. Cardinals are the servants of Golgotha–the Seraphs, you’ll remember.”

Martin looked up at him. Held his breath.

The bird had appeared on the priest's shoulder without a sound.

"They ask me things, and I answer them." A glove slipped out through the robe; a seed was pinched in two fingers. Then it was gone, snapped up in a small, red beak. "And pray the answer satisfies them."

Wings spread and the bird leapt off. It passed behind the Blessed Eye, and Martin expected to see it appear again on the other side… it didn't. It had vanished behind his head.

"Your gun won't kill the cherub. You must have faith. Force it to reveal itself and Golgotha will act through you."

Martin got to his feet. "I'm not going back to that shithole."

"Yes, you are."

"Why not go yourself? Or send the police?"

A pause. "The cherub is shielding itself."

He scratched his head, then his beard. "Can I… Just… Pull Golgotha out of me, then? Put him into you?"

"I'd have done it already."

Silence. Martin shook his head. "Fuck." He stared hard at the Blessed Eye–adjusted his coat, sniffled and rubbed his jaw. "Why is Mr. Crooked making those… fucking… robots. Sculptures, or whatever the fuck they are?"

The light in the tower went red. Some kind of mist began to emanate through the stone gridlines on the wall behind the chancel. It fell like a waterfall. Stray tendrils wrapped around the trail of the priest's robe. "A man longs for feminine company. Even one as malformed and ugly as him. Women can't run if they're gutted and rammed through with metal bones." Shifting in the ambient light made it look like the man's eyes were weeping crystal tears. It conjured images of a mournful Christ.

"I thought he was a cherub?"

Behind the priest was a wash of grain and light. "Mr. Crooked is, no doubt. But the man is a simple farmer, whose body has been forcibly impregnated. A cat farmer, who used to breed cats."

Then Martin blinked his eyes and the Blessed Eye's face was no longer human. It was feline–black cat, with eyes of swirling endlessness. Another blink, and it was human again.

"I…"

He blinked again, and saw the cat. Another blink–the man.

The cat.

The man.

One more blink. Now it wasn't either. He was looking into the face of a woman. A pretty woman, with a comforting smile…

... “If you were a cat, what cat would you be?”

"What?"

"Like... what color?"

He was looking through the bars of a kennel. Under the shadow's cover was a skinny persian. Its eyes were crystal blue.

"I'd probably be a black one."

He looked to his left.

Bonnie nearly had her nose stuck through another set of bars. She wiggled a pale finger–got the cat inside to touch it with a paw. "This guy's cute, though. I like his little mustache. Look here… look at it." Her yank on his arm was bateless. "He's got a little mustache like you."

A wide grin split uncontrollably as she tickled his upper lip. He kissed the top of her head, then peered into the kennel. "He looks like a wet mop."

"Oh my God." She held out her finger. The cat touched it. "He's a nice little guy."

Claws slipped out silently, and the cat tried to pull her finger into its mouth.

"Hey you!" She pulled away.

"What breed is this?" He looked for a tag–saw nothing.

Heat tickled the back of his neck. He heard labored breathing.

"That there's a Selkirk Rex. Y'all like him?"

Martin turned.

The man was nearly seven feet. Rolled up sleeves bared scars running up and down–some deep into flesh. A scratched up vinyl apron was pulled tight over a hefty gut. "Oh… This here's for their claws–keeps em out 'a me when I trim nails or move 'em around." A rusty truck from the fifties sat like a skeleton in the tallgrass behind him. Flaking painted words on the door read: *FORSYTH CAT BREEDER*. He pulled off a glove, extended a hand. "Rhett Forsyth, like it says on the truck."

"Martin Navarro."

He turned to Bonnie. "Pleasure, miss. Are you looking to buy? Business–I have to say–is slower than molasses going uphill in winter. But these critters are all sterile and medicated."

"Oh, well… I don't know. I don't think I have time with work and everything." Bonnie folded her arms into her sleeves.

"You two are… Do y'all live together?"

She smiled. "Uh… No. We just started going out, uh… not too long ago now."

The breeder put a finger in his ear–scratched around. "I see. Just browsin' then. That's alright."

The stack of kennels was alive with noise and vibration.

Martin put his hands in his pockets. "Do you breed them at your home?"

"Yessir. I do. I run the tourist center up the road there as well."

"Oh, okay."

The breeder crushed his ballcap in his hands. "I bring 'em in sometimes and let 'em run around. Kids go crazy for 'em, you know?"

Martin chuckled. "Yes, sir. I can imagine that."

"Y'all should come by sometime. Are you… I don't know if y'all are familiar with the forests around town? Lots 'a trails and places to sit for a picnic, or what-have-you." He refitted his ballcap–wiggled it back and forth until it sat straight.

"Well, I was born here, but I can't say I ever went up too far into the woods. My mom was always scared of bobcats and serial killers and that sort."

The breeder snorted. "Might have some wildlife deep in the brush, but there ain't no serial killers in a small town like this–and I'll eat my damn boot." He threw his gaze onto Bonnie. "You ever change your mind, darling, you come on down to the tourist center and I'll let you have your pick of any little critter you like. A pretty girl needs a pretty cat."

BANG!

It sounded like ricochets from an automatic rifle. One after the other.

Martin looked back at the kennels. The doors had all flipped open. The breath he sucked in was dry and prickly–like he'd inhaled smoke.

Bonnie was gone. The breeder was gone.

"Roman?" His tongue was dry. "What the fuck is this?"

There was a faint noise from the kennels; whatever made it was hidden within beige plastic walls.

He stepped towards them.

"*M.... ti..... He....p....M.....e.*"

A sour odor. It invaded his nose–wafted out from the kennel's mouth.

"*Mar.....in...... hel..... me...*"

Sticky slime began to dribble at the corners, then it collected on the plastic lip in a glossy line. The sun hadn't left the sky, and it beat down on him relentlessly. Heat and smell. A dumpster in the summer, or roadkill on hot pavement. Muscles contracted at the back of his throat.

"*Martin..... help..... me....*"

He bent down–peered into the kennel's maw.

—

The black carpet had left its impression in his palms.

Roman stood upon the chancel, watching. "A memory."

Martin flipped himself and vomited chunks and acid into the carpet fiber. Contractions in his torso–up his throat and chest. The acrid waves sucked tears from his eyes. Three bouts emptied his stomach. Afterward, he lay half-propped up, hair hanging over his face.

"Quite the motivation." The priest stepped closer to the edge of the chancel, hidden boots cracking hollow reverberations. "Perhaps enough to inspire some gumption. Maybe you'll agree?"

Martin got up and headed for the door, all the while feeling the crystal eyes on his back. The image from the kennel had been branded across the gray flesh of his mind. No matter what he did, he couldn't even veil it.

Her body… twisted and broken.

Arms and legs bent to fit the space inside the plastic box, and her face looking out at him–empty, and screaming.

"Snowy Oaks mayor Philip Masterson has died. He passed away at seven-thirteen this morning at the Saint Cosmas hospital after a four day long battle with an as-of-yet unknown illness. Masterson reportedly experienced flu-like symptoms, as well as pulmonary edema–or liquid in his lungs–according to a press release from his P.R. team near the onset of his condition. A spokesperson for an anonymous councilman alleges Masterson was poisoned by members of the Church of the Holy Transcension, who have been purchasing a large amount of property around town for around six months. Council members are calling it a 'plot to overtake the town' and say the death of Masterson is a step in that direction. The church's leader, Roman Ward, answered our request for a statement, denying the church's involvement in Masterson's death and offering his condolences. Last year, the church purchased the Church of Saint Francis from the state of Virginia and have since

begun an expansion and renovation, which is set to conclude near the end of next year. A Catholic funeral for the mayor will be held at the Abbey on Sunday in what Ward is calling a 'gesture of good faith.'"

The Snowy Oaks Herald 2012/04/25

Someone other than himself was staring back at him through the mirror. It looked exactly like him, but missing the spark of life inside a human being. He reached out to touch it–his fingers met on the polished membrane. No warmth. Just a cold, bathroom mirror.

He put the pistol to his chin.

Waited.

Nothing happened.

He turned the gun on the mirror. He could see the darkness inside the barrel–or rather, the darkness inside the barrel inside the mirror. His own eyes stared back at him, until he had to look away.

Snap!

A sudden web appeared in the glass. Paint was smudged in the center–rubbed off the butt of his pistol. "I'm not… kidding around."

Silence.

His drawers rattled open. Junk inside clattered and shook. When he found what he wanted, he shut it with his hip and unfolded his utility knife. The blade hovered over itself, razor tips nearly touching. When they met, the glass was marred. One long slash–dust glass twinkled as it fell into the sink. Another slash. More dust. He drew a long, winding trail, across the cracks–intersecting with itself. A cloud of ice, frozen in the membrane. It grew until he couldn't see his reflection anymore.

Fizzling static.

He went out into the living room. White noise sparkled and popped behind the glass of his television–fly swarm in a jar. The pistol butt cracked against its plastic forehead; signal was restored for some thirty seconds before the analog blizzard was swept up again.

Mellotron. Three notes. It invaded his apartment through the window. He met it at the window sill–leaned out to look over the street. "*Engaging in carnal pleasure without permission from the Holy Lord is the strictest sin, and will be punished with impunity. All underground brothels and dens of debauchery uncovered by police will be burned–and their occupants slaughtered. Those who bring tips on the locations of these dens to authorities shall be rewarded by the Church of the Holy Transcension.*" A snap. A pop. Then the monotone robotic voice said: "*A young woman was found dead under the Patts Avenue overpass. Her eyes were removed, and her lower jaw ripped off. If you see Mr.*

Crooked, find the nearest phone and alert the police."

Ten or so passersby on the sidewalk, going about their business. A lithe young man beat the air with his fist, screamed up at the metal loudspeaker: "Fuck you! Cultist, dirty pigs! Get fucked!"

Martin scanned the horizon. Patches of forest with the occasional rooftop growing out above. A distant wall of mountains, and hills stacked up to meet them. In the distance, a column of black smoke was lifting into the sky. He leaned back in, looked to his left. Mousie the puppet was plunked on the chest of drawers–just as always. "What's happening to me?" No answer to his question. "Feels like I'm dreaming." He marched over to where his coat was hanging by the front door–probed its pocket until he found the pill bottle. The cap popped. He tipped it into his hand.

Nothing.

He looked inside the mouth. Empty plastic shell. "Oh shit." *Plock!* The bottle struck the kitchen floor after a brief sail through the air. His head was aching again. Now he had nothing to stop it.

Bonnie's room was quiet through the vent. He shifted to get comfortable–tweaked his side. Sharp pain, like his lungs were punctured. A rough massage from his one hand did little to calm it down. He could see the vent cover in the reflection of her standing mirror; he stared for a moment. He was staring at himself, though the version of him behind the reflection was hidden by the cover. It was the version of himself he'd stared down in the bathroom. A separate set of eyes. He felt the urge to sit up so those eyes couldn't see him–but he didn't.

There was no sign of Bonnie. Only indications of her presence: the book on the floor beside her bed; a bra thrown aside on the carpet; the bedsheets tangled up and messy. He rolled his gaze around the room over and over again, as if she might appear in his peripheral. But the apartment was dead.

His headache worsened.

"*Martin...*"

From her bedroom door. Barely a whisper. His eyes snapped in its direction. There was a figure there dressed entirely in black. A pale, bald head was facing him straight-on; the skin was almost translucent. It was a face familiar to some deep part of his mind, though his shallow parts couldn't recall it. Wide eyes–lidless. Pinpoint black pupils. It looked as though the eyes were part of the skin–no separation, no ridges. Where there should have grown eyebrows or even lashes was smooth, veiny skin. And where there should have been lips was nothing at all. Skin. Just more skin.

"*Hey...*"

Martin's body stiffened.

"*Hey...*"

He couldn't move.

"*Will you tell me what you saw in the basement?*"

Something external reached down into his throat and pulled his voice out: "It was a man, but he had no mouth. Mama… he's standing behind you." He forced his teeth shut. "Get the fuck out of my head…"

Springs squeaked. The bed. Bonnie was lying there, legs spread open. Her face was twisted in agony as she flailed and bunched the bedsheets in her fists. It looked like she was screaming, but nothing was coming out. Like a pantomime of rage. As Martin watched, a dark wet blob crept out of her vulva, dripping slime onto the carpet. She pushed, wracking her body with spasms. More of the thing emerged, pulling pink flesh apart around it.

All the while, the figure in the doorway kept its eyes on Martin, still as a shadow.

More. The thing was taking shape now–but not any recognizable one. As its wider sections were forced out, Bonnie started to thrash and cry dark black tears that stained the bedspread. Blood was squirted in a jet from between her legs, then more slime. The wall in front of her was awash with viscera and awful color. Another spasm, and the thing started to sag with gravity. A final push seemed to give it life.

Two wide black wings erupted from the shape and started to flap awkwardly, throwing fluids around the room. It was stuck, flapping–wings smacking her legs and beak nipping at her genitals. Suddenly, the legs were out, and the bird flopped into a wet pile on the ground, fluttering and beating madly. Violent sounds were choked out through its beak. Something like a crow's shriek mixed with a woman's screaming.

Martin rolled away from the vent–sprung to his feet. Long, panicked strides carried him to his front door, and fumbling hands threw the door open against the wall of his apartment. A crack of drywall–he didn't stop to look. His fist pounded beneath the embossed numbers on her door; he put his eye up to the peephole and obviously saw nothing. Wrong end. "Bonnie!" He rattled the hinges with each strike. "Bonnie! Open the door!" A pain in his hand. He took his fist away and saw its imprint left on the white paint in slick, wet red. The sight froze him there for a second. He examined his hand and saw his knuckles were bleeding. His breath trickled out of him like a leak.

"Will you shut the fuck up?"

He looked up. A ragged old man in a myriad stained nightgown–stuck diagonal out of his front door frame down the hall. Martin sniffled. "Uh… I'm sorry. My neighbor is in trouble."

"Call the cops, then. People are sleeping."

"It's eleven in the morning."

That observation got an exaggerated middle finger response. "Fuck you. Y'all kids make so much god-damn noise all the damn time. I'm sick to death of it. Fuckin' and screamin' and bangin' around all day long. Call the cops and shut up!" A slamming door punctuated the end of his advice.

Martin flew back through his own door and nearly dove onto the floor beside the vent. It took a moment for his eyes to adjust to the billowing, warm darkness again, and he had to blink the dust away. He was halfway to his flip phone pocket when he stopped. The beating of his heart was felt in his brain–pumping, blood heat.

No Bonnie.

And no mess on the wall. No bird on the carpet, and no skin man in the doorway. Nothing at all but an empty bedroom.

The vent puffed in his face. Tears started from his eyes. He struck the wall above the vent with his fist. Again. And again. "Fucking!..." A roar–almost bestial. The drywall gave way beneath his blows. Insulation guts were ripped free of their wooden ribcage and strewn over the floor. Some of the pink, cottony chunks came away sopped in blood.

He stopped–fell to the floor.

Then he went to the bathroom to wash the eviscerated

flesh and dark red stains off his hands. Instinct had him look in the mirror, but he'd cut the reflection away.

—

Stink.

Rotting stink of dead human flesh being eaten away by bacteria and bottom feeding vermin. Blood and grease had formed a pool under the bum's corpse–wrapped around the base of the box where the television still sat atop. Martin could hardly see the luminescent screen through a veil of skittering flies–all crawling across the glass. He looked down at the man he'd snapped full of bullets not a week before. Animal fangs had torn the waxy skin off his face. It wasn't a man anymore–just a lump of rot.

The picture on the screen had hardly changed. A dead body being recorded. *LIVE* still blinking in the top corner. But time had done its work to the grainy, pixel carrion. A mangy rat bolted across the decrepit cafe bar. Cooking utensils and plastic tubs of cutlery waited around, as if they hoped they might be used again soon. Like the cafe had just closed for the night. Corpse ovens and dishwashers had been torn away from the walls and picked over, until they were no more than metal shells.

Martin took a step–crushed debris under his heel.

"Sorry… I shot you over a ring." His voice carried. "But you did reach for something." Curiosity took him over. He took a few more steps, then stretched to peer around the television.

A cheap plastic water gun–staining in the melting human pool. Rigor mortis fingers clutched in desperation for the bright yellow handle.

His eyes began to blur and cross. "Shit… why'd you do that?"

The rotting thing was silent.

"God…" He fell to a crouch, rubbed his hands together. His new angle offered the sight of a black wire trailing out from the back of the television. It snaked through the blood, behind a counter, then into a yawning, black doorway.

After a moment, he got up–followed it. Flickering white light played the room like a silent film. A bulky camera setup hung precariously above a long, metal table. Reclined there was a corpse–the same corpse from the television. Through the strobing, he could see a wrapped bouquet of flowers withered on a stool. A note was scrawled on browning paper: *For my love, who lives forever in my heart.*

It was all reflected in his eyes as he stood in the doorway.

He approached the camera, found the power button–shut it off. The unblinking, black eye of glass changed somehow. Like he'd freed it from a sentence–put it to sleep.

Underneath it, the corpse's face had sunk into itself. The eyelids were ripped to skin threads by beaks and animal teeth. Once, it had been a woman. Blonde hair–now the hue of old urine. Care had been taken to keep the body presentable, though now the world was picking away at it.

His hands went idly to his pockets–shoved themselves in. "That's your husband outside? Boyfriend maybe?" A pause. "I guess he's with you again, isn't he?"

Silence.

He cleared his throat. "Maybe that's what he wanted." His toe drew a line in the carpet of dirt. "I met a girl here a long time ago. She lost a ring out in the dining room once. Your husband wanted it for himself." A sharp pang in his forehead. He held his palm up to it–scrunched up his face. The room was gently spinning. Tunnel vision. His speech sounded distant–as if he were speaking through a pipe, with his ears on the other end. "Um… So that's what happened to him."

Wind swung the moth-eaten curtains out in the dining room. It whistled against the shards of broken window still wedged into the wooden framing.

He watched the curtains. There were human shapes in the rippling fabric–linen ghosts. "But she was in her apartment… beside mine. And I gave her the ring. And she… took it…" The skin on his hands went white as paper.

He'd pulled them out of his pockets at some point–he didn't remember doing it. "But I picked her lock..."

"I picked her lock...

"I picked her lock...

"went inside to see if she was there..."

"the ring was on the floor just in front of the door…"

"'cause I'd slid it under…"

"and there was no…"

FURNITURE

The scent of decay was beginning to torture him. He stepped out into the dining room and sat down on a barstool. His hands cradled his head. He kept his eyes shut to keep the room from twirling in a colorless blur. "But I saw her through the vent…" At some point, he realized his leg was bouncing, restless. An effort made it stop, but it got back to it again once his mind had drifted. "Mama…"

"Mama..."

"I need more pills."

"I need more pills."

"For my head."

"For my head."

"I keep seeing him everywhere."

"I keep seeing him everywhere."

"And I see your body mangled and bloody."

"Mangled and bloody, Mama."

“Like a puppet.”

“Like a puppet.”

“Ayla gives me Clozapine.”

“Who’s Ayla?”

10

The bus was patched like a ratty pair of jeans–welded plate metal, duct tape, wood planks. He'd sat for its full route once by now, and was halfway through its second loop. Gray silhouettes stepped on, found a seat or a handhold, stepped off after a while. The road rumbled under the floor.

He couldn't see the driver. A welded metal curtain kept him hidden away. Only a thin slot would be filled with the man's eyes when new passengers paid for their ride. Then a cigarette-burned voicebox would utter a brief rehearsal of gratitude.

Martin watched the rolling Virginia horizon beyond the barbed fence and the trees. The hills were more blue the farther they were, like layers in a painting. An endless sky was a field for marching clouds. Powerlines were hung messily from tilting wooden poles rammed into wide patches of unkempt grass.

His head was still pounding.

Wisping conversations lifted above the road hum: “It’s not that I want to fight. No one wants to fight. But I was walking home from school last week and one of them pulled a huge knife. I could’ve taken him down, but I decided to run just ‘cause my muscles were sore from gym class that day–I didn’t feel really confident.”

“You know, something really needs to be done about those people. My family says ‘oh, just ignore them,’ but I don’t care if they’re not bothering me. I mean, it’s fucking annoying sitting on a bus or waiting at a stop with them when they smell like that. Or when they light up some crack and make the whole place reek.”

“What are the police even for at this point?”

“Walking around the border fence with their dicks in their hands, most like.”

A young child was half-standing on the seat beside its mother. High-pitched sing-song chorus–over and over with the same words. Same melody. “*THE SUN WILL COME OUT AND SHINE ON ME. SHINE ON.... ME SHINE... ON ME. THE SUN WILL COME... OUT AND SHINE ON ME... ON ME... SHINE ON ME.*”

The mother sat with her head hung low, ignoring the racket.

A lull in the rumbling. The doors peeled open and moist warmth passed Martin’s left shoulder. He didn’t turn to look.

Plastic and metal sealed over and the bus lurched back into motion. A stiff start.

Then he felt eyes on him. He turned.

Wrinkled eyes. A permanent grin. Yellow teeth. The man's breath was stale and bitter with crack smoke. Then came the stench of unwashed flesh. His gaze passed clean through Martin's figure–traveled on into a distant nothing.

He turned back around, feeling it enter and leave him.

"*THE SUN WILL SHI- COME OUT AND SHINE AND… ON ME. SHINE ON ME SHINE ON ME SHINE ON ME.*"

His shoulder was brushed.

"What's got ya sittin' back here, kid?"

His eyelids pulled apart–heart smacked his ribcage. He felt the metal of his pistol in his belt with rigid fingers. A slow turn. Beside him on the bench was a hulking, black cloak. *His* face–under the drooping hood.

"There ya go with that look again, little bull. Like you saw a ghost–or maybe a devil." It was like a flesh mask. The folds of gray skin were dead or dying. His breath was awful–lizard corpse under a heat lamp. One large hand clamped down on Martin's shoulder. "I knew a girl once, now listen. Mess 'a red hair and heart-shaped ass. Know what she did? Opened her mouth like a snake and fit her lips and jaw around this little kid. Digested the little fuck over seven days–you could see his legs and arms poppin' outta her gut.

Under the skin, ya follow?"

Muscle and veins popped and pulsated under the knuckles near Martin's neck. Heat tickled his beard. Sallow, wet heat.

Thumping laughter. "Gone silent again, have we? Heard ya talkin' in my meat locker. Lots 'a funny sounds come outta that room. But I saw ya walk out with ya gun, lookin' around for me. I was watchin' from behind the door. I was so close I could'a reached out and grabbed ya. I felt your heat… and your smell. Tell me how you cut yerself down, now. I know my knots, little bull."

Martin felt his head swimming. "You… How the… They're gonna catch you."

"Not likely, boy. They don't know what I look like. Y'all little things are dumb as doorknobs. Loud and noisy and stupid." He turned his crooked neck to look at the little singing girl. "I'll bash her brains in. Think that'd be funny?" Phlegm crackled at the back of his throat.

The fingers were tightening on his shoulder. "No… I don't. And then they'll really know who you are." He considered reaching for his gun. Then pictured the gray fingers squeezing his brain out like toothpaste through his ears. His breath was quick and thin–eyes searching in vain for an escape.

The beast heaved and creaked like an old bellows. Its

throat flesh squealed and bubbled. "And how many of 'em would talk? Step in to do nothin'? That's the thing about cattle, boy–you fire a rod through one of their skulls and the others are either too busy munchin' and fuckin' and shittin' on the ground to pay any mind, or they scatter like little birds from a shaken tree… Tell me, then–would you do anything? Or would ya watch me crush that little tune outta her skull?"

"I'd shoot you."

"*HA!* Would ya? Or maybe you'd run out the door once the chance presents itself. Try and get away from me while I'm busy makin' schnitzel." He leaned closer, sniffled and croaked. "You pull that little peashooter and see what goes down, I stamp. Whole mess 'a trouble." Long, greasy strands hung down from his mashed scalp. They whipped at every jerk of his head. "You pissed me off now. Got an attitude on ya, little fuck. And that little girl's racket ain't doin' much to help out. Ya don't think I'm serious?"

The bus stopped. No one got off–no one got on. Martin looked over at the child and her mother.

They didn't move.

The bus started rolling. His heart smacked again. His thoughts were screaming; he tried to project them into the mother's head by stare. "Why kill someone for no reason? Fucking sadistic…" Tighter. Tighter on his shoulder.

The beast clicked its teeth together. "'Cause you squirm

for it. And you're an arrogant bull with balls too big for ya own good. Maybe a man wants some peace and quiet, too. You never thought 'a what ya might do to some little fucking ankle biter while its screamin' and singin' on train or a plane? Makes me hard as diamonds thinkin' of her little skull pop like a balloon." The thing tilted its head, then laughed into Martin's face. Brusque, snapping laughter.

He tried to hold his breath.

"Any time now, I'm gonna reach out and grab her. Any damn time, and then this bus'll get redecorated. But how about we even the odds some? If she quits her yappin', I'll change my mind."

Another stop. The bus settled–people got up and people got on. He looked over.

They hadn't even shifted. The girl chirped and jumped up and down on the seat cushion. It made the plastic and metal creak.

A solid yank on the shoulder brought his attention back.

"I got a proposal for ya. You know my little sneakhole in the fence now–means you can leave ya kennel. You're gonna do that right quick. Get outta town. Leave ya little priest." Dark slaver was pooling behind his bottom lip. It pulled itself in a long strand down onto the nighted cloak. "Find greener pastures and so forth. Hitchhike to Roanoke."

Martin looked at the tattered back of the seat in front of

him–nearly brushing his knees. The world wheeled past behind the scratched window in his peripheral. "And what's out that way? There's nothing anywhere."

"Who told ya that? The priest?"

Silence.

"There's plenty, boy. It ain't a shithole anywhere but this little kennel y'all are stuck in." When the beast saw confusion, it chuckled and coughed. "Yes, boy. This town is full 'a ghosts. Far as everyone outside is concerned, you're probably dead as a fucking doornail."

Martin frowned, mouthed silently. Then: "How is that possible? Think I'd believe some shit like that?"

The bus stopped.

He looked over at the woman and child. They didn't move. "*SHINE DOWN ON ME, SHINE ON ME. THE SUN IS GONNA SHINE DOWN ON ME.*" A jerk and a rumble. Onward down the road.

He wanted to throw something at them.

"Stay here and I'll make 'em right–all those people outside. Dead bull. Dead as a doornail and a dirty hooker."

"But you can't hurt me." His fingers ventured toward the gun. "So you strung me up in your closet instead of gutting me quick and easy."

No answer.

"And I can get past your… barrier, or whatever the hell.

Maybe I can kill you if I tried it." He felt the fingers loosen from his shoulder…

…and snap tight around his neck.

His windpipe started to close. Sound moved like blood through a clotting artery–up from his voicebox to his useless tongue.

"Who said I can't hurt ya?" The beast breathed hot air into his face. "Looks like I can. I can squeeze tighter if I want–watch ya little eyeballs pop clean out ya head. Make hot red blood spill out ya mouth and out ya nose. Look me in the eye little bull–real hard."

He saw moist, black balls tucked amongst swollen skin. Empty glass pearls, with something behind them that looked like nothing at all–and everything all at once.

"I am your hell. And I'll burn ya while you scream. I'll melt the skin off ya muscle and turn ya bone to charcoal, boy. And for the rest of your time livin' in this town–'til you decide to listen to what I instruct–you'll see me in the corner of your eye whenever you ain't sleepin'. Behind every tree. In every reflection. And I keep my word. I'm a man of honor, ya see–more than most."

The fingers peeled apart and Martin clutched at his bruising neck. Coughing racked his ribcage. Blood rushed up and made the world spin.

Then the bus stopped.

His eyes darted over.

First the mother stood, then the girl–still singing. "*SHINE ON ME... ME... SHINE ON ME. THE SUN'S GONNA SHINE ON ME-E-E-E-E-E-E-E-E!*" They shuffled into the aisle.

He let out a breath, tried to calm his thumping heart. They passed by, headed for the door.

...And the beast caught her.

"You fucker!" He tried to fumble for his pistol, but folds of his jacket and shirt got in the way.

The singsong was cut short. Brain splattered across the back wall of the bus. Screaming. The mother lunged–then she saw the face of the thing now holding the erupted head of her daughter... and she fell back onto the ground.

Masks of pale horror in every seat were craned back to watch. When realization took, they all flooded into the aisle and spilled out the door. Screaming. Crying. No one helping. Hands grabbed and pulled and boots stepped over legs and arms and heads. Stampeding cattle, with an open gate.

The pistol finally worked its way out into Martin's hands. He aimed.

A smack–strong and quick. It leapt clean out of his fingers.

All the air in his lungs was pushed out through his mouth. The back of his head smacked the metal window frame. An iron grip had him–pressed him up against the window.

Mr. Crooked had blood on his face. Ravenous breathing, like a predator. His permanent flesh smile seemed a little wider. The dangling corpse was still clamped–fingers tight around the skull. He lifted it up to Martin's face. "Shine on me." The single blow had pounded flesh into paste. Every facial feature was gone. The heat rushing out from the internals licked his face up and down–reeking of blood. "Shine on me," said the beast. "Looks like she missed her stop."

The macerated corpse struck the edge of a seat on its way to the floor.

"The woods are nice this time 'a year. Plenty 'a places to have a picnic or take a hike. You never followed my advice back then, did ya? Still interested in that little kitty?"

Martin slumped down into the seat when the heavy fist let him go.

Heavy footsteps rocked the bus as the cloaked hulk made its way to the open doors. Then it was gone.

—

Red and blue lights crystallized in the bus windows. They'd been fast. It couldn't have been twenty minutes since the monster had fled.

The bus rocked gently; a beige campaign hat peeked up from behind the thin plastic railing by the doors, followed by a pinched face–then a pistol. "Back of the bus there–you in the jacket. Get your hands up over the seat."

Martin obeyed.

"Ma'am? Hands up, too."

The crying mother never heard him. She was huddled down over the puddle of gore that had been her daughter. Tears rocked her arched back. Her hands ran back and forth through blood-soaked hair.

"Ma'am!"

"Her daughter's dead, are you blind? Open your fucking eyes." Martin couldn't look down at her, or the caved in face of the corpse.

"Quiet! Speak when you're spoken to, boy!" The officer stepped up farther into the bus, revealing his tail of companions–all armed. They moved as one mass of tight gray shirts and trousers, tall black boots. "What in the fuck happened here? Someone called us in–was it you?"

Martin blinked. "No, sir."

"Said Mr. Crooked was here. Killed someone. Looks about right to me." The officer kept his gun aimed at Martin. His companions split their aim between him and the crying mother. "Tell me your name, boy."

"Martin Navarro."

"You see how this looks, don't ya?"

He frowned. "I… What? Mr. Crooked ran out just before you showed up. He's probably around here somewhere close."

The officer turned to his tail. "Can you call in a ten-fifty-four and request backup to search the area? Thanks, Thomas." He turned back to Martin as the other cop shuffled out into the sunlight. "I'm gonna need you both off the bus. We're gonna ask some questions."

No response from the mother.

"Ma'am?"

She touched her daughter's face. The flesh depressed under her fingertip. Structureless and nearly liquefied. "Baby… my baby…"

The officer approached slowly and placed a hand on her shoulder. "Can you hear me, ma'am? I need you off the bu-"

"-HIM!" Her finger was aimed at Martin. Fire roiled behind her eyes. "It was talking to him! The fucking thing that killed my baby! It was sitting beside him and talking to him before it… it's his fucking fault!"

The officer looked up. His hand went down to his belt of tools and fumbled. Then he brought out a pair of handcuffs, dangling noisily on a thick chain.

—

Fluorescent hum, like a swarm of flies hanging over his head.

The walls were gray brick, dripping with condensation. No windows. Stinking carpet. His hands were cuffed to a pipe bolted to the table. It was a bare tabletop–a dented field, scratched to hell near the pipe by hundreds of agitated handcuffs. Across the field sat a weary detective. Martin could see his nametag: *Det. K. Carr.* He leaned lackadaisical over a notepad and pen. "Why was he talking to you?"

Martin sniffled. "He, uh… He told me what he was gonna do. I don't know… It was funny for him, I guess."

"But you have no relation to him?"

"No." He fingered the cuff chain–wondered if the detective could hear his heart snapping against the edge of the table.

"So he just picked you at random? Out of those ten people on that bus."

"That's how I understand it. I don't know, sir. Maybe."

The pen tapped the notepad. "So what were you doing on the bus? Were you heading somewhere?"

"No… I was just trying to clear my head."

"Couldn't do that at home?"

He looked down at the paper cup in front of him.

"Definitely not, no."

"Why definitely?"

"Uh… Just having lady problems. There's things in my apartment that remind me of her." The light flickered over his head. It sparkled in the silver of his necklace–caught his peripheral. Its chain felt tight around his neck.

"That's a nice necklace." A nub eraser pointed–pencil finger.

He smiled weakly. "Same lady gave it to me."

"What's that pendant on it? Like an animal or…"

"A Cardinal."

The officer nodded. "You like birds?"

"Uh, yeah… I have a tattoo of one on my arm. She pointed it out when we first met."

Pencil scratching. "So… what's the problem with her? Why are you needing to clear your head?"

A pause. "I… feel a little distant."

"Like… was there a fight or anything? Argument?"

"No. No, uh… I'm just trying to find her again." "She lives with you?"

"No."

"Do you have her number?"

"Yes."

Graphite impregnated the paper. Microscopic flakes sparked off the lead. "Can you tell me how everything went down? Start from getting on the bus, maybe."

"Alright. Uh… I was sitting–just about ready to get off once my stop came around. The girl and her mom were sitting across the way. The girl was singing something and standing up on the seat. Then, uh… I feel something next to me; I turn to see who'd sat down. It was him."

"What did he say?"

"He, uh… started yammering on. Told me he was gonna kill the girl 'cause her singing was pissing him off."

"How long did he talk to you?"

"Must've been five minutes."

"Alright."

Another pause. The officer was quiet, so he kept talking. "Then the girl and the mom got up to leave. I thought he was gonna let them go. But he didn't."

Light flicker. Pencil scratch.

"*Hey.*"

The blood left Martin's face. Cold wind clawed at his back. He turned–saw a yawning stairwell descending into shadowy nothing. Wooden railing, carpet stairs. There was something at the bottom. He could sense its eyes touching and feeling him–prying off his clothes and skin. Leaving him naked in space. But he couldn't see what it was.

"*Hey.*"

His mouth went dry.

The voice in the basement was wrong. Sucking in every word instead of breathing it out. Slow, measured tempo. Attempting to construct language. "*Martin.*"

His temple started to ache.

"*You are letting him get away, Martin. My t-t-t-troublesome child... needs discipline. Killing and feeding his urges. Tearing the l-l-l-legs off of insects.*"

The darkness was a roiling, swirling pit. He saw shadows a billion feet tall colliding and splitting into fourth dimensions. Behind them and around them and in front of them was absence–beyond the expanses of the stars and planets. Whatever existed before.

"*Split open his flesh-matter so I can pull him out. Do it fast now, and no more d e l a y . M a r t i n , d o y o u h e a r m e , M a r t i n?"*

Saliva on his tongue tasted sour.

"*M i s t e r N a v a r r o . L o s t l i t t l e p u p . M i s t e r*

m-m-m-m-m i s t e r

m i s t e r

m i s t e r

"Mister Navarro?"

"I live in the Townshend… Sorry." He cleared his throat. Dry flesh pinched–started to ache. He looked up at the hanging light fixture. A moth beat its wings, pushing itself through the air in a messy orbit around the bulb. Martin could hear the electricity pumping through the filament. Blood cells in a vein. Sparking yellow light, hot like lava.

Scratching pencil. "Do you need some water?"

"No."

Silence.

"No thank you."

The graphite tapped the paper–three times. “Uh… Alright, do you have family in the area?”

“My mother, yeah.”

“Where is she?”

A pause. “I… uh, sorry.”

The sergeant looked up.

“I don’t… remember.”

Tap... tap... tap... Eraser struck paper. “You don’t remember where she lives?”

“Uh…” His stomach was constricting.

“That’s okay. So you don’t have family in the area, then?”

“No, I… My mother…”

Scratching pencil.

The door handle across the room started to jiggle. Lights flickered.

“I’m gonna be honest with you, mister Navarro. We have DNA off the girl’s body. You understand?”

He frowned. “No…”

“Okay, do you wanna start telling me the truth? Or do you want the night to think it over in a holding cell?”

Jiggling handle.

The door swung open. Into the room flew a bird–red feathers. It circled around the ceiling, then landed on top of the hanging lamp shade.

"What the fuck?"

The detective turned in his chair, looked up, then down, then spun back to face Martin. "What are you looking at?"

Martin tried to pull away from the table–the cuffs jangled.

"Mister Navarro? Do you need a doctor?"

A humanoid figure peeled around the doorframe, entering the room. Him. Pale, bald head. Veiny. The skin man. His eyes were wide saucers–locked squarely onto Martin. Only a couple long strides carried him across the room and to the detective's chair. Then he was gone–if he'd been there at all.

"Officer, I th-"

BANG! The detective's face came down against the metal tabletop. It stayed there for a moment, and the room went quiet.

The bird on the lamp chittered.

And the detective lifted his head off the table. Blood and puss were streaming out of every pore on his face. "*S e c r e t s a r e l i k e f i l t h i n y o u r s k i n . G o t t a s q u e e z e ' e m o u t .*" The pencil buried itself in his forehead, then two fists got a solid grip on it–started pulling down. Flesh was pushed by the blunt force–started to bunch like fabric.

Martin pulled on the cuffs with both hands, tried to find

some weakness in the chain. He rattled it violently; it bit into his wrist.

The pencil snapped. Viscera-covered hands dug into a massacred face, trying to tear the rest of the way through the skin. Bone fragments flew like sparks as the skull gave way. "*I can make an insect crush its own face*." Something else spoke through the detective's split mouth.

He tried to find something to cut the chain. There was nothing.

"Holy fuck!" Two officers stood in the doorway, pistols drawn. They rushed in, one aiming at Martin, the other at the flailing suicide. "What the fuck happened? You!"

Martin was standing, arm extended to get distance on the table. "Unlock the cuffs, jackass! Now!"

One of them fumbled for his keys as blood and the body's other liquids splattered onto his uniform–onto his cheek and neck. "Fuck fuck fuck!" When he found the right one, he gripped Martin's arm and slid the key around like a nervous teenager until it caught and plunged into the hole. A click, then metal teeth clattering. Martin fell onto the carpet–crawled on his side to get clear.

Gunpowder snapped four times–its scent joined the melange of blood and sweat.

Limp body falling out of its chair, piling on the carpet amongst its shedded gore.

An alarm had been triggered. It screamed in the background as the two officers gathered Martin and held him up against the wall. A hot pistol mouth exhaled against his cheek.

“What the fuck happened? Huh!”

Martin sucked in the foul air. “I don’t know! He just started clawing at himself!”

“I don’t fucking buy that, asshole!”

“That’s what happened! Watch the security camera!”

“God-damn!”

They yanked him roughly out into the hallway. He looked up at the hanging lamp as he was passing, looking for the bird. It was gone.

11

It felt like an invisible hand had a hold on every part of his body at once.

SLAM! Into the thick, metal cell door.

His shoulder was starting to feel tender and wet. "STOP IT!" No response. Sentient legs ran him at the door another time. Another crack on the metal. His sole slipped on the concrete–down in a heap.

The invisible hand let go.

"Fucking… shit." He lay on his back–reached across himself to feel his shoulder. Blood had soaked through the sleeve.

He hadn't been in the cell ten minutes.

WASTING TIME.

OPEN THE DOOR

WITH YOUR BODY.

"No! I can't fucking do that! I'll die before I put a dent in it!" His head was pounding. "Leave me alone!" A whimper came out involuntarily. It made him feel like a child. He ran his hand under his shirt sleeve, then pulled it out coated from palm to fingertips in glister. He looked up–saw the skin man in the corner of the cell, sitting on the bench bolted to the wall. Martin took a breath–remained crumpled on the floor. "I remember you. The man in the basement–the bad man in the basement." A long groan, to distract from the pain.

Under the white hot fluorescents, the figure was made more pale–more glassy. Its skin-eyes were piercing, and unrelenting.

"You stood at the back of my classrooms." The headache flared. "Watched me blow out birthday candles. Watched me through the glass door while I took showers. I fucking remember you now, you pale fuck. Are you happy I ran out of pills? Now you can follow me around again?"

Silence.

The lock snapped open, then the hinges croaked. Into the room came the sergeant–the man he'd met on the bus. Beige campaign hat, gray uniform stinking of starch and cologne. Martin was eye-level with the man's tall, black boots–stained by salt and mud.

He looked up from the floor–up the sergeant's nose.

"Gonna bust your shoulder, boss." A shadow under the hat brim looked vaguely like a mourner's veil. "Why don't ya get yourself up and have a chat with me?" He didn't extend a hand.

Martin sat upright, then navigated into the chair offered up by the sergeant. He looked–the skin man was still in the corner, on the bench, watching quietly.

"My name's Sergeant Toledo. We've got some things to talk about." A pause. "Hope you don't mind, I've got some eyes on my back."

Another gray uniform hovered by the closed cell door, thumbs looped through a leather belt.

"Fine." Martin's eyes flicked between two faces. Then three.

Toledo groaned as he sunk into his own chair. He groped his nose with his thumb and index–sniffled. "So what the fuck happened back there with detective Karr? Did you say something to him?"

Martin stiffened. "He just started clawing at himself… You guys need better background checks on your officers. Guy was clearly a nutcase–not to… speak badly of the dead." He felt his muscles–loosened them. Cramp.

The sergeant was staring with a down-tilted head, chin and neck smushed together. "Hmm… Right." Sniffle. "He was a bit depressed, if I recall. Wife left him for some burger-flipping, pox-faced college kid–near ten years younger than her. Imagine that shit."

"Yeah, awful." Martin adjusted his legs.

"Maybe he thought he was just an ugly bastard and dug his face out. A final 'fuck you' to the world and to God for doing him up like that. Wild to think about, eh?"

"Absolutely."

A pause. Toledo took his hat off–set it down on his lap. "Now what's the actual story, boss?"

Martin blinked.

"I've watched the security footage, talked to the officers who were watching you through the two-way mirror. Nothing odd. Bastard just drove that pencil into his forehead. How much force would that take?"

A pause to think. "Uh… Quite a lot, maybe."

"Yeah. I think, *maybe*." Hard eyes squinted. "You were lookin' around the room, though–like a little mouse in a box. Think I heard Karr ask you what the fuck was up, then he just… *bang!* Weird."

Silence.

"So what were you looking at, boss?"

Martin felt his throat seize up. "Uh… you didn't… see the bird? Or the…"

"Yes?"

"The, uh… There was a bird that flew in through the door."

"Door was closed. It didn't open 'til the officers opened it."

The room was spinning. "That's what I was looking at… I mean…"

Toledo sat forward in his chair and sucked in through his nose. "Alright, Mister Navarro. I'll be real with you… I don't have any evidence to say you did anything in there, but we have you in as a suspect in a murder case, then my detective finds that talking to you is his latest and greatest reason for a *DIY* lobotomy."

"Yes, I understand."

"Do you? I hope so. 'Cause you're gonna spend the night in my concrete hotel, pissing in a bucket. Your questioning wasn't concluded, and now we've got a couple more to tack on."

"Can't I get a lawyer?"

Toledo snorted, stood up from his chair with a scream of metal. "Where do you think we are, boss? I'm the law, as they say. Judge and jury. You leave when I say you leave, whether that's out the front door or in a bag." He stepped closer to his prisoner, grabbed his collar–ran his fingers along the fabric. His breath was hot. "That's a nice shirt. Handsome shirt. I could make you take it off–if I'm scared you have weapons on ya."

Martin felt every hair stand on end. His throat was dry.

"Enjoy your sleep." The sergeant let go, then walked to the door, shifting something in his pants. A slam of metal, then two sets of muffled retreating footsteps down an unseen hallway.

Martin shifted his gaze from the door to the bench–to the figure still sitting there. It seemed he had a permanent cell mate.

—

There was a painting up in the hallway outside the cell door. Martin could see it through the little barred window cut into the metal. A flickering amber light kept the painted image dancing on the line between visible and gone–but the paint was so dark anyway. Blacks and browns and blood reds. It was some kind of hell angel with a bald, red-flesh head and massive shadow wings. A swirling hurricane poured like an avalanche from a hole in the sky, down to earth where the spires of a pale building were half enveloped. Bony, skeletal hands were positioned with pointers aimed skyward on one hand, and earthward on the other. *As above, so below.* White painted runes were drawn at the tips of the digits. Martin couldn't recognize them. They formed a diagonal with a three-pronged hook dangling from the goliath's open, screaming mouth.

Footsteps.

Martin tried to peer through the bars. Eventually, a form came into view.

"Ain't that something."

He stepped back, rubbed his jaw.

"*'Anyone ever try and run a truck through it?'* Ha! Fence-boy, ain't it?" The officer touched his hat brim–nudged it up and out of his eyes. "So you're the guy who made Karr a shish-kebab. Small fucking world."

"I didn't."

The officer passed a plastic bag from one hand to the other–used the free hand to re-tuck his shirt. "Right. Innocent until proven guilty. I'm here to get ya for your phone call. You get one, so hopefully you've got a honey or a sweet old lady." His eyeline fell beneath the little window. Rattling keys.

"How about a lawyer?"

"Ha!" Silence.

The door snapped and creaked, then it swung heavy out into the hallway. Martin could see the officer fully now.

Same stern brick of a face. Black hat. Flashlight hung from his belt. Martin said: "There's a–uh… in the fence by the overpass, in the treeline…" He trailed off.

"What?"

He pushed strands of oily hair out of his eyes. There was heat on his cheek now–just the left one. The painting on the wall, in his peripheral. All the air around it was humid. "Sorry…"

"Sorry, what?"

A pause. "I… saw an ad for a lawyer there. On a bench."

"That right?"

He didn't answer.

"Same ad's plastered up all across town, genius. Roy Callahan. Scumbag fuck got lots of degenerate methheads and rapists and robbers and all sorts outta jail time. Some guys I arrested myself got off 'cause of him. Know what they did?"

"I don't."

"Transcensionists cut his tallywacker off and fucked him with it. Stuck a metal rod in to stiffen it beforehand, you know? You heard that?"

"No." He felt his palms getting wet.

The keys jingled. "That's the rumor. Anyhow, he's part of their fucking pajama-wearing sorority group up there in the church. All of 'em are snipped."

Silence.

"Maybe not their leader, some people think. He's still swingin'."

Martin blinked. "I don't know."

"Yeah, me neither. Fuck me, man. Let's go. You got me talkin'." He grabbed his prisoner by the arm and started him walking. "All of this to say, you best quit daydreaming of legal representation. We don't do that anymore. Haven't you ever been in trouble with the law?"

"Uh… not since the fence got put up."

"What was it before?" A keycard excited a wall mounted card reader–made it go green and squeak. Deadbolt, sliding free. He gripped the thick metal handle and yanked the door open. Pushed Martin through.

"I… can't you find that shit out?"

"What, you diddle a kid or something?"

"No."

"Then spill it. I don't care."

They walked past mahogany doors, beneath humming amber ceiling lamps. Plastic plants conjured images of mummified corpses stuck into wide pots–soil dry and covered in a layer of dust. They passed beneath a sign: *DETENTION.*

"I, uh… got caught with some coke."

"Yeah? Got some in the fridge here, no problem."

Silence.

A smack on his shoulder. It hurt. "Just fucking with you. You an addict or something? Degenerate junkie?" He frowned at the blood-soaked sleeve.

"Not anymore, no."

"Know how many times I've heard that?"

More officers passed by, all clad in their hats and gray outfits. Martin felt a tug and came face to face with a locked, wooden door.

"Here we are, Montana. Hope you've got a number." Out came the keys again. One slid in and turned, then the knob jiggled free. The room inside smelled like printer ink and piss. A stained, fabric chair with a broken arm was tucked under a counter. A dented, black phone was bolted to the wall, and Martin was left alone with it. The door shut tight–locked–then there was only ambient muffled chatter through the walls.

He stepped up to the phone–didn't sit in the chair.

And waited.

He tried to think of a number. He didn't know many. But there was only one that really mattered.

The buttons were coated in flaking chrome. He had to tell the numbers by counting. Each one clicked in–stuck–then sprung back. Ten times. A dial tone–got louder as he lifted it to his ear.

A long breath out. The air was thin.

"*Hello?*"

"... Mama?"

A pause. "*How are you, hijo?*"

"I'm alright, how are you?"

"*I'm okay. I had my paintings in a show yesterday, and some people bought a few.*"

"That's fantastic. How much did you make from that?"

"*I think it was six-hundred, or something like that.*"

"That's great."

"*How is Bonnie?*"

"She's alright." Silence, then: "What paintings did you sell?"

"*Oh, it was one of the landscape ones, and I think... uh, I think some portraits. I know one of them was Clark Gable.*"

"Oh, okay. That's great."

"*I'm so happy. And then, you know, you showed up afterward and helped me load all the rest back into my car.*"

"Great, that's good of me to do that."

"*You were asking about your father, like you always do. I just wish you'd let it go.*"

"Well, mama, it's hard for me to understand when I'm half blacked-out."

"*Don't say that about you, hijo. That's not nice.*"

"It's true, though."

"*You just need to find something to do with your life. You had a little bit of money, though, and you bought me some lunch. That was nice to see. Maybe you have a job.*"

"No, I doubt it. I'm a deadbeat. Probably stole it."

"*Why do you talk like that about you?*"

"I'm just telling the truth. I don't wanna hear it to my face."

A sigh through the phone. "*You know you have mental health issues. You have to have some patience with you. You told me you're going to a therapist.*"

"Yeah, I think I said her name was Ayla."

"*Well let's see how that goes, then.*"

"That's provided this therapist is actually a real person. I wouldn't put money on me actually telling the truth."

"*Well maybe you can go and do some research about it. See if she's actually where you say she is.*"

"I did, mama. Went to the building I told you about. Nothing. No therapist in the basement–just a bunch of boxes and shelves and shit. Know what was there? Lots of pills."

A longer pause. "*God...*"

"I'm sorry to tell you, mama, but that's what I saw. I think I'm lying to your face."

"*We need to do something about you.*"

"Like what?"

"*Well... Your aunt lives in Roanoke. She offered to help*

me find a nice apartment there."

"You wanna move away from me?"

"*I don't see what else I can do... now that you told me about this... that you're lying to me.*"

"I mean… maybe it would smarten me up if you did move. I don't know."

"*It's better to move into a bigger city anyway. I'm getting older. There's more services there.*"

"That's a big decision."

"*I know.*"

"Well… uh… tell me what you decide, mama, okay? I can help you move if you decide to."

"*You're so sweet, hijo. I'm gonna have dinner now, okay? Maybe you'll call me tonight before I go to bed.*"

"I wouldn't put money on that, mama."

"*Yeah. I know.*"

"I love you."

"*I love you, too.*"

The phone snapped back onto the receiver. He stood for a moment, looking down at his reflection in the dark plastic.

Keys in the door. He heard it open behind him.

"Are you going looney?" The officer stepped in, spinning his keys. "You didn't call anyone. Just talked to yourself for like ten minutes."

Martin stepped away from the phone. "Yes… I know."

"You know?"

"I've always known."

The officer frowned, then grabbed Martin's arm. "Okay nutbar, let's get you back. Boss wants another chat with you."

The door shut tight, was locked with a key, and Martin was brought back to the cell.

—

Rain hammered low and muffled against the roof. Thunderclaps shook the room. A clock on the wall clicked endlessly, marking the meaningless passage of time. Martin ran his fingers along the metal pipe to which his cuffs were bound. He hardly paid attention to what the sergeant was saying to him.

"Told Renfield you liked to sniff blow, huh?"

A pause. "No. Not now."

"But you did."

The cuff chain sparkled like a windchime.

"More time you spend with me, the more I'm convinced you're a looney." The sergeant licked his finger–pulled a page on his notepad. "You ever crash in a cardboard box? Sleep alongside a meth-mouth, toothless hooker and pray you wake up with your wallet?"

"Is that a serious question?"

Toledo's eyes hardened–glass marbles in deep sockets. "Is that talk-back? You're a real geeker, you scrawny little cocksucker. You're supposed to cooperate with police, you forget that lesson from preschool? Too busy pickin' your nose and shittin' your pants?"

Martin looked at the man. He could feel the expressionless mask on his own face. His eyes were crossing the longer he stared. "Would you shoot me if I asked you to?"

The sergeant sat up straight. "What's that?"

Silence.

"Feels like I'm talkin' to two people at once. I can't say I've ever met a son-of-a-bitch like you, boss." He clicked open a pen–tried to scratch something onto his notepad. The ink wouldn't come, so he tossed it down onto the tabletop. Another came out from the cigarette pocket in his shirt. "How much do you weigh?"

"What?"

"Did I stutter?"

Some time to consider. "Um… I haven't checked in a while." He looked over at the corner of the room. The pale shadow was still there, staring.

The sergeant clicked his tongue. "Don't look like a muscular guy. You're a little thin, boss. But you're toned."

Silence.

"You had sex in the past couple days?"

"Am I at the fucking doctor?"

Scratching pen. "Just curious. Said you had a lady at home. Most slender young men like you that dress well and keep your hair nice are homosexuals." His eyes flicked up to meet Martin's–they were probing. Against his will.

He shifted in his chair. "Apparently not all." There was bite in that answer.

"You like both, then?"

A frown. The air in the room was growing thick. It was hard to breathe it in. He glanced at the corner–got no solace in the pale thing's empty expression. "No."

"No?"

"Did I stutter?"

Now the sergeant frowned. "Most young, thin guys say 'no' before they try it. There's something feminine about a kid like you. Dresses well. Talks well. Groomed well. That's just my experience." He scratched his mustache.

Martin cleared his throat. The handcuffs chittered. "Haven't seen many women working in this building."

Pen scratching. Lines and lines of indiscernible black lettering. "That bother you?"

"Saw a few young boys around. Running papers and cups of coffee."

The pen stopped. Its wielder sighed–sat forward in his chair. His breath smelled of coffee. "Maybe. We've got some guys around here look young. Baby faces. Full of energy." Something made the man's face break into a grin. "Feel free to report my conduct to a superior if you find it to be… uncouth." He blew in Martin's face as he relaxed back into his seat. "You're a tits man, or an ass man?"

Martin sniffled. His face felt oily. "Personality."

That made the sergeant cackle. He slapped his knee, summoning a hoarse fit of coughing. "Fuckin' geeker. Only a fucking fag would say something like that, now. Ain't no man I ever talked to with balls gave that answer." Back to scribbling. "I'm starting to wonder about you, boss. Surely you would've had me fuck my own eyesocket with this pen by now."

"Surely."

That got no response. The sergeant took a long while to write something extensive, then he looked down at his watch. The time didn't seem to startle him. "Got other matters to attend to. Gonna have to continue this little chat some other time." He got up from his seat–collected his things. "I think I might just keep you, boss. Take you home with me and feed you twice a day."

He was gone through the door. Martin let out a long breath–eyed up the figure in the corner. It hadn't shifted position in hours. Not even a flinch. There was a bed hung against the wall with chains, but the sergeant hadn't uncuffed him from the table. Gradually, he fell asleep on his folded arms.

12

Sparkly buzz.

A snap of the lock, and the door was swung open. A nameless officer entered, gripping a ring of keys. He selected one, then undid Martin's cuffs from the table. "Come on with me. Change 'a scenery after you drain the one eyed monster." He snapped the now empty half of the cuffs on the one cuffless wrist, then pushed the prisoner out into the hallway.

The washrooms were not far down the hall. Martin stopped at the door.

"Well, go on. I'm not goin' in with ya to change your diaper." The keys spun and crashed on their ring.

"Can you take the cuffs off?"

That summoned a wry expression to the officer's face. "Don't need full range 'a motion to piss."

"And if I'm not pissing?"

"Then it'll be good exercise."

The door groaned as he left the officer to wait out in the hall. Inside the bathroom, all was yellow. One fluorescent spit and whined–its light rotted the white colors of the tiling. Edges and grooves were sprouting mold that climbed in webs up the walls. He pushed on the single stall door, which revealed a cracked and stained toilet. Tools unknown had scrawled spidery messages into the navy blue paint of the stall.

Don't forget me, God.

I'm gonna be executed tomorrow. Better than having the chief's baton up your asshole.

Fuck the cops. Fuck the cops. Fuck the cops. Fuck the cops.

Once he'd finished, he crossed to the sinks–single units bolted and caulked beneath a long mirror. The tap sputtered and vibrated like a runaway engine. Cranking the *hot* knob only got it lukewarm. The whole time he washed, he never looked up from his hands. He didn't want to know what he'd see if he looked in the mirror.

Outside, he was swept up by the waiting officer and marched down the hall past windows into offices shuttered behind aluminum slats. Phones rang like nighttime crickets. Lawmen drones meandered all around. Gray, gray, gray. Black boots and black hats.

K-9 UNITS.

Ravenous barking, sealed behind a door. For a second, it sounded like yelling. Angry outbursts.

He was halted in front of a nondescript wooden door. There was a small window at eye level, but there were more aluminum blinds. Whatever was on the other side remained hidden until the officer turned the knob and cracked the door.

Toledo, sitting in one of around thirty cheap, plastic chairs. Dancing specters rose from out of his coffee cup, occasionally catching the light from the projector. The lights were down. "Bring him in." A sip of coffee. "Sit him there."

Martin's eyes were adjusting.

"Morning, boss."

Silence.

"Thought we'd fire up the old projector to take a good look at this–get you out of your kennel for a little field trip. You like that?"

He watched the sergeant through hanging strands of hair.

"This is quite a special day for all of us here."

"Why?"

There was a clipboard on the sergeant's lap. He used his pencil to gesture towards the front of the room, where the projector's blinding image had now gotten a little more friendly to Martin's eyes. Displayed there was a shot from high up–likely a security camera. It had been zoomed and cropped in–focused on a grainy figure robed in black.

"You recognize that *thing*?"

He had to squint–sit forward in his chair. "I do."

It was difficult to draw detail from the fog of grain, but the face was defined enough. Masticated flesh–gray and deformed. No eyes were visible. There was only a pixelated brow of shadow. Tendrils of long hair emerged from beneath a wide hood, swept in the figure's motion. Around its silhouette, the image looked off-color–burned, somehow. Burned pixels in a digital photograph.

"You said yes? You do?"

"Yes, I do."

Toledo cracked a grin and vibrated in his chair. "Motherfucker, that's him. God damn… This is from a camera near where the bus stopped. That's him. *I* got a shot of Mr. Crooked!"

Bodies were pouring in through the door, curious. Murmurs. Pointing at the projection.

"This here, gentlemen–take a good long look at it. You are the first in this town to set your eyes on this ugly motherfucker and live to tell about it. Come on, now." Up from his chair. He set the coffee cup down and threw the clipboard across the room. "Look at that!" From where he stood, up near the wall, it seemed as if the beast in the projected photo was staring back down at him.

Now the officers were trickling towards the front.

Children at a zoo, peering through the glass at a lion. Martin remained in his seat, head down, eyes on the dirty, mashed-in carpeting.

And they all started to laugh and chatter. Toledo grabbed one of them by the neck and pressed the boy up against the wall. A flat palm struck ass through khaki pants. The sound of their cacophony rose in pitch and volume. They all touched the wall–touched the grainy image of the beast, then they began to embrace and some began to cry. All this while *his* face looked down over their heads, made large in light on its background of chipping paint.

—

The donut caved in under teeth. Crunch of sprinkles. Still, umber liquid filled half a glass that could have been crystal. Its facets sprayed light everywhere–messy, like a murder. Even in this isolated room, the voice of the church was heard; three mellotron keys, from the cage speaker up in the corner of the ceiling. Then: "*Today is a momentous occasion. Due to the deft investigative work of Sergeant Toledo of the Snowy Oaks Police Department, an image of Mr. Crooked has surfaced for the first time. He is hidden no longer. All are welcome at the Red Abbey, where his grotesque visage will be bared to the public. Blessed Be,*

King of Heaven."

Toledo brushed crumbs off his shirt. "Mister Ward has these made for me. Ships them in along with this-" Up came the crystal glass, to a pair of smiling lips. A sip. "'Cause I do my job so well." What remained of the donut plunged in past strings of saliva.

Martin was slumped in his chair, blinking.

"I'd offer you some, but it's not cheap." He flicked the rim of the glass. Sharp tone, like a bell.

"Are you gonna interrogate me, or did you come for a lunch buddy?"

A chuckle. Out came a pen, which started skittering across whatever was pinched in his clipboard. "You'd make a fine addition to my force, boss. Fit right in. You ever considered pinnin' a badge to your chest and making a difference in the world? Or you too busy huffin' nose candy to even know what day it is?"

He smiled–looked away, towards the copy of the sergeant in the cloudy one-way mirror. It occurred to him now that Toledo could have been a bit-part in an old Western film: sunken cheeks, thin eyes, thick mustache.

"Eh?"

Martin looked back. "At what point do you determine I'm free to go?"

"That'll be when I feel like there's no reasonable doubt."

"But you got a picture of him."

Toledo leaned forward. "Yes?"

Silence.

Ticking clock.

Martin balled his fists. Then he heaved out of his chair and pushed the table into the sergeant's stomach, sending him back flat into his chair.

"You…" Out came a gun. It was up against Martin's temple. *Click!* Back went the hammer. Locked in place. The sergeant was up close to his prisoner–hand on his neck, breathing words into his ear. "Firey little fucker, ain't ya? Huh? Don't like how I'm treatin' you, boss? Well I can do a lot better." He pulled Martin off his chair, tried to get him on the ground, but he was still cuffed to the table.

A yelp of agony–the cuffs bit into his wrist. He hung from them, kicking his legs.

"Fucker!" Keys, jingling. He pulled Martin up by the collar while he undid the cuffs from the table. *Chick!* Rattling metal. Now he dropped Martin like a sack and kicked him in the ribs. "You're bleeding on my boots, boss!"

His wrists were weeping. The steel of the cuffs had torn through. He made a weak attempt to sweep the sergeant's legs out from under him, but a thick leather heel stopped him halfway–pressed down on his chest.

"I should'a known. Should'a known if you keep your

dog locked up, it gets a little antsy. You were smart, before, boss. You shut yer trap and took what came to ya. *Lets-*" A solid kick. "*Go back-*" Another, to Martin's stomach. "*To that!* Eh, boss? Be a good dog, now. Sit!" He used both hands to pull up on Martin's shirt. Then he dropped him in the chair–the legs squealed on the concrete. He went back to his own chair, rolling his shoulders–stretching his arms. Before he sat, he hoisted his crystal glass and downed what remained inside it. "*WHOO!* … Gets ya goin', don't it?"

Blood ran down the handcuffs where they hung at Martin's sides. Liquid rubies formed–collected in puddles on the floor.

"Now… where were we?" Flipping through notes. "*M-m-m-m…* Ah, yes. Detective Karr. *Mr. Pencil.* You were telling me the door opened up before he stabbed himself, yes?"

Silence.

"You gone deaf now?"

A cough. Bubbles popped and sputtered in Martin's throat. "Yes."

"I watched the security tape a couple times over, and had one of my guys analyze it. It wasn't tampered with–no doctoring, nothing. That door did not open."

Through tears and blood, came: "It was Golgotha."

A pause. Then Toledo leaned forward again, as far as he

could manage. “What’s that?”

“Golgotha… It- was Golgotha, fuckface.”

A smirk turned to a grin–turned to laughter. “That right? Golgotha? Now listen here, boss. I may work with Mister Roman Ward, but there ain’t a chance in Hell I believe what he preaches. There’s one God, and that’s the Christian God. Praise Jesus Christ. The only thing that’ll make me believe what he says is if I see a damn miracle happen right in front ‘a my eyes. And even then–you gotta convince me it wasn’t Christ that did it in disguise. Understand me?”

There was no answer to that.

“Ain’t no such thing as Golgotha. What the Hell makes you think Golgotha killed my detective, boss?”

“Why… do you- have that painting…” A loud, racking cough. “Up there in the hall?”

A squint. He straightened his crooked tie. “That painting is sacrilege. Hear me? But I’m required to hang it. All around here, in every room. That means nothing about my beliefs.”

“I saw a cardinal fly in through the door.”

“I saw no bird.”

“But it was there. It sat right up there on the light while your detective killed himself.”

“Cardinals are messages from God. From Christ. Let you know he’s with you.”

"They're me-"

"*EH!* That's enough about that." Scribbling pen. Frantic notes. There was a sudden chirp from Toledo's breast. He reached to up squeeze the walkie. "What?"

It blew static. "*Call for you, from Ward.*"

"I'll take it in my office." He looked hard at his prisoner. "Sleep tight, boss. Don't let the bed bugs bite. I'll be back in the morning to see if you've bled out." Before he fled the room, he reattached Martin's cuffs to the table. A buzz, a click. The door swung open, then shut.

And Martin stared up at the popcorn texture on the ceiling.

13

He dreamt he was hanging by his legs again, in that room with the dead women. Somewhere outside the room was the wicked monster, trudging and dragging its heavy mattock. Doors opened and slammed shut. Wind rapped on the walls, like children playing ding-dong-ditch. A knock–walls shaking–then nothing. Shadows from the corpses trickled over the furniture–the cluttered desk, the garbage bag lumps pushed against the floorboards. Flies everywhere–especially around the lumps.

His eyelids struggled to stay open. Even after he heard thin, desperate breathing from behind him. It sounded like a crushed windpipe struggling to perform. Air leaking out of a tire.

Forceful, trembling fingers grabbed at his dangling figure. Pulling at the cloth of his shirt. There was no warmth in the fingertips; they could have been rubber–mannequin digits. At once, they locked on and yanked hard, spinning him around. He demanded his eyelids part.

She…

Colorless skin. Eyes pulled wide open. Smiling.

"*He fucked me. He pulled out my guts. Look at me, Martin.*"

He couldn't take his eyes off her face. His peripheral caught sight of her shriveled, naked body. Blood dripping down her belly and between her breasts. Into her melted wax smile.

"*Look how he made me beautiful.*"

Before he could speak, her left arm joint gave out. A thud. No blood leaked out from the shoulder stump, and the meat inside was gray and cold. Then her other shoulder followed suit. Another thud.

"*I can't touch you anymore.*"

Laughter.

Her mouth was still creased up in glee–still giggling–as her head fell off.

—

The table jumped in fright as he woke. Pain coursed through his knee. He'd shot bolt-upright, surprising the sergeant–scribbling notes on his pad.

"You twitch in your sleep, boss."

His forehead was slick when he rubbed it. Unwashed hair hung in clumps; he felt like an alley rat, just woken from sleep on a bed of garbage.

Confirmation came from across the table: "You're starting to stink like a hairy asscrack. Think we'll let you shower one time, but I'll have to keep an eye on you from the door."

"Fuck off."

"Say again?" A creak. The sergeant leaned forward over his clipboard. "If I was you, I'd keep that tongue locked down. You wanna make a good impression, now–else I'll decide to keep you in jail 'til you're back aches and you smell like Bengay."

The hanging lamp flickered.

Martin looked over at the expansive, looming mirror. He wondered if there was anyone on the other side today. Since his arrival, the clock on the wall had frozen on seven thirty-two. It ticked, but didn't move–somehow. It was the only thing to look at. *Seven thirty-two.* Concrete walls. His shadowy reflection in the mirror.

Seven thirty-two.

The cuts from the handcuffs had sealed over. Now they hurt. His eye started to itch; he leaned forward to get it in reach of his fingers.

"I enjoy watching you."

Silence.

"Seems I should thank Mr. Crooked for bashing in that kid's brains in the right place at the right time. Funny how the world works, isn't it, boss?"

Silence.

"You seem distracted today."

Martin looked to his right. Another chair had been brought up to the table, and was now inhabited by the mouthless thing. Rigid posture, like a demonic blow-up doll–but a pretty pathetic one with its lack of anticipating lips. Up close, Martin could inspect its all-black suit, and the veins running beneath its membranous scalp. The eyes, as he'd thought, were indeed made of skin–or at least connected directly to the skin around the sockets. The pupils were little divets, cored out as if with a little spoon. They were black as rot.

"I keep a chair open for Jesus." A pause, then an eruption of laughter from the sergeant. "Naw, I'm just getting ready for a guest. Should be here quick now.

The skin man kept its alien eyes stuck tight to Martin.

"Chill out, boss." A chuckle–it could have been nervous. "He's not actually gonna come down on a ray of sunshine and take a seat. Look over here, for me, would ya? … That's right. Wanna see those deep brown eyes 'a yours." Pen skittering. It ran a little long and fell off the page, but stayed in his grip. "Shit…"

Martin stared at the sergeant hard. For a few seconds only, he felt something like patronizing confidence as the man fought with his utensil.

"Before Roman Ward moved in to Saint Francis up there on the hill, I was a detective. Long time ago now. You were probably still swimming in your daddy's nutsack. There was a guy who lived on Holloway and Main–right at the corner there in that big house with the round tower-looking piece. You know that one?"

Silence.

"I get a call to come by with my partner: some dumb bitch I can't remember the name of. Now this guy who lived there used to walk around town dressed up as a schoolgirl; he was like fifty-something, and had these heeled boots, tights, skirt–the whole fucking thing. He spent his days on park benches across from the school, eating peanut butter and cucumber sandwiches with the crusts cut off–watching the kids playing at recess. Back when he first started this shit, I was just finishing my sentence as a beat cop–about to get my big boy cherry popped and graduate–and I had to arrest this guy two or three times and take him in for questioning. Had this white face paint on and bright red lipstick to make him look like a girl. He talked in a high-pitched voice and kept telling me: *'No mister cop, sir! I'm a*

little girl! I'm a little girl!'"
The handcuff chains jingled. Frozen, ticking clock.

Seven-thirty-five.

"I go to his house with my partner and we find a meat freezer full of little Timmys and Tinas in his basement–all cut to bits. Some pieces were missing, and we were wondering why, right? I found a leg in the oven and a toddler thigh casserole in the fridge. Fucker kept talking and acting like a little girl 'til they lugged his ass off to Roanoke jail." A long period of silence went by while the pen went to scratching. "I got a commendation for that… Tracking him down."

A door shut somewhere–beyond the walls.

Toledo clicked the pen shut, then set it down with the clipboard on the table. Sighed, then made his chair squeal under his weight as he leaned on the backrest. "That is to say, boss… I've got experience dealing with schizo fucks, bipolar freakazoids, kid fuckers, wife beaters, gang rapers, cop killers-" He paused there–lifted his eyebrows at Martin. "-and everyone in between. I can't place where you fall on that list, though I can hypothesize. There was a serial killer up in Charlottesville who used a young kid to bring people back to his house. Then he'd pay the boy five bucks and a *Mars* bar and send him on back home."

Martin's skull was vibrating. Like it was about to erupt.

"I didn't have a *Mars* bar in my pocket, did I?"

A smile. "Bless your heart, boss. Today's the last day I get to have fun with you. Who am I gonna talk to once you're gone?"

Martin felt his heart snap across his ribcage.

"That's right. You're going home, big boy. Our visitor is here to pick you up from school. You excited?" A wide grin was pulled very slowly out of the malleable white clay of Toledo's face. He went to reach for something on his belt of tools–fumbled with it. Snapped open a clasp. There was a flash of reflectivity.

BANG!

Martin felt pain–looked down at the table. A wide bowie knife was rammed through the back of his hand and into the thin metal tabletop. It took him a second to register what had happened–then he yelped and the handcuff chain danced a noisy, wild dance.

The sergeant was cackling like a hag. "*Ha!* Look at you squirm, boss! Like I pulled yer pants down! *HA-HA-HA!* Come on now! Look at this geeker, my good God! And his blood is red, yes sir! He bleeds! Red as rubies!" He let go of the blade–left it embedded where it was. It stuck up out of the table like a birthday candle. "Couldn't let you go without a parting gift to remember me by, eh? 'Cause you bet I ain't done with you, boss. No, sir."

Martin felt the sergeant's hot breath in his face. He looked up and found him leaning over the table.

“Saved by the bell. But next time you do something, just you watch. Big Brother has his eye on you now, boss. One of my detectives is dead ‘cause of you. I don’t know how or why, but facts are facts.”

Martin held his breath. Clenched his teeth. He didn’t struggle, or the knife might slip. Pain ran up his arm–through every finger. The knife tip was staining. It kept slicing slowly, separating. Splatters and a pool of crimson on the tabletop. Rivulets ran down over the metal pipe–snaked through the handcuff chain.

Then it pulled up.

Martin fell back in his chair. There was a wobbly line from his wrist to his knuckles. It was weeping everywhere.

The walkie clipped to the sergeant’s shirt chirped. He waited for a moment, staring, before reaching up to strangle it. “Yeah?”

“Visitor for Navarro. Are you ready?”

A pause. “Send him in.”

From somewhere in the room screamed the loud buzzer, then the door swung open. In came a red silhouette, floating beneath his robes. The scent of incense and oils followed close–overpowering.

Toledo got up, took his knife. A little key undid the cuffs, and he tossed them across the table. "Don't forget about me, boss. 'Cause I won't soon forget about you." He reached down to grab Martin's chin–pulled his head up to face him. Then he let go, and headed for the door. As he passed the hooded figure, he bowed his head, then he was gone.

The door slammed shut–locked with a snap.

Martin clutched at his hand, air fizzling out between his teeth. "Fucking psycho son-of-a-bitch!" He forced the chair away from the table with his feet–doubled over.

"You'll need stitches. There will likely be severe tendon damage." The priest had his hands hidden beneath blood red fabric curtains. "I've seen everything that happened in this cell from the day you got here. Golgotha provides this sight to me."

"Why didn't he fucking help me?"

A pause. Then: "I am his agent in the physical world… And your failure was worth punishment."

"Failure?"

"The cherub is aware of your efforts to destroy it–and your ability to pass through its barrier. A task that should have been simple with the element of surprise is now complicated. It was emboldened to seek you out in daylight. That is toying with prey. You are a mouse hunted by a cat. Where before you were meant to be the hunter, you are now something to be swatted. Are you understanding me?"

Martin sat up, looked down at the wide red stain spreading through his jean leg. He used his uninjured hand as a clamp to keep the flesh on its partner closed, but that squeezed out more pulses of mess. "I understand jack fucking shit. And who's this? I'd bet you can see him."

"This is a rendering of our Lord." The priest kept his distance from the table–never moved from where he stood by the door. He hadn't been acknowledged by the flesh man, and never looked in its direction. "Manifested for your eyes–using your thoughts and memories. A more tangible reminder to do what you are told." The crystal eyes fell upon the massacre spread across the floor and table. Red puddles and delicate red tongues stretching out from the table edge–dripping down onto the tiles. "Will you come with me, please? Before you bleed out."

He got up from his seat and followed the priest out the door. As he did so, he glanced down at the clipboard Toledo had clung to. He expected to see detailed notes with how often he'd scratched it with his pen… but there were only swirling, nonsensical lines. No words. No notes.

He was then led through the police station hallways, tracking gore into the carpets. The priest handed him a roll of bandages produced from out of his cloak, and he wrapped his palm as best he could. Cops followed him with their probing, curious eyes until they reached the front doors.

Behind mud-splattered glass stood two figures in outfits Martin had never seen before. Gloved hands yanked on the door handles, and the cold morning air swirled viciously against the stagnant, air conditioned heat. Warm breath fogged out through the slits in two helmeted faces–pig face style. Medieval. The sigil of Golgotha was stamped multiple times into the blackened metal.

“One of my congregation will stitch your hand and give you food and water when we reach the abbey.” Roman descended the police station’s concrete front steps.

The helmeted figures let the doors go and hurried behind. They were an encroaching wall that Martin had to stay ahead of. Both were strapped into bullet-proof vests over their baggy, red shirts and trousers. Antique Sten guns hung from straps across their shoulders. They parted and walked ahead of the priest as they came to an old thirties-looking car parked on the street. Its back door was opened and Martin was ushered inside with Roman following. A snap. Door shut. The priest reached over to flip the lock. As the car swayed back and forth, it’s suspension accommodating the helmeted men getting into the front, Roman said: “I never use this car. There are few times I leave the abbey these days.”

Martin sucked in air as pain rocketed up his arm.

“Please don’t bleed on the seats.”

The engine sputtered and kicked, and the car was moving.

14

Drug-clouded eyes. Vacant expression. The man was wrapped in rags–an old blanket with tassels along the edges. They hung into opaque sidewalk puddles, feeling with their dangly threads through the mire. A kick from the ancient engine. The man outside didn't flinch; his eyes were boring through the bullet-proof window, into Martin's.

The pedestrians ahead of the car were clear now. Lethargically, the wheels went to rolling. Smoke ejaculated from the modified hood exhausts, drawing a cloud around the hood ornament: seal of Golgotha.

Martin watched the bum slide away beyond the edge of the window.

"This car was a retirement gift. Nineteen-thirty-two *Daimler Double-Six*."

A low drone from Martin's left. He turned to see the priest looking out the window.

"It was modified, you'll see… to keep me safe from the

rabble. There are some who hate me."

The bandages had fully soaked through. But the bleeding was lessened if he pressed the wound together. His first attempt at speech came out in a pathetic sigh. He cleared his throat. "Retired from where?"

A pause. "I was a neurosurgeon. In the nineties, at Cardinal Medicine. My employer was Osian Molina, who I'm sure you've heard of."

"I think so."

"He was killed when the F.B.I. raided our building in Roanoke. I was there, organizing samples of gray matter collected from… *monkeys*." As they passed under an overpass, the priest's crystal blue eyes were mirrored in the window. His reflection was looking at Martin–had been, perhaps. The whole time. It vanished as the car lumbered into the daylight again. "The whole event confirmed to me what I'd been growing to suspect. Each day prior–for perhaps a month–I'd been uncovering things in my research that did not abide by our laws of science. Then that day, the answer was revealed to me." He trailed off, took a long breath.

Rumbling of tires on the road. The engine vibrating the car.

"While the authorities were questioning me, I felt something enter the room. It was a beautiful and horrifying presence, taller and larger than physics' three known dimensions could contain–it was invisible to me." Another breath. Unsteady. Martin wondered if there were tears in the man's eyes. "The King of Heaven, there in the room. For me. He spoke in my head, and showed me visions of endless, spiraling pits into shadow–like storm clouds, spinning infinitely large beneath me and around me. Pillars of even darker shadow rising up through them. Heaven… so beautiful and awful. A domain where an Old Testament God might dwell with his angels, beyond human understanding."

Martin felt his hairs stand up on his arms. "I think… I-"

"-You've seen it. I know. Golgotha shows very few a window into Heaven. It's separate from even the plane of reality I was tasked with studying for Doctor Molina–connected, of course. But I would not be able to explain it. Not even a man with a degree in every known field of science would come near to wrapping his head around such a thing. It must be shown to you."

Through the car's windshield, Martin could see the Red Abbey on its hilltop. They were closing in, passing now through the town's main street. Pedestrians mulled about–some walking in the road. A barrel pushed up against a brick wall licked at the mortar with flaming tongues, turning it black. Four husks of men huddled around it, warming their hands.

"That sounds like what I saw in the police station. When the… I guess you've seen that, haven't you? … Tell me what happened when I got in there."

"With the unfortunate detective?"

Silence.

"Golgotha made the man claw his face to shreds–with a pencil. Is that right?"

A pause. Then slowly: "Yeah. That's right."

"A display of his power."

"Then why didn't he try and get me out of the cell? Couldn't he kill all the cops in the building if he killed that one guy?" Stab of pain, right up through the arm. He winced, then pressed tighter.

"Not necessarily. You did not want him to."

"What?"

"You wanted the detective to die–your questioning was unfair. You didn't kill the girl on the bus, but the police were blaming you. A week ago, I told you that you were perfectly capable of breaking through Mr. Crooked's heavenly barrier, and that you did. I said you were capable of defeating the cherub and bringing him back to the Abbey, but you did not want that, did you?"

Martin watched the streetlamps flash in the red cloth of the priest's robe. Every dark shadow that passed across the window would reveal the ghostly impression of his face in the glass, always staring into Martin's eyes. He tried to muster up an answer. "Why wouldn't I have?"

There was a response ready and waiting: "Because you want to sit in your apartment and waste away into nothing. Falling back into addiction and rotting under a heat lamp made of memories."

"Why didn't he kill Toledo? He was torturing me."

"And that's what you deserve, is it not? In your own mind?"

"I… Mr. Crooked threatened me on the bus-"

"-And you wanted him to kill you."

Silence. Then: "Excuse me?"

"But when you were hanging from a rope in Mr. Crooked's meat locker, you desperately wanted to be free and run home. Not to fight. Not to capture the monster who strung you there. Just to be let down." Now, finally, the red robed head swiveled to face who it spoke to. "Golgotha dwells in Heaven. He has only a finger on you–pushed through the curtain at a time when it was pulled back for him. He can only act through you, Mister Navarro, not for you. Do you understand me?"

A drop of blood fell through the bandage. It struck his jeans and spread through the fabric. The gates of the Abbey were open, so the car drove through onto the incline road leading up the hill. Martin felt a pain deep in his chest. "He can let me leave… Turn your head into a mess on the window if I wanted that… He can burn down your church."

Wrinkled lips smiled in the halflight. "But Golgotha is not a pet, nor a weapon. And when he came to me that day, back in ninety-eight, and showed me the truth, I pledged myself to him fully. And I wanted to serve him… *wanted.* I was not forced, nor gently coerced. I am his earthly body, Mister Navarro. My will is his, and his is mine. So what is it that *you* want?"

"'At a time when it was pulled back for him,' what does that mean? When was it pulled back? And why did he cling on to me instead of any other bum on the street?"

The car took a dirt road alongside the broad wall of the abbey. At the end was an industrial garage door retrofitted into the bricks. It opened slowly–and loudly. Black birds took wing from off the crenelations high up.

The priest shifted slightly. "There is a reason. Perhaps I'll tell you. But only if Golgotha wishes me to." As the car rolled under the door, he was hidden by a blanket of shadow–crawling up from his legs to his cowled face. "But first, your hand must be stitched."

A key turn shut off the engine, and the garage door came down behind them, slamming home with a reverberating boom.

—

"I love you."

"I love you."

"I love you."

"I love you."

"I...

"...love..."

"...you..."

"...Martin. You're such a sweetheart." She sat on the edge of the dining table, covered by a long t-shirt. *Evanescence.* The printing was old and flaking away. Charcoal and laundry detergent danced through her air, spinning circles. "I didn't see any pills in your drawer today. Or in your bag."

His hands ran up and down the smooth warmth of her legs. She had her feet propped on his chair on either side of him–her hands playing with his locks of hair, bunching them up in a hairdresser's pantomime. He smiled. "Oh so you were looking through my stuff, huh?"

"Mayb-" Giggling, uncontrollable. Attacking fingers found her armpits. She doubled over, crushing the skittering flesh spiders between her ribs and biceps.

Then he embraced her, and held her tightly. Her chest lifted and fell gently against his. He lost himself in its rhythmic movement–listened to her breath traversing her windpipe, up from the lungs and out her nose. Kitchen window sunlight was brushed through her hair. Loose strands tickled his cheek. "I'd give up anything for you. I'd give up my whole life."

She hugged him tighter.

"I love you."

A long silence, followed by: "If I was a bird, would you take care of me?"

He chuckled, then pulled away to get a clear look at her face. She'd put on black lipstick, and it was smudged a little on the left side, right in the corner of her mouth. Her coffee eyes were moving beneath their shroud of bangs, searching him for an answer. He gave one: "Of course. I'd make a little bird bed and put it right on my nightstand, and I'd learn to knit so I could make you bird clothes."

Her eyes widened, and her mouth rounded out into a quiet "Woah."

"What if I was a bird?"

"Well, if you were a bird, then I'd try to turn myself into a bird. I'd go to whatever evil wizard made you one, and put a gun to his head. Then we'd be birds together and we could make a nest out of sticks–like those little guys that look for shiny stuff and bring it back to make their houses all fancy."

"That's crows, I think."

She slid down off the table and into his lap to hug him tighter. "Okay, then we can be crows together." After a second, she sat up straight. "No! We should be cardinals, 'cause you like them the best. They're your favorite."

"But then I'd be all pretty red and you'd be beige."

A puzzled look.

"The females are beige and the men get the red feathers–so they can prance around and attract the girls. But the females can sing pretty, I guess. "

Her black lips came down to kiss him. "You're so cute when you talk." She reached down to tug up on the bottom of his shirt, and he lost sight of her as it was lifted over his head.

—

"Let's have a look at your bruises."

The shirt stuck on his ears, then slipped off. It was

thrown on the table beside him.

"The cop really had his way with you, I see." Doctor. An older man with hanging jowls–like a bulldog. Glasses with thick lenses magnified his bug-eyed countenance. "This shoulder may be broken, or close to it."

Martin coughed. "That wasn't the sergeant."

Squint. "We'll x-ray it. First, we stitch the hand, or you'll bleed out." A toolkit snapped down onto the doctor's rolling table. An opening lid revealed a set of surgical needles–long and curved like animal talons.

"I hope those are sanitary."

The doctor scoffed. "I'm not a back-alley wastrel selling root canals for ten dollars. Have some respect."

A groan: "Sorry." Martin surveyed the room: brick walls; gothic decor; seemingly high-end medical equipment. Better than what the town doctor had in his broom closet practice. Two heavy bookshelves flanked a large oil painting, under which stood Roman Ward, gazing up into the image. It was the same painting from the police station: a winged colossus wielding glowing runes.

The priest's voice bounced off the walls: "Doctor Ito was one of my colleagues at Cardinal."

Martin wondered if that was meant to ease his concern. Doctor Ito began to unwind the gore-soaked bandages from his hand, revealing the raw and angry wound bisecting his palm. From out of nowhere came a cloth soaked in something; it clamped down onto the wound and shot seething pain through every nerve. A yelp, echoing over and over.

"Scream if you like. I've got to disinfect it."

The cloth remained until the pain had slowed to an ache, either from disinfection, or because Martin's body had numbed itself in shock–he had no idea. What was once clean white came away redder than the doctor's cloak. Then the needle swung into view, and it pierced the skin fast and deft. Each pull on the string brought the two flesh halves toward each other.

"I can't tell if there's tendon damage. You've lost too much blood to start poking around." The magnified eyes popped up to look at Martin's face. "White as a bone, mister. You should pray to Golgotha that there's no infection or lost mobility in the hand–well, that's extremely likely with a wound like this…" He trailed off. His attention was focused on the needle.

"Fuck…" Martin ground his teeth. He looked away from the needle, fearing he might pass out. His wandering eyes settled on Roman, who just now turned around to face him. The priest was hard to distinguish outside the room's hanging lamp light–save for his crystal eyes. Light always managed to find them somehow.

"Golgotha will save the hand," he said. "If you want him to."

Martin felt tears creeping through his ducts. There was a hard pressure on his chest, and his skull. The room suddenly seemed vacuous and dark, and he felt like an ant under a magnifying glass.

"You saw this painting in the police station." It wasn't a question. "This was painted by one of my congregation, using descriptions I gave to him of our Lord. There are three runes, you see?" A burgundy gloved finger extended toward the rendering. "The Dog, the Bird, and the Rusty Hook–there, hanging from his mouth."

"I see them." His attention was half focused on the feeling of his skin being cinched. The priest's descriptions were hardly distracting.

"The Dog represents guidance from Heaven. It is an omen meant to communicate the will of Golgotha."

He felt his breath catch in his throat. *Dog.* The dog. The jackal leading him to the underpass, the tourist center, the bus.

"The Bird is the angel which visits us on earth, though I've explained that to you, if you remember."

Bird. Cardinal.

The needle yanked tight, pulled flesh.

"And the Rusty Hook. Once we are hooked, we belong

to him, and we must do as he commands–in exchange for the first two. Those are the base tenets of our religion."

Martin felt the air around where the doctor was seated change–temperature, or heaviness. A head turn, and he saw the mouthless skin man sitting on a chair in the shadowed corner. He tried to recall if it had always been there–since he'd been ushered into the room–but he couldn't. The room held a shroud of darkness over the figure's upper half, obscuring its flesh eyes–its popping veiny scalp. Whenever he looked at it, all sound in the room would be sucked into a vacuum–all light blotted out–and only the soft sound of breathing would whisper to him. It was sizzling breath. Mucus. Coming from that corner.

"Bonnie..."

"Bonnie..."

"Bonnie..."

"Bonnie..."

"She wasn't in her room, was she?"

The doctor snatched a pair of scissors off his utility cart–snapped the suture string with long, stainless steel teeth.

Martin looked down now, at the hand. Thread was holding it together, pierced through the crimson-bruised, swollen mess. "I… um… She was never there." He could feel his blood pumping through the veins beneath his temples. "I saw her so clearly… through…"

"Her vent."

"Yeah…. Yeah, the vent. I don't know why I started looking through it in the first place… or when. I don't remember." It felt as though he was reclaiming his hand–like a shirt from the dry cleaner–as he lifted it off the doctor's cart. He turned it front to back. The palm was stitched as well. Frankenstein's monster. Two hands sewn together, from two different people. "But I can't remember now… where she is–really. I think she moved out a long time ago. A few years… maybe that's not a long time. But why did she do that?"

Roman's eyes glew under his cowl. "Perhaps you might ask Golgotha."

Martin's brow scrunched in. His heart kicked up. "If he knows, why hasn't he told me?"

"You should know it by now."

"Why?" He stood up out of the chair and entered the shadow under which the priest was standing. The crimson figure stood taller than him by a foot or more, but he stared up into the maw of the cowl, resolute. "That's bullshit. Of course I want her. I need her. At no point did I stop needing her."

"But you thought she was in her apartment."

"I wanted her to talk to me. To come into my apartment, or for me to see her in the hallway, or out on the street. That never happened. Only through the vent."

Silence.

"Huh? What's your explanation for that?" He saw no change in the priest's stoic features–nothing to indicate what might be occurring behind the swirling crystal eyes.

"Such a stubborn man, you are."

That took him aback. "What?"

A long pause before: "Of course she never appeared in your presence."

"Why?"

"Because that's not where she is physically. Golgotha only sho-"

"-then where the fuck is she?"

"... Golgotha only showed you a mirage. You wanted to see her through the vent, in her fully furnished apartment, and so that's what you saw. But Golgotha is a caring Lord. He hoped you might grow suspicious and question why she never came out into the hallway. Why she never knocked on your door anymore. Do you understand me? He wanted you to catch his hint that she is not safe and at home where you wanted her to be."

Martin moved his mouth around his stuttering breath.

"You were starting to. Were you not?"

"You're talking in circles now." He blinked fogginess out of his eyes. Tools clinked against glass. Urgency began to manifest in his tone: "Tell me. What are you not telling me?"

Roman huffed. "I do as Golgotha commands."

"You said your mind and his are the same."

"No, no. My will is his, and his is mine. He can speak to me only when I pray and open my mind." After there was no more rebuttal, he said: "After all that you've seen, you still don't believe me. You question everything I tell you."

Martin felt the warmth of a gloved hand on his shoulder.

"Mister Navarro, I have your best interest in mind. You must believe me. What have I done to lead you astray from your path?"

He'd never been able to stare into the priest's eyes, but something now gave him the strength. He took the time now to examine them–searching back and forth, up and down. The irises were webs of sapphire, taking his mind away from where he was now and lowering him gently onto the tranquil bed of a shallow ocean. Rays of sunlight danced and twirled in the ripples on the surface, playing that movement onto the sandy floor below like a projector. In all directions was water–dark as the immeasurable volume pressed onto itself. Opaque, like a frosted window. But that vast emptiness gave him a sense of tranquility. Colossus shapes dwelt there, moving slowly, beyond the constraints of time–nearly impossible to perceive with bodies that moved through four dimensions instead of three.

The priest blinked.

And Martin was back in the infirmary, his lungs attempting to recall how to breathe. His headache had cured itself. "Where… is Bonnie now?"

"In Mr. Crooked's abattoir."

"Mr. Crooked's abattoir."

"Mr. Crooked's abattoir."

"What? Dead?"

The hand slid off Martin's shoulder. "I don't know, Mister Navarro. Golgotha can not see beyond the Cherub's barrier. But she was taken there."

"When?"

Silence.

"When was she taken there?"

Silence.

He stepped away from the priest and stormed over to the

door. His hand went down to his belt to make sure he felt metal–a hammer, a sight. Loaded. The door was thrown open–struck the interior wall–then he left the priest and the doctor and sprinted full-tilt down the stone corridor.

—

“Why are you running so fast?”

The train came to life, spewing smoke. As it began to move, he slowed down–feet clapping pitifully on the platform concrete. He bent over, hands on his knees. Breath. Fall air–cold and wet.

Then she touched his back. He straightened and turned to embrace her. “Sorry. I thought I could hold the door for you.”

Fallen leaves rustled and skittered in clouds over the tracks.

“Why the rush? We’ve got all the time in the world.”

He smiled. “Yeah, I guess you’re right.”

“Sit with me, speedy.”

Her cheek was warm under his fingers. Dark hair whipped in the wind. He led her to an open bench and they sat there, his arm around her shoulders–watching the leaves fall in sheets of amber.

15

Creaking hinges.

The delicate hum of gears and clockwork mechanisms swirled about the room. It recognized the now-open escapeway and took it, bumping into Martin on its way out into the Virginia dampness. Odor followed it. Formaldehyde and rot. A can of air freshener sat on a shelf just inside the door. Bloody handprints had hardened on the plastic label.

He met the same greeting figure from the last time he'd come. But her skin seemed as if it had tightened a little more around her parts. Out came a flashlight. The white glow explored the wrinkles and stitched incisions–delicately sparkled in a pair of empty, glass eyes.

Chink... click... chink... click...

Her arms waved at him. Stiff.

He looked closer at her face. Lipstick had been applied messily, and smudged in multiple directions. The light ventured down, to the neck. Bruises forever stained purple in the gray flesh.

"Fucking… God." Martin threw the light, let it land on another automaton. This one was lying on her back, arms lifted over her head. Rotators in the hips moved her legs up and down. The knees were bent. Maybe a yoga pose, or something very different. With each movement, the whole body shook, like a fish out of water. But aside from this singular motion, the thing was dead. Blank face. Mechanical.

Martin's heels were loud on the hardwood floor. A primal warning in his mind expected one of the automatons to lunge at him. Quick glances in all directions. There were too many of them to count–and each was stitched together from the cuttings of multiple carcasses.

Ten women.

Twenty women.

Sixty women.

A hundred women.

His chest started to ache. He could feel his heart striking against his ribs. The pistol in his hands preceded him in every turn–every move through the crowded lobby. A tall, peaked ceiling echoed the clockwork symphony happening beneath it. Skylights were boarded up, but let in slivers of warm sun. It wasn't enough to reveal the full scope of the room to the naked eye. A chandelier of buck antlers hung quiet from a joist, along with hundreds of lengths of fly paper–all of them nearly stuck full. Taxidermy animal heads were bolted to the walls high up, looking down. He imagined they could have been amused at the irony of what they saw beneath them.

He stopped just before he reached the reception counter. *SNOWY OAKS TOURIST CENTER.* It was painted on the front, just beneath an interpretive symbol of three snow-covered trees. Beyond the desk was a set of doors and a hallway leading into the back rooms. It was a dark portal.

"I'm here! Come out, fuckface!"

No answer.

He waited, spinning in place constantly, trying to focus on the figures in the darkness–in case one of them was living. He felt eyes on him, and turned to see three automatons seated in a row along the wall. Their arms were down at their sides, hands gripping the edge of the bench. Each had their legs crossed in the exact same pose. They were older than the rest–at least compared to the ones he had seen. Skin was beginning to sag and come unstuck. Stitches were loosening. When they all turned their heads back and forth in sync, the mechanisms lagged and stuttered.

Now he felt exposed. He snaked through the mechanical crowd, his eyes lingering on each figure. Morbid curiosity. A car crash–too horrible to look away from. One had her crotch messily sawn off and retrofitted with the mouth of a wolf. Fangs hung open in wait of prey. Another had been facially defiled with needles and thread: face posed and secured in a wide grin on the limit of human capability. The eyelids were sewn open over glass eyes–widely, like the automaton was scared of something, but forced to smile anyway.

Martin reached the corner of the room, and pressed his back against it. He could see it all now. Half his mind wanted to scan the mechanisms–search their zippered up skin shells for her face, or legs, or whatever bit had been used–and another half couldn't look at them for fear of what he'd see. Images filtered into his consciousness of her warmth made cold and stretched over metal ribbing. Vomit waited in his throat, asking to come out. He denied it.

In this half-conscious daze, he nearly missed a change in the room. A primal sense took over–pointed it out. Directly across from him, in the opposite corner, was a hulking shadow. He'd never heard footsteps. Never saw it enter. But it was staring at him, the massacre of a face crosslit by the sun that filtered in between the boarded-up windows. Long hair hung like a cowl.

The pistol locked in on its target. Waited.

"Don't fucking move."

No answer.

"I thought you were gonna follow me around."

Through a wet throat rose its voice: "Didn't take much for you to get picked up by the pigs, little bull. Like a stray dog, you are. Yessir, I was watchin' that. Checked your apartment every day to see if you'd come home. Checked your bedroom. Checked the shitter. Checked all up and down. But the pigs had ya still."

No response.

So the thing went on: "I must say, I didn't expect you to return the favor. You're like a dumb bitch whore who gets beat on by her man. Always comes right on back. That's what you deserve." It paused–waited to see if Martin would answer. He didn't. "But I can read a room. I think you done grown some balls. You're not gonna run this time."

"No."

A malformed smile. "Guess we'll see, won't we?"

"I was told there's a woman… here."

The mattock shifted slightly forward into the light. Its head stamped on the floorboards. "Got a lot of 'em. They just love me, little bull. Ain't none here wanna leave."

"She's small, with dark hair. Bangs. We…" He trailed off. Tried to collect himself. "We came to you to look at your cats. A long time ago."

"Selkirk Rex," answered the thing. "A pretty girl needs a pretty cat."

Martin felt a weak breath trickle out his mouth.

"Such a pretty girl."

"Where is she?"

Silence.

"Where is she, you ugly fuck! Answer me now or I'll put a hole between your fucked up eyes!" His finger slipped down onto the trigger. Tremors in his hands kept him from aiming straight.

"I remember her. Yessir." Unnatural laughter, punctuated by phlegm-filled coughs. "When I saw her that day I was smitten, I must say. God-damn, I ain't never seen a girl like her in my life. Young and smooth. Tight like a screw. I could picture them bangs flyin' up and down. Up and down, up and down, up and down. She unlocked something in me that day I saw her."

Martin tightened his grip on the pistol.

"I was an old man. And the little bull with her was a young, handsome specimen. I bet he made her scream like a banshee whenever she felt the need. Bless your heart, but that just ain't right. Old farmer Forsyth ain't never felt the love of a young, beautiful kitty. Not anything like her."

Martin felt his heart speed up.

"I was a lonely man, you see. No pretty girls wanted to talk to me, now. So I followed you back to your apartment, and I went up the elevator with my here tool–got it right outta the back of my truck. I'm surprised you don't remember."

Tunnel vision. The room was fading away–the ticking and clicking of the mechanisms shifting into a dull, constant drone.

"Broke down her door, yessir."

Martin couldn't breathe.

"Broke her ribs with only one swing. Got blood all on her pretty white bed."

Thumping, in his skull.

"Saw you in the doorway with that shiny gun you got. I wonder if you heard her tryin' to breathe with her chest all caved-in. Sounded like music. And what a terrible shot you are, little bull. Hit my arm before I got to ya. Knocked you out with a fist to the forehead."

"... Liar."

"And I took her pretty body back here, and I made her bangs fly up and down. All damn night. God, it was beautiful. She took my virginhood, you know that?"

"That's a lie."

"I can show her to ya if you want. Do ya want that? She's just in there." A long, gnarled finger emerged from the darkness, pointing at an inconspicuous door. *STAFF ONLY.* "I'll stay right here, little bull. You walk on over and open that door. You can see her from the doorway.

Martin didn't move.

"Butterflies in ya stomach, little bull? She ain't as pretty as she used to be. Nothing to scare at."

He took in breath in a long, sputtery draw. Then he moved, almost unconsciously. One step at a time. The pistol stayed pointed at the hulking thing, though it was jumping like a scared cat. When he got to the door, he reached for the handle. It was old and flaking gold paint.

He turned it.

And saw her.

Bonnie...

Bonnie...

Bonnie...

The room was very small. Only a little bigger than a closet. Candles were placed in nearly every available space on the floor, every one a different length. Flies explored the ceiling, scared of the heat from the candle flames. Placed up against the back wall was a chair–one likely pulled from the lobby. A large halo was painted on the wall behind it–framing it. Dead, shriveled flowers hung from nails hammered into the yellowing drywall. And seated bolt upright in the chair was a body with skin that looked like wax. Preserved by chemicals, but still rotting with time. Clumps of her black hair had fallen out, and her eyes had been replaced with glass marbles. She was stripped naked. The same paint from the wall had been used to place runes and symbols onto her lifeless flesh.

"My Eve. The origin of all." The voice sounded in Martin's left ear, muted. "Kept whole. My undying wife."

Candlesmoke and the putrid air made him feel dizzy. He stepped away from the door, into one of the automatons. It fell over, striking the ground with a clatter that reverberated against the insides of his skull. The vomit that had questioned before now demanded. It sprayed out of his mouth and ran down his chin, but he stayed standing. "You… murdered…"

The beast said nothing.

"You…"

SNAP!

The mouth of the gun began to smoke. The beast reeled and stepped back against the wall. Martin advanced.

SNAP!

Black slime leaked from out of the wound now square between the monster's eyes. But it didn't fall.

SNAP!

Martin broke into a run, and as the third bullet punched

a hole through Mr. Crooked's chest, he slammed into the hulking beast and grappled him to the ground. It reached for the mattock, but a well-placed boot sent the tool skating across the floorboards. Long greasy hair flung back and forth as a rain of fists came down onto the beast's disfigurement. It tried to fight back, and Martin felt the strength of its grip. He was ripped away with incredible force, but lunged again to get on top.

The gun pressed hard against a lumpy temple and spit four rounds through the skull–into the brain. There was a roar–like that of an animal, before the hulking thing grabbed Martin and lifted him into the air. It got to its knees, then to its feet, while its head snapped violently with the force of a string of gunshots. All into the brain. But it kept moving.

Martin was pressed against the wall, hard. Hot breath wafted in his face. Then words: "Little bull really did grow some balls. But guns don't hurt me, son. Might as well throw that little peashooter away and put your fists up." Then he was thrown across the room, knocking down four or five automatons that started a chain reaction. Cracking and striking of metal on wood–dead flesh muffling it sometimes. Mechanisms breaking and spraying little gears and tensioned wires. Martin groaned and tried to roll over desperately. He realized the gun had fallen out of his hand; now it was lost somewhere in the darkness, amongst the taxidermied feet.

Instead of bullets, he shot his flashlight beam at the heavy, moving shadow. It was bent over now, grabbing at something. The mattock head dragged heavy on the floorboards on its way up. The beast got a good grip on the leather-wrapped shaft and cocked its arms–tensioned its bulging, gray muscles.

Then a swing. A wide arc that tore through the Frankenstein crowd. Falling automatons knocked over their neighbors. Metal faces crumpled around the flat end of the swinging head. Over the clamor came: "All ruined! Ruined! Ruined! Fucking rat touched you! God damn!" Each phrase was punctuated by a sweep of the tool–a grunt and another batch of destructive noise. "Touched you… with his… dirty… fucking… *HANDS!*"

Martin wrestled with the junk pile he lay on top of–leapt stumbling to his feet. The mattock's flat tooth nearly nicked him, but he dodged, falling into another automaton. The air by his head was cleft into two vibrating gusts of wind, left in the weapon's dust. He could feel the weight of it–the power and the rage. He kept low, then sped clear of the whirlwind, just missing another swing.

"I told you not to touch my girls! Don't touch 'em, you fucking rat! I'll shatter those little fucking ribs!" The beast stopped mid swing and turned around to locate its target.

Then it broke into a charge, and the room shook with every footfall. It was an unstoppable force. Any dolls still standing were swept aside by the mattock, or a swinging arm.

The reception desk tapped Martin on the lower back. He spun quick and leapt over it–catching his foot on the ledge. A spill, onto his shoulder. Pain, coursing like fire through his flesh. But his cringing body saved him from the sharp tip of the mattock. It came over the desk and embedded itself into the back face. Deep. Inches from Martin's neck.

And it stuck.

Frantic wrenching from the beast's awkward angle couldn't free it from the layers of wood, metal and drywall. "Motherfucker! Come here, you-"

A grab at Martin, over the desk. It missed.

The thing was like an angry animal stuck behind a fence. Martin kept far back out of its reach, though there was only just enough room. Its fingers were in his face, clawing and snapping. They were thick, mangled fingers, forcing him back harder and harder against the wall he'd flattened himself against. Once the beast gave up, it slunk off away from the desk and stood there, breathing heavy. "Run, little bull. Left or right. Which way?"

Most of the mechanical sounds had been smothered. Now the room was almost quiet. Martin could hear the beast's bubbling, mucus breath being forced out its flaring nostrils. Its mass blocked his view of the front door, and the boarded windows backlit it in pallid glow–kept its grotesque features concealed in shade. So enormous. It must have been over seven feet tall. His mind offered him images of Bonnie's petite form being ravaged. He saw blurry speckles floating over his eyes. Blink. They struggled to focus.

He looked to his left. To his right. The thing would catch him either way. It was faster than its body should have allowed–its size. He looked down at the mattock embedded in the back of the desk. Its flat end was buried all the way.

But…

"I'll skin ya, little bull. Hang you up in the ceiling with your back cut open, like the Vikings did."

The beast had been pulling up on it–trying to free it from the desk. But it looked able to come out horizontal. He pondered the distance. How fast the beast would move. "You shouldn't have touched her."

It smiled. "What's that, little bull?"

He inched out his boot. Pushed off the wall. Radiant heat from the looming figure embraced him. There were speckles of sprayed saliva on the top of the desk, absorbing particles from the layer of caked-on dust. Martin blinked a stray beam of sunlight out of his eyes. "I'll fucking kill you."

The poorly lit face across the desk chuckled.

"And I'll pulverize your ugly fucking face." He felt

warm tears roll down his cheeks. "I'll do it right in front of her. So she can watch you die."

The chuckling gradually faded. "Then do it."

Silence.

Then the beast suddenly came to life, and Martin's mind was made up for him. It grabbed onto the desk and hauled itself over, snapping the edge of the wood where its hand was clasped.

Martin reacted quickly.

He ducked under a clumsy attempt to grab at him, then snapped both hands onto the shaft of the mattock. It came free horizontal, just as he'd hoped. Though it was heavy, something gave him the strength to lift it. And he lifted it high.

Mr. Crooked was across, planting his feet. The mattock struck him center in the chest, and there was a loud crack. Broken ribs. But it kept going. Deep into his rotten flesh, until it could go no farther. Martin yanked hard, with strength that surprised him. The mattock head came loose, and he swung again. A perfectly aimed blow to the same exact spot. Another, louder snap. The spine.

The beast went down, control of its legs stolen by the metal tooth. Black and red mire escaped through its wound, leaking down its trousers to the floor. It tried to suck in breath, but its chest had collapsed. Another strike shook its paralyzed meat. Whether the monster felt pain, Martin couldn't tell. But it didn't matter. He paused his assault to survey what it had done. What had once been a tall monolith was now a trembling sack of flesh and noise. Awful noise. Like chunky liquid leaking out of a set of bagpipes. The monster retained partial control of its arms, and it grabbed at Martin feebly as he walked around the desk to the other side.

He didn't utter a word–just grabbed the hulk by its long hair and dragged it. The door to the closet was still open, and Martin dropped his conquest in front. Bonnie's upright, wide-eyed corpse watched as he smashed the monster's head to pieces. Chunks were bitten off with each swing. Skull fragments shot off in all directions. Inside was a shriveled, black brain. It turned half to dust as it was hit by metal. He didn't stop until it was all paste, and the decaying blood that had leaked out was filtering through the floorboards–down into whatever might be tucked down in the basement.

Then he stood, breathing hard.

At some point, willpower turned his head to look through the open closet doorway. He tried to think of something to say, but there was nothing.

—

He'd filled the truck with a jerry can found in a back room–

likely used for the outside generator feeding power to the decrepit building. *FORSYTH CAT BREEDER*. Time had eaten most of the decal off the door, but it was still legible. He was shocked the engine started, though the noise it made was dubious. Now he drove in silence, not talking to his passenger.

She'd had her spine replaced with a thick, metal rod. That kept her upright in her seat. He'd never forgotten the scent of her charcoal perfume. She didn't smell like it anymore. The face was still her own, but it was tightly hugging. Discolored. Lifelike enough that it looked as though she were just sleeping–as she used to whenever they returned from a road trip. But the beast had cut off her eyelids.

So Martin had wrapped her with a blindfold.

The truck rolled around a bend in the road, and a view of the border fence appeared behind the treeline. They'd opened the gate–Roman Ward, and a company of cars and red-robed ghosts. Police waited around amongst them, leaning on their cruisers. Their postures could be read clear from a distance as they noticed the approaching truck. Some drew their pistols, but didn't raise them.

Martin hit the brake, then turned the key. He stared down through the windshield at the cowled priest, wondering what he might see in the man's face. All he got was a slow nod, and a crystal blue flicker. Then he felt the truck bow as a group of cops climbed into the flat bed to examine what was stowed there.

Mr. Crooked. Some bloody, desecrated remains. Brought back, as instructed.

16

He found the pop can buried in the grass–plucked it out and turned it in his hands. The bullet hole she'd made was still there. Fringes of aluminum bent outward. *Co– Cola*. A little stream of rainwater leaked out when he turned it. He put the can on top of the fencepost, like he had back then, except this time there was no one to shoot it. At the base of the post was the mound of disturbed dirt he'd backfilled with his shovel. Under that…

Dirt crumbs shook off the flat step of the shovel head when he pried it out of the ground. He'd gotten blisters on his fingers from the aged wood handle. He cupped the handle with both hands and leaned his weight–rested his chin on his knuckles. Not far off, human figures filed like world-weary ants through the doors of the Red Abbey. Tall stone towers nearly blended with the whiteness of the sky.

Three ascending mellotron keys, crammed through the speaker bolted to the crowning stone of the abbey's front archway. The echo from its brethren were carried up on the wind from the town below. Then came the voice: "*The might of Golgotha has delivered unto his disciples the body of Mr. Crooked. His spree of terror is ended, by the grace of our Lord. All are welcome to attend the ceremony which will banish his corrupted host from this earth. Come now to the Red Abbey. Blessed be, King of Heaven.*" It ended with a snap of electricity. In another ten minutes, the message would repeat, as it had done since dawn.

Martin stared into the odd collage of dirt and patches of grass he'd made. She was under there, and they would be face-to-face if not for the dirt. A hard gust made his hair fly. It was longer than he'd ever let it grow. Sniffle. He cleared his throat. "I remember everything now… And I let it all out on him. Three years of it. This, uh… whatever's in my head was trying to show me. I remembered us looking at those cats… and then I saw your body in a kennel. I saw you hanging from a hook… and other shit. But, uh… I guess I wasn't paying attention."

A bird traced a half-circle against the pale sky, then came down on one of the vacant fence posts. It was black as night. Crow. The head tilted back and forth as it studied the solemn man it found.

"I taught you to shoot here… or I guess I tried to show you anyway. Remember that? …Then I missed him. Hit his shoulder. When it mattered…” He trailed off. The crow vocalized softly. He blinked in its direction, then sniffled again. The tip of his nose was pink. “I broke my promise. I took pills again… Your mother screamed at me on the phone, and she was crying… I didn't make sure the front door to the apartment building had locked; I guess it got hung up on those seizing hinges it has. So he got inside. Isn't that ironic. You called the landlord about it the night before.” He felt convulsions in his chest. They played his voice like an out-of-tune piano. “…I wish I hadn't wanted coffee that one time… I should've gone straight home.” His fingers came up to his eyes. They left them wet. He collapsed to a crouch, hands still wrapped around the shovel's stem, as quiet, pitchless moans escaped him. They racked his body, each time pulling a well of tears down his cheeks.

The abbey tower bell started to chime. Red light was emitted from the great, stained glass eye. What remained of the town's population pooled around the doors, unable to find room inside.

On the fence post, the crow fluttered and squawked. Then it buried its beak into the soft down beneath the feathers, and started to preen.

—

He'd entered through the abbey's side door, which had been opened for him by a shadow in a red cloak. The nave was fully packed to bursting, and he had to push his way through to get a view of the chancel–upon which stood Roman Ward in special finery he'd never seen the man wear before. An enveloping headdress extending up like a spade-shaped mitre, sprouting the crescent moons from the seal of Golgotha. Beaded tassels hung from these elaborate branches, all studded with flickering jewels. Martin couldn't see the priest's face–it was hidden behind a black mask carved to resemble its wearer. Strange runic symbology and patterning was etched into the dusky skin. As the man moved, golden trim and embroidery from a new red cloak sparkled in the light of candles–along with a chain of golden bracelets hooped the full length of each gloved forearm. Even still, behind the mask he wore, the priest's glowing blue eyes shone clear.

Placed around the perimeter of the chancel, Martin could see near twenty black iron candelabras. Smoke had gathered in a slowly rising cloud that climbed the gridded back wall. The lectern was gone. There needed to be a clear view for the crowd, or else they might miss the abomination placed in the center of the scene.

It was a stone–ancient looking. Something that might be found in an Egyptian necropolis. A hole was drilled, or carved, through all four feet of its length, wide enough to fit a body. And indeed, it did.

The beast was stuffed inside, headless–flaps of neck skin drooping like wet paper. Limp arms were cranked at an unnatural angle, pointing skyward, where the wrists were bound to the ankles of legs bent at the knee. The sight inspired thoughts of slaughterhouses and gutted pork.

Suddenly, the room was flooded with the sound of choral voices, singing in Latin. An amplified mellotron played underneath. *Glória in Excélsis Deo*. The melody was in a major key–cheerful. Much of the gathered throngs joined in the song. Those who did knew every word. Martin didn't, but he could tell certain lines were strange based on how they matched the timing of the organ. It was like someone had cut the song's legs and arms off, then sewed them back on–except one of the arms didn't match. As it came to an end, a short period of silence followed.

Then a singular booming voice shattered that silence to pieces. "For three long and terrible years, our town was tormented by a malevolent angel broken free from heaven. Our women were butchered, and they were raped. Mothers of our children. Daughters of our mothers. They were taken by this maleficent sprite to the old tourist center beyond our borders, wherein their bodies were violated–dissected as if they were animals. Turned into a mockery of life."

Behind the priest, one of the robed figures waiting at the edge of the chancel came forward and pulled a blanket off what had previously been a covered silhouette. As the covering fell away, revealing the automaton, the crowds began to murmur and grow restless. Martin recognized it from the tourist center; one of the only automatons left untouched by the rampaging mattock. The robed shadow reached out to tap the elbow of the mechanical woman, which started her jittery dance. Arms lifted. *CA-CHUNK.* Lowered. *CA-CHUNK.* Over and over again, making the whole framework rattle. The mock chicken, hands over its breasts, and eyes held wide open by rigor mortis. Its head turned left, then right, then left–smiling down at the crowd.

Someone screamed, and started to cry. “That’s her face! My daughter! Oh my God, Jessica.. my … baby…” It was drowned out by the overflow of chatter and shuffling bodies.

“The face of Jessica.” When the Priest spoke again, the room went quiet, fast as a blink. “And the legs of another woman, the arms of a third, and the breasts and torso of a fourth. Stitched together with course leatherworking thread… forced to enact this profane pantomime. The limbs of one hundred and sixty women were taken. Our brave policemen found them all. Some were hung up in a small room, so that the blood would drain. Others were sculpted into these effigies. The rest were stacked in grotesque piles in the basement of the visitor center, callously doused in formaldehyde. What lay at the bottom of these piles was rotted away. Eaten by insects and rats."

There was an overall ambience of despair. Martin listened, trying to keep his eyes on the ornamented priest. If he turned to look at the weeping faces around him, he knew he would break.

"This is what became of them. Each distant scream in the small hours of the night. Every virgin defiled posthumously. Every girl who did not come home when she promised to." The dark mask turned then, and met the face of a watching Martin. "By the grace of our Lord… now avenged." Out came a glove, jangling with bracelets. "Come."

A blink, back into consciousness. Martin hesitated, but the gloved hand beckoned again, silently. He took a step… then another. Whoever stood in his way parted without a push. He felt naked. His knees wobbled under him as he forced them to carry his body up the chancel steps. Once he'd ascended, he crossed over to Roman, glancing at the stone altar–the twisted body he'd mangled the day before wedged inside. Firm, gloved fingers molded onto his shoulder and locked tight.

"This man… was given a task by Golgotha. He was weak, and ensnared by his sin, and the task was hard fought. But he was the only one among us able to complete it. For the King of Heaven is within him. His divine hand guides him to do what is right. He, too, lost something very important to the malevolent angel. His love carried him the final stretch."

Martin looked down at his feet–blinked hard. He wanted to leave. But he'd walked under a spotlight… and the priest's grip was unyielding.

"Martin Navarro struck the angel down using the talisman that gave it power–allowed it to walk among us undetected, and possess its inhuman strength. Golgotha gave mister Navarro the strength to lift it–the power to swing a damaging strike… Blessed be, King of Heaven."

And the room echoed. "*BLESSED BE, KING OF HEAVEN.*"

"And now, mister Navarro." the priest spoke quieter–just to him. "You will be the one to banish the sprite back to heaven, where Golgotha may tear it apart. Punishment, which is earned."

He tried to recall the face of the priest standing before him, but the mask was striking–and dark. It felt like he was speaking to a different man entirely. But the eyes were the same. He knew, without a doubt. "How do I do it?" He looked up, away from the mask. There was writing on the curved headdress moon-horns. *Rex caelorum beatus labiis meis loquitur. Beatus oculus sanctitatem suam videt.*

"Repeat what I say." A pause. A breath. "Exalted King who walks for two."

He repeated. All of it, as he was told. The room followed suit; hundreds of voices speaking in unison.

"Center of our worldly form; Grace above all other things; Guide in what I'm wont to do, Guide of hand and fire rod; Sword of Heaven 'gaist the storm; Touched me in my mother's tow; So I knew the Word of God."

Then he felt something, just below his chin.

He frowned, looked down, and saw a knife in Roman's gloved hand. Its blade was tipped in a globule of crimson, edged with a long streak of blood.

His next breath sputtered warm in his mouth.

From under the mask, the deep, sonorous voice continued. "Give the blood of he who walks; Knowing of the word of God; Acting with the hand of God; Heaven's grace in twenty drops."

The hand on his shoulder suddenly came to life, and he was thrown against the altar. Two robed figures rushed forward to puppet him and keep him restrained. They lifted his head to expose the neck, then dragged his open wound across the edge of the altar, leaving a trail of glinting red.

"Penitent shall be the sheep; Savior of their women bled; Rest assured Golgotha grins; For the root of pain is dead."

Once done, Martin was thrown aside onto the ground,

and he clutched desperately at his open throat. His vision was beginning to blur and grow dark, but out of the corner of his closing eyes, he thought he saw the body of Mr. Crooked begin to seize and rattle in its bonds. The headless corpse vomited a brutal noise to accompany the cloud of black mire coming from its neck stump. It was liquid, boiling with large bubbles that popped and sprayed, but it lifted into the air like smoke–up into the high cathedral ceiling.

"Witness the cleansing of our earth! As was foretold, Golgotha has rid our realm of this evil parasite! Blessed be, King of Heaven!"

"*BLESSED BE, KING OF HEAVEN. BLESSED BE, KING OF HEAVEN.*"

As Martin's eyes shut of their own volition, despite his struggle to keep them peeled, the voices of the crowd faded away into a piercing tone–heart rate monitor. Going flat. Then eventually, that too faded into silence.

17

A man entered a pitch black room, somehow visible against the backdrop of nothingness. He was enrobed, which obscured any recognizable human forms below the neck. Above it, however, a grinning sunface squinted with glee–bore its perfect rows of white teeth.

Vision cleared… details sharpened.

Not a sunface. A pale visage framed by the rim of a baldcap yellowed like sundried plastic. The sun's rays sprouted from a sort of headdress, along with dangling lengths of golden beads hanging low across the figure's chest. Two of these connected up at the face–to the tear ducts; it was impossible to see how.

Water was leaking somewhere–out in the void. Each drop was like the tick of a clock.

The figure came to stand before a massive display: a waiflike humanoid hung suspended amidst a web of black ropes, naked, but lacking any human protrusions. The head was elongated, skin smooth onion paper. Out of its shoulder blades, massive winglike spreads of black thorns hung limp. Though instead of resting on the ground, they hung down beyond it, exposing their full length. The waif was motionless, not fighting against its bonds–or if it was, the bonds were tight and unpliable.

WITNESS YOUR WORK.

It came from the sunface, through its monstrous grin. Words made by sucking air instead of pushing it.

MY WAYWARD CHILD REQUIRES PUN ISHMENT.

The darkness of the figure's robes gave birth to a pale hand with five-jointed fingers. Four curled up like spider legs, leaving the pointer digit outstretched. Up it came, until its tip was pressed into the hanging waif's paper stomach. Then it walked up, over the ribcage, over the breast where a nipple should have been, depressing the flesh beneath it. The waif tracked its progress desperately with wide, unblinking eyes that rolled wet in their sockets. When the finger passed below its view, the eyes kept rolling–inward beneath flesh. Mucus gathered at the corners, where the lids connected.

Then the finger pushed through. Nothing leaked–the waif was bloodless, it seemed. A corpse. Skin split and peeled into itself, giving view of rubber band tendons and fibers of muscle snapping and thrumming like guitar strings. The entering finger moved down, and the matter it passed through parted against it without much force at all.

RETURNED TO THE VOID.

A scream. Long and painful–heard above the sudden roar of energy. Black tentacles of flame erupted from the hanging waif, rocketing upward at an almost unintelligible speed. Flesh was turned to dust and flakes peeled away with the force of the blast. Before long, where the figure had been was now nothing. The restraining ropes fell away, swinging like pendulums. The sunface retracted its hand back into its robe and turned to face…

YOU SHOULD BE DEAD.

DEAD.

DEAD.

MARTIN.

—

He sucked on the stale air, finding it no longer slipped in and out through the cut in his throat. Fondling fingers, searching… Gauze and bandaging. He took his hands away–tried to blink focus into his eyes. There was blood on his fingertips, but it was a thin coat.

Thundering reverberations occasionally sounded from above–somewhere far over his head. They shook the floor, and whatever he lay on… a cot. Burlap stretched across wood struts; they squeaked as he shifted around, probing the fog for images amongst blots of color. This room stank of candlesmoke and blood. A gentle sound of disturbed water suddenly made itself clear to his right. He turned. A red robed figured, handling scissors over a small tupperware–dragging a cloth across the blades to soak up a blotting slick of blood. Drippings fell down into the container: seeds that sprouted into rapidly expanding clouds of darkness. From under the figure's cowl came a familiar voice, "He's awake, Vowess."

Doctor *Ito*... The firelight slashed across the thick lenses of glasses.

A waft of air and warmth–and incense. Something dark and encompassing. Thin cloth, filling his view. Behind it, a woman's breath–faint feminine tones. "You've saved him, it seems. Or is this muscle twitching?"

"Roman was sloppy. He did not hit the carotid, nor the jugular."

The woman continued to breathe and study him. Martin felt her hand touch his face, then move down to his neck to search for a pulse. He tried to speak, and his voice was raspy–almost a whisper. "*Take... your hand... away.*"

She did so.

"*I'll... rip... your... fucking eyes... out.*"

He got quiet breathing in response. It felt like he was half dead in a forest with a bobcat snuffling over his face. His muscles rejected his requests to sit up. He could only watch with slowly clearing vision, and wait.

Before long, the woman spoke through her veil: "Doctor Ito dragged you off the chancel while the congregation was focused on the cherub's banishing–before you bled out."

Scissors clicked against wood. The Doctor plucked up a scalpel now, and began its cleaning. Another reverberation–trembling stone, far above.

The woman's voice was mature and eloquent as the rest of the cultists. Her veil was sewn around the brim of a wide hat–one that evoked images of gunslingers and Annie Oakley–but decidedly more formal. It was red, as was her robe. Beaded ornaments hung off the brim alongside the ebony veil, each strand with a capping bead molded into the Seal of Golgotha. She remained kneeling by the bedside, like a worshiper. "Golgotha will speak to the Blessed Eye very soon, I imagine. He will know that you are alive."

Martin coughed hoarsely. That seemed to wake up his voicebox. "Where am I now?" His eyes had cleared up well enough to see the stonework walls of this miniature room.

"If I tell you, then Golgotha will tell The Blessed Eye."

Another cough. "Am I in the abbey?"

Silence.

"Who are you, then?" He blinked hard. No manner of intense focus he tried allowed him to see through the woman's veil.

"I am Vowess Neve."

"I've never seen a Transcensionist woman… I… maybe I thought you wore the same robes–all of you. Why are you different?" His head was thumping hard. Every word and every breath sent sharp prickles up and down the soft flesh of his inner throat.

"The women are called 'Vowess,'" she said. "Men are Apostles. But we women dwell beneath the abbey, and must not enter the nave. We are… virgins. Or if we were sullied by a man before, our virginity was returned through Golgotha. The unholy that dwell in the town can not see us."

Another metal click. Ito now began on his forceps. The

water he used was opaque now, but he continued regardless.

"You are unholy. But… you are the holiest of all. You are the vessel of the Lord."

Martin felt a surge of strength. He pushed hard and managed to lift at his hips. The pain in his head objected–his brain felt like it was sloshing around. A sudden urge to vomit shot up out of his depths, then retreated just a quick. He bent forward and leaned against the burlap with his arms. "Horseshit. Holy enough to cut my fucking throat."

The woman sniffled behind her shroud. "There was no more need for the vessel."

Martin turned on his ass and put his feet down on the stone tiles. His boots were still on–their heels clicked, making him feel like a horse, or something else with hooves. A hard lump in his belt announced itself like a cold tongue against his hip when his untucked shirt lifted a little. He grabbed at it clumsily. Racked the slide on the way up with his other hand. The cultist woman's veil depressed against the pistol's protruding nose. "I don't wanna hear about your cult bullshit again. Quit. I'm gonna leave now, and if I see another red robe, I'm putting five holes in it. Especially Roman–and you can tell him that to his face if you like. Unless he can already hear me somehow… I brought your fucking killer, now get whatever's in my head *out* of my head. Take it back, and don't bother me again."

Metal click. The forceps went down beside the scalpel. Ito was watching out the edge of his cowl, glasses alive and flickering.

Silence.

Then the woman said: "We saved your life." And her voice nearly cracked. Her breath came faster beneath her veil, gently pushing the fabric up and down. "We saved you."

"Why?"

A pause. "I… h-had a son. In Roanoke. And he married a girl… before I left them. Or… they left me. My husband and my son. I watched you from a window when you buried that girl outside. I'm sorry."

Five fingers tightened around the pistol's grip.

"We should… get you out of here. Before you are discovered." She slowly rose to her feet. The faint ghost of a face was just visible now behind the veil as light rose like warm air up underneath it. It was a world-weary face, cut by wrinkles just beginning to form. "But… we'll need to blindfold you."

"I'm not going anywhere with you." He blinked. Another tremor. Something fell off the doctor's table–a boxcutter. Martin stared at the retracted blade–the blood stain. "You can tell me how to get out. Give me directions. Then I'll decide whether to smoke you both and let your freak friends find you in here."

A splash of water. Ito shook the tupperware upended over the floor. Then he went about sliding his utensils into a roll-up bag meant for kitchen knives. A cough–to clear his throat. "No need for that."

The pistol found a new target.

Ito straightened his glasses. "I will be leaving with you, boy." Bony fingers strangled the knife bag with its velcro-ended tail. "And then you will never see me again. So long as you carry Golgotha inside of you. I have betrayed Roman, and he'll put me to death if he gets his hands on me."

"Why?"

"I was a Catholic many years ago. My relationship with Roman led me to worship a false god, which is not the true God. It is a devil, boy–what you carry inside you. We have all gone and worshiped the Golden Calf, with Roman Ward as our Aaron." An absent hand came up to scratch his jowl. "I knew it when I watched him cut your throat. He is a deceiver–*Antichrist.*"

Martin watched the doctor place the knife bag into a knapsack that leaned against the wall. He lowered his pistol a little. "I put my trust in him."

"I know."

"You think I want to put my trust in *you*?

Ito straightened, turned in place. "I've saved your life

two times now, boy. I could have let you bleed out on that stage, or from that split in your hand… You don't deserve this, son. I don't know how this came upon you, but it was of no holy method. You're cursed, boy."

The adrenaline keeping Martin's arm up gave out, and he let the gun fall to his lap. He felt pain again, in a hundred different places. His throat was throbbing. "Fuck… I don't…" Hot tears gathered in his eyes, thick like blood. "I want it out of me… I want it fucking out of me now."

Ito snatched up his knapsack and approached the bed. He knelt and grabbed Martin's knee with firm fingers. "*Koketsu ni irazunba koji o ezu.* My mother said that to me all the time, boy. You know what that means? 'If you do not enter the tiger's cave, you will not catch its cub.'"

Martin met the doctor's spectacled gaze.

"You only have to trust me once." A long length of cloth appeared in Ito's hands. "So Golgotha is blind… yes?"

The woman was still standing there. Martin looked up at her, but the ghost of her face was no longer visible. He said: "What about you?"

A pause. "My name is not truly Neve, but that's what you must call me. The Blessed Eye will not know which of the women helped you–he does not see our faces. I will remain here." As Ito tied the blindfold, she continued: "When you're out, The Blessed Eye will likely come for you, and he will know where you are all the time. He may send the police, but they won't arrest you. They will shoot you. Golgotha was supposed to be released from you when you died. You… are not a valuable host anymore."

Martin put his gun back through his belt, and tried to ignore the screaming in the back of his mind. When he opened his eyes, he saw fabric. He could only place the two figures in the room by hearing.

"You must find a way to force Golgotha out of you before you make a mistake–and die."

He felt a strong hand pull him to his feet, then lead him to the door–or what he assumed was the door by the click of the lock.

Ito spoke point-blank into his ear: "Go where I lead you, and do not speak."

Then the door was shut behind him, and he heard their two pairs of footsteps bouncing off unseen stone walls. Occasional buzzing of fluorescent lights passed by on his left–giant mosquitos all equidistant. The tremors that he'd felt in the room continued out here, shaking dust from the ceiling and onto his head and shoulders. He wanted to ask what it was causing them, but he caught himself before he did. *No speaking*. They passed through a gossamer cloud of gregorian choral with its grandeur shrunken by small, cheap speakers. A radio, maybe. But it was distant–or tucked into a side room, spilling out into the hallway. Soon enough, they stopped, and a door was opened. Wind and the scent of pine greeted Martin's nose. He nearly tripped on the threshold between stone and grass. The door shut, and they continued on. Car horn, far off. Birds, and grasshoppers.

"Golgotha speaks to Roman at nine *AM*, noontime, and six *PM*."

The sudden voice made Martin jump.

"Expect that at these times, Roman will know your location, and everything you've done during the day. If he wants, he will phone the police station and relay it to them, then they take some time to get there and search. Understand, boy?"

All he could muster was: "Yes."

"Don't stay anywhere longer than you need, and once these times come, wait a little while before moving, or Golgotha will see where you're going. And don't think about where you want to go before you go there… throw a dart at a map."

"Alright."

"Once I'm gone, you won't see me again, boy. Do you have questions?"

He considered. "No… no, I don't think so."

"Good luck, son. Wait thirty seconds, then take off that blindfold."

"Thanks, doctor… Same to you."

After thirty seconds, off it came. He looked around and saw the road leading towards his apartment–some six blocks down. The occasional pedestrian went about their grim business, clothed in patched rags. It was pleasant morning weather.

And Ito was gone.

18

Mr. Crooked had indeed entered his apartment, just as he'd said. The door he found blasted off its hinges. The furniture, in pieces, he stepped over carefully to avoid tripping on a table leg or a fragment of a picture frame. He felt as if he'd stepped into a wartorn country–an apartment shelled and long abandoned. An idle hand came up to feel the bandages coiled around his throat. For the first time, he felt little bumps running the full length of where he imagined the cut would be. Stitches. He swallowed, coughed–the racking pulse of each pulling at the flesh being held by those stitches. He hoped they were strong.

Boot heels crunched debris against the hardwood. He drifted further into the apartment, surveying what had once been intact–now turned to dust. His fridge had its doors ripped off and thrown into the living room. Rotting food sat amongst piles of splintered cabinet wood, crawling with flies and squirming larvae. He knelt down as he passed the kitchen island; something was lying in a clear space between angles of destruction. Flip phone. It was sitting now in the exact spot he'd used it to call his mother weeks ago. He couldn't remember checking if she'd replied to the message he'd left… maybe he did.

It was coated in dust; his fingers drew long streaks over its face. *Motorola.* He pulled it open and felt the plastic snaps of the buttons through his fingertips. On it came, flashing a bold *M* on a dim, fuzzy screen. The battery displayed in the top corner, with just a line of pixels worth of energy left.

1 NEW MESSAGE

He clicked around, navigating to the notification. Then the phone's thin plastic voicebox began to vibrate. "*Hi, Hijo... It's alright. Call me back when you're ready, okay? I love you.*"

Not her. She was… not in this town.

What left the message, then?

Click... click click. A dial tone. He put the cold plastic up to his ear and waited, surveying the room without really seeing. "Hello?"

"*Hijo... You haven't called in so long.*"

A pause. He rubbed his fingers together. "I'm… sorry."

Static. "*It's okay, sweetie. Did you find Bonnie?*"

His heart skipped. "She's dead, mama. But I killed the

man that murdered her."

"*That's good. Very good. It's good that you remember now.*" When the phone got no response, it waited.

And he waited. But it didn't say anything. "Who is this?"

"*Your mother.*"

"No, you're not. I'm… talking to myself."

"*I'm your mother.*"

He grit his teeth. The flies in the kitchen began to buzz louder. He thought he could hear the squirming and writhing of the maggots boring tunnels and pits into the decaying organics. Large worms pulsating inside the meat. Flies pushing white eggs onto the empty spaces where their brood could gnaw at the mold and break down what remained beneath.

"*Your aunt visited my house again. She was banging on the door until her hands were bloody and raw red. Then she used her forehead. She shook the door with every strike, and they were fast strikes. Before long, I heard her skull snapping against the wood. Like a snare drum... And the screaming. It was so loud. And angry. She beat her head until her brain was smeared across the door, and she kept going.*"

"Tell me who you are. Now." He felt sweat between the phone and his tightening fingers.

"*I'm your mother.*"

"No."

"*I'm your mother.*"

"I haven't seen her in years."

"*I'm your mother.*"

SNAP! He broke the oyster in two. Its wire guts tied the two halves loosely together, dangling. "No… Be quiet." A sideways toss added another piece of junk to the ruin. He got to his feet. "No more."

Mousie was sitting, where he'd always been, on the table by the windows. Surrounded by havoc and decay, he was the only thing untouched in the entire room. Martin walked over and saw the framed pictures of his family shredded and smashed, the plastic flamenco doll dismembered, and the plastic Jesus on his plastic cross missing. One glance back at the kitchen found it quickly, forced between an element on the stovetop, melted and interlaced with the metal–blackened by a gas flame.

But Mousie hadn't even been nudged.

"Too cute to kill." He took up the puppet and turned it over numerous times. "Or maybe you scared him off. Did you remind him of something? … If that's even possible."

The windows were frosted over at their edges. Sunlight glinted in the scratches left by the gnarled branches of the tree outside. At any gust of wind, those gray fingers would tap noisily, asking like a bored child for someone to pay attention. And Martin did pay attention. “The… fuck.”

She was down there on the sidewalk across the road. Black clad, and still as a shadow. Dark eyes were fixed unblinking at his apartment window. Deep coat pockets swallowed her hands.

He set Mousie down–drew his pistol. The window was stuck with ice, but he broke the seal with a hard push. A biting chill took the opportunity to push past his exposed face into the already cold apartment. He stuck both hands out into the white sunlight, stacked around the grip of the gun. It was quiet outside; he heard her voice as if she was standing only a few feet away.

“You’d shoot your *Tia?*”

The safety clicked off. “I don’t know if you’re real. I don’t think so.”

“Are you on your drugs again? Typical.”

He checked behind, over his shoulder, then looked back. “How did you get past the fence?”

“What fence?”

A smile. “I see.”

Silence passed between them, then: “I didn’t know you had grandpa’s gun.”

“He gave it to me.”

“No he didn’t.”

He frowned, used one hand to push the window up a

little more–to its limit. "It was a gift for my birthday–when I turned twenty-one. How do you not know that?"

"I wasn't there. Your bitch mother probably stole it from his house when he died. Along with that doll. I thought she sold both of them like the dirty rat she is. But no, she gave them to her cokehead degenerate son."

The tree reached over to tap the glass, but it met Martin's face. He snatched it and broke the limb off. "At least she didn't kill her parents."

"You…" Dark eyes grew somehow darker. "She *did* kill them. The fucking dirty cow bitch. She refused to help them when they were getting sick. Who was there? Me! I fucking helped them! I did everything and more while your worthless mother was dealing with *YOU!*"

Martin felt warmth in his cheeks. His chest was hammering. "You refused to put them in a home. They needed help, and you refused, 'cause you wanted control. You wouldn't be able to tug their leashes if they were locked behind a wall of nurses. They'd find the bruises, wouldn't they? Fucking cunt. And you accuse my mother. You *dare* accuse my mother… Now you leave this town and you leave my mother alone, or I will put a fucking bullet between your eyes. Do you understand me, you abhorred fucking cunt? Am I perfectly fucking clear?"

SNAP! Concrete dust spouted up from the sidewalk

beside the dark figure's feet. Not a flinch.

Snow began to fall, first a scant sprinkle. Wind pushed at the tree, but it no longer had an arm to tap. Martin heard every breath leave and enter his lungs. Tunnel vision. It blurred space around the dark figure outside, demanded he give every ounce of attention. He nearly jumped when she started to move. Closer. Crossing the street to the base of the apartment building, then along it in the direction of the front door.

He grabbed the window and slammed it shut, shattering the glass into wedges and fractals. "Fucking…" Fumbling hands reached for Mousie, then he barreled across the room to the closet by the entrance. The destruction had bypassed it, so he found his backpack exactly where he'd placed it however long ago. In went Mousie, then he slung the straps over his shoulders.

And tripped over a table leg.

He cracked his head on the wall and felt a bolt of pain fizzle back and forth across the wound in his throat. A groan, to vocalize the new agony returning to the bruising on his shoulder. It had dulled, but no longer. Despite himself he was pulling up on the kitchen counter, trying to find footing. Once he did, he was out the empty door frame and in the yellow glow of the hallway.

When he'd arrived, he'd never checked the door to

Bonnie's old apartment. But now he noticed the glint of sloppy lettering painted in blood: *YOURS FOR AN HOUR. COLD AND LIMP*. He turned away, started down the hall towards the elevator.

There was an ad board bolted to the wall where the hallway bent left. Flyers and notices were flattened behind a pane of glass, long out of date and discolored under the fluorescents. *BEST PIZZA IN SNOWY OAKS... DIVORCE LAW... TRASH COLLECTION SCHEDULE REVAMP...* In the reflection of the glass, projected over the printed flyers, he saw her–walking fast, beyond the bend in the hall. The longer he waited, frozen, the larger the reflection became. He searched frantically: apartment doors, one after another; a fire hydrant bracketed into the drywall; a janitor's closet with the door cracked open. Without much thought, he pounced at it. The closet was dark, and the door was missing a handle. He gently guided it closed and pressed his full weight on. Then he waited… and wondered why he was hiding. She was unarmed.

But the way in which she'd crossed the street… the speed.

Before too long, he heard footsteps on the hallway carpet. They approached the closet door, and then they stopped.

Silence.

He put the nose of the pistol up against the door. Micro sounds taunted him from out of the darkness: creaks and swaying, droplets of water. Something touched his leg. Insects–crawling up the door: a cockroach and a spider. He tracked them with his eyes–watched as the spider grabbed the cockroach and wrapped its thin, spasming legs over its shell. His breath was leaving condensation on the blue paint of the door. He tried to hold it, as a sudden feeling that she could hear it strangled him hard. His eyes wandered. They passed over the cockroach being consumed, to the rusting hinges of the door, to the hollow hole in the wood where the knob had been pulled out.

In that hole was her wide, glassy eye–peering in at him.

Something was suddenly forced through the hole, just thin enough to fit. It bounced against the edges with violent urgency, catching occasionally as its lump joints negotiated the opening. Wiry hair grew from each segment. Claws raked the paint off the door as they searched for Martin's flesh. He fired a volley of shots through the door and heard a shriek. The hairy stalk began to retract through the hole, catching and banging and flailing like a fish on a line. Once it was fully out, the sound of running feet on carpet fled from earshot.

Martin waited a minute, then leaned off the door. It swung slowly inward, letting in a wash of yellow light. His gun was out first. He looked left and right, then checked the bend in the hall. Malosa was gone. She'd left no blood, but six bullet holes were punched through the wallpaper. He put his gun back through his belt and went for the elevator before anyone came looking, summoned by the gunshots.

19

The main street of the town had been cleared, and grey-clad policemen walked up and down the sides grasping batons–eyes on the crowd of the destitute. The iron mouths of the church were made singers atop their wooden poles, blaring triumphant orchestral music in place of the usual deadpan morning announcement. Making its way down the awaiting street was a procession near a mile long–a river of blood red shifting forms. Some raised tall banner poles hung with black flags–all bearing the Seal of Golgotha. The rest kept their arms folded into wide, overlapping sleeves and their heads downturned.

A thump. Vibration through the earth.

The red river was led by a rusting, white pickup with a massive drum in the flatbed. Every minute or so, its tight skin was struck with a mallet–wielded by a tall figure in ceremonial garb. Bells hung from the figure's headdress, which sparkled wildly with the motion of each swing.

Birds took flight from telephone wires drooping across the road.

Martin sat on the roof of an abandoned three storey complex, peering down at the passing parade. He had his gun in his hands, playing with the hammer and safety switch. Six boxes of *.40 Smith and Wesson* were stacked up by his leg. They'd been rammed into a gun safe two floors down–by him, his past self, a year ago. An emergency stash he'd stolen just in case. He imagined there was no better definition of emergency than what he faced now. Out came the magazine–dropped from the butt. There were two bullets still inside; he topped it off with fourteen. "Are you frustrated?"

Silence.

"I wonder if you feel emotion." He looked up at the skin man, who sat on the knee-high parapet across the roof. Some thirty metres away. "Roman is down there. I'm up here. If he knew that… I'm sure you're screaming at him. But he's not listening, is he? He's busy with his subjects." He snorted, then slid the magazine back into place with a click.

Now the main event of the parade came into view: a gilded palanquin resting heavy on the shoulders of twelve men. Golgotha's seal was cut out of metal sheeting and welded to the back of the chair–crescent moon wings, as if the chair was able to lift off and fly away. And sitting there, held down by ropes…

The beast… headless. Nothing more now than a husk. An empty balloon with the air let out. Motion from the palanquin's twenty-four legs jostled the corpse violently. Its brutalized neck flesh flapped back and forth like the ears of a giddy dog. Sections of the watching crowd in turn erupted into cheers and jubilation when the display was lugged into their view.

Just behind the first palanquin came a second, more modestly adorned. There was no chair on this one, but an upright wooden frame. Seatbelts held the Blessed Eye to the frame–tightly, so he wouldn't fall off. Wine-red gloves waved with something like bashfulness at the sea of faces. The headdress Roman had worn during the banishing ceremony took its place on his head once again. His elaborate robes did a poor job of hiding the wooden frame beneath themselves, but from a distance, one could imagine he was balancing on his own.

"I could try to hit him." Idle fingers cocked the hammer, then released it slowly. "But they'd shoot back."

Flanking Roman's palanquin was a company of six guards–pigface helmets, Sten guns. The same ones who'd driven his car. Their breath was released in clouds out the punched eyeholes in their helmets.

"Maybe it's worth it." Martin pushed hair out of his eyes.

The early winter wind blew it right back with a sharp kiss. "What do I have left? That you haven't taken away from me? Bald fucker."

Silence.

"You could push me off the roof, can't you?" He squinted against the cold. "Like you pushed me against that cell door… right?"

A silent, fleshy stare.

"Why don't you?"

It gave no reason.

"You give me what I don't want… make me suffer–and you find it funny. I try everyday to give you up, but I always see you sitting there–somewhere. You make me do things I don't want to do. And I can't shake you. But if you need me dead now… why don't you push me off this roof?"

As the sun reached its zenith, the crimson eye of the Red Abbey shone down upon the moving procession. All was turned to roiling blood, and the music from the metal speakers crescendoed at the coming of noontime. Martin opened his backpack and pushed Mousie to the side to make way for the boxes of cartridges. Then the zipper whined sharply. He got to his feet and crossed to the roof entrance door, looking to the parapet where the skin man had been–now vacant.

—

Life became a routine that wouldn't seem to end. His watch was digital–he set alarms on it to never forget. *Nine, twelve, six*. The night allowed brief respite, apart from the constant presence of the skin man. It was always somewhere: behind a tree; sitting perched atop a rooftop; peering at him from around the corner of a hallway. When he slept, it would watch him sleep. He pulled his tattered blanket over his head and felt like a child. Once, he collected courage out of his weary hatred and approached the bald, mouthless ghost. Close. Enough to examine every aspect of it. This gave him the same tightening in his chest he'd experienced at the funeral of his grandmother, when he'd been made to approach the open casket. The sight of waxy death–recognizable, yet wholly different. An effigy, or a sculpture made to approximate what once was. Back then, he'd felt an unconscious bolt of expectation that the corpse's eyes might suddenly flit open while he hovered over. Now, he feared the apparition might move a limb–reach out and grab him.

But it only spun its head to keep him in its sights, just the same as it had always done. And it reeked of sulphur–rotten eggs, mixed with ozone. Maybe a metallic hint of blood. Its black suit was too textured to be made of fabric–too plush. There were patches of discoloration, like age spots on a geriatric. Pulsations. Blood flow, moving *through* the material. He thought he could see the faint whispers of veins.

There was something pinned to the lapel: red circle. A bird. He'd seen that logo a long time ago on the sides of trucks passing through town. *Cardinal Medicine*, from Roanoke. He frowned, looked up into the figure's eyes–skin covered and dilated. "God: the employee."

Silence.

He scoffed.

The skin over where the figure's mouth should be seemed to push and pull with phantom breath.

Martin pulled his map of the town out from the zipper jaws of his bag, then unrolled it. On cue, he felt the little vibration of his watch–heard its chirping. There was a coin in his hand–a quarter. It fell onto the map and bounced crooked, landing on a spot near the glossy paper's far corner. *SNOWY OAKS TRAINYARD.*

—

Spiders belonging to the Thomisidae family will utilize camouflage to hide from, and ambush their prey. Ant Mimic spiders, for example, will go so far as to mimic the behavior and appearance of ants. Some will wave around their front appendages to imitate antennae. Can you find any along your walk?

The sign was lying in the dirt, enveloped in a web of tallgrass. The same cartoon cardinal he'd seen on a sign by the tourist center was waving a paint-chipped wing. It was smiling, even under a layer of dirt–curling the edges of its beak. Made him think of the automatons with their sewn and stapled grins.

His boot heels crunched gravel, finding uneasy footing. Blackened metal rails cut through, stretching off in opposite directions: one way into the center of town, the other off into a distance barricaded by chain links and barbed wire. Three box cars and one engine sat silent and picked over–skeletons in the underbrush. The engine had been gutted, and whatever labeled useless was strewn haphazard in the vicinity of the car. *NORFOLK SOUTHERN* was stamped onto each of the metal hulks. Stray tongues of wind swept through the yard, smelling of old diesel.

He approached the furthest box car and jumped up onto the side. The rolling side door shook, didn't move, then started banging as he wrenched wildly on the handle. "Fuck you!" He nearly went head first through when the door suddenly popped and skated along its rusted tracks. Now he saw into the car, and out the other side–the other door was already open, on the other side of the car. "Son-of-a-bitch."

The boxcar floor smacked hollowly under his boots; every step vibrated the whole wooden frame. Empty beer cans started rolling again after time collecting thick topcoats of dust. They left trails in the filth–little aluminum snails. Up in the corner of the car was a vacant wasp nest with its wall peeled off. Six layers of comb would have housed hundreds of squirming, translucent larvae, scratching with their pincers for sustenance. Martin could think of that sound–his father's barbecue had made it decades ago. It was loud–impossibly loud. It stopped once his father turned on the gas. He'd asked to see the remains, and his father had obliged, pulling open the metal casket to let the wind carry away large, black flakes. Shriveled kernels that had been humming and alien. Larvae that had popped with the heat like pomegranate seeds.

He kept away from the empty nest, kicked one of the cans out the open door.

A soiled mattress was rammed into the corner of the car, fabric impregnated with stains of every color. It gave off occasional whiffs of feces and urine. Something crunched under Martin's boot. He lifted it and saw the dried up shell of a wasp. Then he noticed the rip in the side of the mattress–the second wasp frozen in a state of panicked flight. Threads had wound themselves around the insect's legs and head, keeping it fettered halfway out the torn hole. Web. An intrusive impulse gave action to his foot, got it hovering over the mattress. Then he stepped down. A crunch. Hundreds. Like bubble wrap made of candy brittle. He stepped off–wanted to vomit.

Even from where he stood, he heard the sudden singing of the mellotron. He hadn't seen a speaker nearby, but the sound came from everywhere at once. "*He who was once an agent of Golgotha is now a betrayer. Martin Navarro had once wished to be sacrificed to rid the world of its black angel, Mr. Crooked, yet when the time came, he was taken by co-conspirators who arrested his natural death. He is an undead blasphemer keeping prisoner one vital hand of our Lord. He is an abomination equal in wickedness to Mr. Crooked, and must be killed without question. If you are able bodied and armed, keep your eyes to the woods and dark places, for he may be hiding there and watching you. Kill him before he begins another bout of violence to take what remains of your loved ones away. Blessed be, King of Heaven.*"

The world began to spin. His breath came in short, difficult bursts. "What… Jesus Christ." He fell to a crouch, keeping his eyes on the warped floorboards of the car. "You… fucking snake."

It was standing under the wasp nest, arms at its sides, skin eyes gaping.

"Just leave me alone… get out of me. Why don't you just fucking leave?"

Silence.

He got to his feet and jumped down onto the gravel. Walking to the fenceline was like walking through water; his feet were pulled and pushed by the sea of tiny rocks. No check for patrolmen–he imagined they were here, somewhere along the fence. But tunnel vision had a grip on him again. He looped his fingers through the holes in the chain, scanned back and forth, up and down. Wide loops of barbed wire ran along the top, double wound. There was nowhere to grab or throw a leg over without slicing crotch. And it was ten feet up. He didn't have boltcutters to snap the thick links; even if he did, they would need to be strong cutters. Mr. Crooked's hole would be patched now, and guarded.

No way out. There had never been.

He could have continued down the road a week ago instead of stopping at the tourist center. "Why didn't I fucking… why?"

The dog.

And the rusty hook.

"That's bullshit." His fingers unwound from the fence and he started back to the train car, passing the skin man where he now stood watching. "It's all bullshit. None of it is real. *You're* not real."

An urge came over him to…

The figure reeled with the punch, stumbled on the gravel, then found its footing. It continued to stare.

Martin sucked in breath rapidly. His chest was thrumming. He got close and pushed with both hands–all his weight. The skin man stumbled again, then regained its balance. Nothing further. "Fall." He pushed again, and the same thing happened. "Fall, you bitch!" Again, the same. The same. The same. He was pushing it back towards the box car, further every time. A moment to think, and breathe. Then a boot heel to the figure's knee. Its leg buckled and brought it down, but it sprung back up almost instantly. He wanted to use his pistol, but the sound would attract the patrolmen–if there were any. Instead, he pressed the little nub on his switchblade; the blade flipped erect. "Do you bleed, prick?"

Metal bit deep into flesh, and never hit bone or struggled to pierce. It was like stabbing a block of gelatin.

And bleed, it did not.

"I don't like your eyes."

He grabbed the figure's throat and drew near its head. The knife went in twice, came back out. Both cuts sealed over when the foreign metal left. He used the tip of the blade to dig back in, then he pried. The opening widened; he squinted to see inside. There was eye-matter there, as there should be, but it was jellified–solidly. Nothing leaked out the incision–no fluid, no blood.

He pushed the knife deeper.

Cut the optic nerve. Got through to red flesh. Fingers on his free hand entered the opening now, and pulled. The skull was soft–the same texture as the brain inside it. He replaced the knife blade with his other hand, then he pulled with both. Flesh and cartilage parted with minimal effort. He felt the climax of force and tension–pulled his face away. Then the whole head split like a watermelon. The chunk he'd prief off went sailing through the air before it struck the gravel and lay there undulating. He could see the inside of the figure's head now–a jagged cross-section. But still, no blood.

He stepped away, panting. "You'll catch a cold walking around like that."

It continued to stare with only one eye. Half its head was now gone, but it still stood.

"Ha!" The knife went back into his pocket, then he walked back to the box car with nothing left to do but eat his lunch. It was canned ham.

20

Eyes open.

He was facing the back wall of the box car; if he looked up slightly, he could see the wasp nest. It should have been pitch black under nightfall, but he could see the nest–and the wall. Shadows danced and seizured, carving strange forms out of the foreign orange lamplight.

His pistol was clutched between his hands while he slept. He slowly slipped one hand into place around the handle.

Lamplight.

Sleep's veil was falling away–gradually. Each micro movement announced itself against the nylon skin of his sleeping bag. He fumbled for his pocket, where he kept a small salvaged makeup mirror–snapped off from its base. Useful for checking corners–and backs… useful right now. He lifted it, turning back and forth to find the right angle over his reclined shoulder. A reflection of the soiled mattress across the car… the first door, still shut… second door–

cracked just slightly. He tilted the mirror down and saw the blinding glow of a lantern.

Then he heard muffled voices, and muffled pain.

"*Dirty fucking pig. You'd 'a shot my drummer with this, now.*"

"*No... please. Please don't! PLEASE DON'T!*"

CRACK!

Hysterical laughter from some ten or twenty voices.

" 'No! Please don't!' *Ha! Piggy likes to squeal when it ain't him with the big gun.*"

Martin undid the zipper on the bag and crawled out onto the splintering floorboards. He crawled slowly on his stomach–got to the box car door. One wide eye peered out into the night. There were ten or twenty, indeed. Most wielded electric lanterns and rusted machetes–some had guns of different types. They were gathered in a circle around a central figure, who had a fence patrolman's hair locked in an iron grip. Every hole on the cop's face was a blood faucet, including his swollen tear ducts. Life was leaving the man with each passing tick.

"Whattya say we let Dino play a little, now?"

An eruption of enthusiasm.

"Come on now, Dino. Blow his mind with that guitar 'a yours!"

At that, one of the figures around the rim of the clearing

came forward. He had what looked like an electric guitar resting over one shoulder. As he got to the kneeling cop, he lifted it off and down. He put one hand on its head like a cane–bent at the hips to peer into the man's bloodied face. "Mister policeman, my name's Dino."

A whimper.

"Shake my fucking hand, pigshit."

Up came a trembling hand to accept the guitarist's. Two solid shakes, up and down, then the hands came undone.

BANG!

And the cop's head was macerated by the edge of a swinging guitar.

The crowd erupted into cheers and hollering as the guitar went about lifting and falling, pounding the skull and brains into the gravel.

"Jesu–"

Martin fell back on his ass as the sliding door started to shake and rattle. The expanding doorframe maw brought more of the light in, and the cold night wind. He lifted his gun at the face looking up at him, but didn't pull the trigger.

A mask. Not a face… but it was a face–sewn onto leather. The face of someone else.

"Boy!"

The guitarist ceased tenderizing the meat. All went quiet. All turned to look at the man in the box car. Grasshoppers chittered, somewhere in the dark.

"Come on down here, boy! Put down that gun!"

Martin scanned the blanket of grotesque masks. They were all uniquely vile, some leather or ratty denim–others skin. Flayed faces with skin gray and jagged eyeholes occupied by intruding eyes. Closest to him was one of these, the stolen face desecrated across the forehead with a sloppily carved cross.

He got to his feet, then lowered the pistol. They were more than his stock of ammo, even if he could fish it out of his bag before being shot. Leaving his things, he took a seat on the edge of the box car floor and slid off. The masked bodies gave way to him, creating a path to the center clearing. He took it, and soon came to stand a few feet away from the man who'd called. A glance at the guitarist. Blood and spongy, wet matter dripped slowly off his guitar.

"You a bum?"

Martin coughed. "No… Uh… Though I guess I would be now."

The man wore a button-down pinstripe shirt and muddy wool vest. Both arms were inked past his rolled up sleeves. He had bright green eyes tucked through the square holes of his leather mask. A rust-caked metal choker cinched the leather around his neck; it was spiked, with what looked like syringe needles. He said: "What's your name, son?"

He took some time to consider before he spilled out: “Martin.”

“Martin…” He pulled up on his waistline, straightening his suspenders. “That’s a hot name around here as of yesterday noon. You hear that speaker squawkin’?”

“Yes, sir.”

“Might be I can guess your last name. Wouldn’t happen to be *Navro*?”

“No.”

The man studied him intently, looking him up and down. “Navarro.”

A rough finger came up to wag beside the grotesque leather mask. “That’s the fucking one, now… Navarro. That’s Mexican.”

Martin looked at the guitarist again. He was stock still, clutching his instrument. His mask was made of stained denim. Leather devil horns grew crooked from his temples, beneath what could have been an approximation of a halo. His technicolor, stripy pants were dulled by blood and filth. Back to the leader: “No, but that’s alright.”

“Cultists want you dead, son.”

Silence.

“You hear that?”

“I did.”

An eyeball was wedged in the dirt by the man’s feet–and

a shard of skull. He noticed, bent down to pluck it up between a forefinger and thumb. "Everyone's got an eye out." He held it up to his face, turned it back and forth. "*H-A-H-A-H-A-H-A-H-A!*"

His fellows joined in.

Martin waited. His palms were wet.

"Ain't no one come through this trainyard in a brick, son. Know why?"

"No."

The man came forward and wrapped his arm around Martin's shoulders. He reached and pulled open a jacket pocket–plopped the eyeball in. Martin could feel the warmth and moisture against his breast. His ears rang with the voice of the masked man, close up against him–not quieting his tone: "This here yard has been claimed by my band. Cult fucks stay out, and the cops don't bother sniffin' around. No point in it." He patted Martin's pocket. "No Man's Land. It's the line 'a fire they're walkin' through. You understand me?"

A blink: "Think I do, sir."

"And this sum'bitch came snoopin' around. First time in a long time I've seen one 'a Toledo's boy toys. There's a change in the air, son." *Ting!* He flicked one of the rusty needles on his choker. "Time's about come for a reckoning."

Ambient coughs–sniffles from the encircling horde.

"You killed Mr. Crooked?"

"I did."

He looked over at the guitar player, and got: "He have a wallet?"

Martin reached into his pocket and pulled it out–flipped it open. "What, you want money?"

"No." Snatch. He flipped through the various loyalty cards to stores that no longer existed, pictures, debit and credit cards with no money–stopped. Driver's license. "Says here: *Martin Navarro.*" He held it out to the guitarist. "See. Look there."

A pause, then: "Alright. Fine."

"Hm." The man reached out to grab Martin's shoulder. "What say we head inside and have a little talk, son. Get outta the cold."

Martin got the impression from the force of the man's grip that it wasn't an option.

—

The man's name was Zakaria Reese, Martin guessed–'cause he sat beneath a tattered concert poster which bore a photograph of a figure dressed in nearly the exact same outfit. Pinstripe shirt, cotton vest. *ZAKARIA REESE AND THE CONSEQUENCE. LIVE AT THE ROADHOUSE 3/24/2010.*

A hanging bulb sputtered yellow light. Its gasoline generator heart could be heard rattling and coughing beyond the thin office walls. Down in the belly of the warehouse, the rabble of masked men made a racket. The guitar player, Dino, shut the door, smothering the sound. There was an ambient stench of mildew, cigarettes, and alcohol. It was a wet smell that clung to Martin's skin.

"Want a drink, son?"

"Uh… no. Thank you."

Crown Royal bubbled out from the glass lips of a bottle. "Mister Toledo, King of the Pigs, likes this shit. Cultists have it brought in on their trucks with all the rest of the foodstuffs, so he's all nice and obedient for 'em. Know that?"

Martin adjusted himself in his chair. "I did, actually."

"Sometimes we confiscate a bottle or two off them delivery pickups while it's parked outside the station. Ha! … fuck that prick." Back went the cap, then he slid the bottle to the side of his desk. The rippling alcohol reflected light from the overhead bulb. Liquid umber, like before–in the police station. He took up the glass he'd just filled and drained it in one swig through the leather mouth hole in his mask.

As he swallowed, Martin said: "I went to one of your shows."

A wide smile, wafting whiskey. "Got your eyes on the

room, eh?" He lazily gestured over his shoulder toward the poster. "I can't sing no more. You're lucky you got to hear." A pause, then he open-palm smacked his chest to relieve a belch. "When the cultists came in here, they didn't like us too much. I had a couple songs about religion. Shittin' on the church, and what have you. That was the Catholic church, mind you. But it didn't matter to 'em. Maybe they thought it was about them." A glance at his brother, who was now sitting on a plush couch with his guitar across his lap and a bloody rag in his hand. "They went and kidnapped me, then they opened my throat up and fucked with it. Now I can't sing for shit, and I sound like a chainsmoker." He coughed hard, then reached for the whiskey again.

"Can't have no secular music, no sir," came from the couch.

Zakaria put the glass to his lips and struggled with a flap of leather.

"Why are you all wearing masks?"

From the couch came a snort. The whiskey glass clicked on the tabletop. "Wonderin' why I have to drink like a geezer, eh?" His free hand came up to yank down his shirt collar. Red flesh, bonded to leather. Heavy stitches drew a messy line all the way around his neck. "This was the second half of their punishment. All four of us got new faces, 'cause our old ones were famous, see? Can't have that. That's threatening. There's only one God in Snowy Oaks."

"But you could pull the stitches."

"No, no, son. These new faces are more important than our old ones. All those people downstairs follow *this* face. They made masks of their own–some of 'em cut the ugly mugs off of Toledo's pigs, or off an unsuspecting cultist. Used them instead of leather. My band is near thirty strong–all of 'em everyday people, or even cultists who turned–smelled the fucking coffee. Those cult fucks are gonna rue the day they stitched these faces on." He drained the rest of his glass. "That's why I wanted a talk with you, son. Understand?"

Martin blinked. "No, not really."

"Well, I want you to join my band, son. You're public enemy number one, it seems. Mister Roman Ward wants you dead–I want Roman Ward dead. Or arrested, even better. Tried and sentenced to a life of taking it up the ass in a prison shower- Dino, pass me that, now."

A groan of couch leather. Then a clear plastic shell slid onto the desk, filled with donuts. It was opened–Dino snatched one, then went back to his seat.

"Got this off the same truck as the whiskey." Zakaria hovered over the pastries, fingers twiddling indecisively. They latched onto one with pink icing. "You want one? Take it–there's twenty more packs of 'em."

Martin stared into cloudy icing.

"Go, take one."

He bent over–extended his arm. One was plucked up out of its plastic slot. Red icing, black sprinkles.

"Get Mister Navarro a glass, Dino, will ya? For his whiskey. You can have some, too if you want–no, the small ones there. By the sink."

Clep. He looked down at the glass now placed before him. Crystal–light fractals. They went gold and shimmery as the whiskey was poured. He lifted it to his lips–alcohol wafted up his nose. Sharp and warm. A sip. Another. Then he smiled and took a bite of his donut. He'd never tasted anything better.

"King Piggy has fine taste–least as far as drinks are concerned. Can't speak for what he likes to stick his dick into." He cleared his throat. "Damn. So what's your answer, son? Will you come aboard?"

"I… don't see why not."

"Good then. Now I'd best let you in on what we're planning to do, seeing as we're all in order." The donut disappeared through leather-rimmed lips. "I've, uh- been organizing this band for… what, now?"

"Three years."

"Yeah, three. Ever since they did to us what they did. As far as the pigs and cultists are concerned, we're a little community of hermits and bums holed up in this warehouse. But we've been growing steady. Probably have more bodies here than they've got up in their ugly church. Now that's perfect–perfect to overthrow 'em."

Martin put his glass down. "Overthrow them?"

"Unless you'd rather live under their boot 'til you're dead?"

"What's your idea, then?"

Stretched across Zakaria's desk was a map of the town–an old one from the tourist center. His pointer came down on the Church of Saint Francis, visible amongst coffee stains and dust. "Some of the ex-cultists in our band are claimin' there's a signal jammer on the roof of the Abbey. Say they've done maintenance on it. That's why no cellphones work here. It's a big one–powerful. I wanna tear it down, then call in the cavalry."

Then Martin felt something enter the room.

Warmth brushed his ear, and he turned in his chair to look. The couch had gained a second sitter–right beside Dino, who was just finishing cleaning the viscera from his instrument. What Martin had cloven from the figure's head had reformed; its face was now whole once again. Its sheer skin picked up the yellow light–made it look sickly. Jaundiced. Martin said, "Wait. You can't tell me anything."

"Why?" from across the desk.

"I've been running for days. The thing inside my head can speak to Roman Ward. You shouldn't tell me anything else."

Laughter.

Martin turned back around and gave the man a puzzled look.

"Thing in your head? What's in your head, son?"

"Golgotha."

Another bout of laughter. "Golgotha? Fuckin' serious? Then he slid his glass of whiskey aside. "How's he listening, son? Eh? You don't have a bug on ya now, do ya?"

He turned again. Now the horned devil mask was staring. He was being watched from all sides. The guitar tapped heavy against the floorboards.

"I've never found one."

"No?"

The silence was suddenly heavy. He still felt the heat on his left side, as if the skin man were freshly come from the pits of Hell, still offgassing.

"You'll open up that bag at least."

It was lying against his leg. He looked from the couch to the desk, then back again. The guitar tapped the floorboards–a thump that cued him to action. He lifted the bag, then handed it across the desk.

"Too kind of you."

He slumped in his chair.

Zakaria peeled apart the zippers, then hovered over, searching with eyes first and hands second. Out came the boxes of bullets, which rattled when stacked on the desk. Next came Mousie. He held it up by the tip of its crochet hood.

It made Martin shift, restless.

"Nice little toy."

Silence.

"You have a kid?"

"My grandmother gave it to me a long time ago."

"Why carry it around?"

He paused to think. "I don't know."

Mousie was put atop the stack of bullets, lying face down. Like a hungry bear at a campsite, Zakaria emptied the whole bag, piling tins of food and various trinkets on his desk. He asked questions of some, and none of others, then he sat back and studied his guest over the stacks. "Dino."

Martin was lifted out of his chair. Quick hands pushed and pulled his limbs, positioning him like a doll. Then patting–up his legs, down his legs. Along his sleeves and around his torso. The guitarist even checked inside his ears.

Then: "Nothing, don't think."

Martin caught the empty backpack. It felt like a shell of something–a gutted pelt.

“Nothing to worry about, then.” The whiskey glass was drained, then turned over on the table map. “Sit down, son. It’s near sunup. We’ll have a room made up for you to stay in, since you’re part of the band. Yes?”

Before Martin could answer, the office door was thrown open. A masked man stood there, hand on the knob. His voice was frantic. “Zak. There’s pigs outside. A lot of ‘em.”

Martin felt two rough hands latch on to him, and he was dragged out the door.

21

He hit the dirt and rolled over twice before catching himself with an elbow. The sun had come up over the blue-shrouded mountains, and the air tasted of snowmelt over mud and dead leaves. He pulled his hand out of a slick–wiped it on his already filthy jeans.

"Ain't that something, now." Zakaria strutted along the wooden track ties–kicked a stone off the rail. It rang against the broad face of a decrepit box car. "King Piggy's sniffin' for truffles outside 'a his jurisdiction."

Martin elected to remain low, propped up on his arm.

A set of *ATV*'s were parked in a line, some bearing grey-trousered asses and others dismounted. Slung over every shoulder was a black metal *AR*. They seemed like a Renaissance painting, how they were all positioned–with a campaign hat over a scarred, weather worn face at every height. Toledo stood at the head of them, one boot up on a track rail, the other in the mud. He said: "My jurisdiction is every patch of grass and rathole inside the fence–and I own the rats in the holes, too."

A chuckle beneath the leather mask. "You know, I said to myself–and my boys–that if you ever put a foot down on my property, I'd cut ya face off and have a new mask. It'd be mine. No one else gets their hands on it. No one else gets to put their knife up under your pig ears."

Toledo snorted mucus, then coughed a puff of warm breath. "You're a crazy fucker."

"Only thing, though," continued the mask, "I'd see what it's like to look through your eyes. Might start tryna' stick my dick in little boys." He cackled madly, and his posse joined in. Their laughter was brusque and venomous. There were ten of them who came out into the yard with Zak–three being his bandmates.

"That's enough, freak!"

It didn't come from Toledo. A young man was standing a few feet or so away, clenching his jaw til the muscles in his neck were tight and bulging. His pointer finger was fidgeting up and down the trigger guard of his gun.

The laughter cut off. Those ten pairs of eyes were synchronized–found the kid's face in an instant. Zak pulled something off his belt–a knife. Switchblade. The sharp end snapped free in a flash, emerging from the handle. He extended his arm full length, using the flaring tip of the blade to draw an invisible line between himself and the kid's face. "You sucked his dick?"

Silence.

"Let him fuck your ass? Your voice trembles like a housewife–gets her cheeks all bruised when she don't dance like he wants you to." The hovering knife traced the perimeter of the kid's face. "King Piggy likes to talk, boy. You shut that mouth and let him do so, now." *FLICK!* And the knifeblade retracted. He turned back to Toledo. "Mister Navarro was hiding up in a box car. Found him watching us while we turned one 'a your boy toys to marmalade."

Martin felt a plume of dust slither down his throat. He breathed heavily.

Toledo looked down at him, eyes small and reptilian. Back up to Zakaria. "Done well to cooperate, Zak. I didn't expect that from you."

"Boy said there's a demon in his head. Roman Ward can hear what he hears. You bug him?"

A blink. "Naw… That's Golgotha."

"Thought you were a reluctant lapdog?"

"I used to be. Then I watched Roman pull some kinda devil out of a headless corpse. The corpse moved, just like it was still living. But you didn't see that, did ya? You were in your hole, jerkin' off."

Zak ground a dandelion into the wood with his boot.

"Churches attract people with small brains–don't wanna think about reality. There is no God, and there ain't nothing in that boy's head telling Roman Ward what time he shits and what time he eats."

A pause. "You shoulda seen it, Zak."

To the West, a dark thunderhead spit momentary fire, distant and muffled.

"You came for him?"

"We did." The sergeant shrugged his rifle strap back into place. "He's been running around for days. But you helped us out, Zak. Kept him holed up in one place long enough."

"Where's he headed?"

"Back with us to the station."

"For what?"
"Didn't you hear the announcements?"

"Hmm…" He pushed a finger through an eyehole to scratch the bridge of his nose. "I can only imagine what kinda treatment he'll be gettin' from you."

"Only the best I can offer. Just what he deserves." After a moment, Toledo motioned with his head for one of the officers to approach Martin. Boot heels crunched gravel at awkward angles, like the man was a baby just learning to walk.

CRACK!

The rocks sparked, whizzed off in random directions.

A heavy smack; the officer was on his ass, kicking his legs and trying to flip over. He tripped over his gunstrap before lunging to his feet and peeling back behind the line of *ATV*s.

Toledo didn't move.

Neither did Zak.

Martin searched the treeline, then the tops of the box cars. Behind them rose the warehouse where Zak's band resided. A flicker of sunlight winked from the roof. Scope.

"If I give him to you, of course." The dandelion had been turned to green and white paste.

The sergeant clicked the safety off his gun. "You wanna do that?"

Silence.

"Is he worth the lives of your men? Or your brothers?"

"Might be."

"You don't know him from Adam."

"No, I don't. But at least it'll piss you off if I keep him around." He tapped the handle of his knife on his collection of metal bracelets. A jingle, drawing Martin's attention. "Come on back, boy. Get up."

He did so, rising slowly. A flick of his hand got some globules of mud off it.

"Don't you fucking move, or I'll shoot you dead." Up came the sergeant's gun. He had the butt pushed into his shoulder; his muscles were tensed.

Martin kept still.

"You need him dead, don't ya? Just shoot him here."

No response.

Zak continued: "Why don't you? Huh? Pop his head… Now your head'll pop right after his, but at least you were a good dog." When Toledo kept quiet, he said, "Come on, boy. Don't mind King Piggy."

Martin could feel the gun barrel aimed at his back. He prepared for a sharp pain–tensed up his body. Each step towards friendly lines seemed to take an age, and tested the bluff of the trigger. Only when he felt Zakaria's hand on his shoulder did he remember to breathe.

"I have more officers than you have men."

"Do you?"

"I do, Zak." Then to Martin, he said: "We had so much fun, didn't we? Why don't you come on back and we'll pick up where we left off."

Martin rubbed his fingers together.

"You've got plenty 'a boys to play with, piggy." He slapped Martin on the back. "This one's with me. And if you try to come back here lookin' for him, I'm not gonna let you walk like I am today."

A pause. "Clearly, I've let you fester here for too long."

The switchblade tapped one of the needle tips on

Zakaria's choker. "Back to master now, Pig. Be a good dog."

Toledo lowered his gun and turned around. His company broke formation to mount the *ATV*s. Engines sputtered and snapped to life; exhaust pipes breathed black clouds.

"Toledo!"

The sergeant looked up…

…To see the switchblade pointed at him. The blade traced the perimeter of his face, then retreated like a snake into the handle with a click. "Remember, Pig."

The *ATV*s revved their engines and were away, fleeing along the railroad tracks.

—

A small gas lantern exhaled a constant tone. Its light was flickering–serrated against the ribs of the shipping container walls. Martin had sunk into his cot; his flesh gratefully succumbed to the embrace of a mattress. He spent the night sleeping, then waking in turns after images of flayed corpses and Bonnie having her chest caved in chased any sense of comfort away. Each time he shut his eyes he heard the crack of a mattock turning ribs to splinters–smelled the rotting perfume of the monster. His quick, sparse dreams had him walking through fields of Frankenstein mannequins. At the climax, every time, he came to stand before *her*. Malosa.

Darkness wearing a bloodless face. Rusty hooks were pushed through her cheeks, just behind the edges of her mouth, connected to two long chains that pulled her thin, spray-tanned visage into a joyless molestation of happiness. Then the appendages, sprouting hair in coiled, pubic clumps, would rise up from behind her back–they were gripping the chains. They were pulling on them. Arachnid limbs.

And then he would wake.

And the lantern would be breathing, washing the shipping container with its orange light.

A window was sloppily cut into the outward facing wall, through which Martin could see the ceiling of the warehouse and a shifting fractal bath of light gently twisting from below. He was in one of the highest makeshift rooms, tucked into the top corner of the building. Beneath him, a crooked, mismatched monument of shipping containers and support scaffolds made of logs and wooden planking was alive with the ant-like movements of more than a hundred masked figures. Gas lanterns sparkled in most of the windows.

Martin stood up off the cot and went to the window. His clothing had been washed and hung on a rack; they'd given him a moth-eaten bath robe to sleep in. He'd showered under a cold spray, but the temperature wasn't a bother. Filth and blood had shed off like a second skin. At the window, he leaned on the wall and held his stitched hand under the light.

Some of the thread had come undone, but most of the outer skin had healed into a pink, scarred ridgeline. He made a fist; the middle two fingers wouldn't curl all the way. He let it fall back to his side. In the center of the warehouse, many feet below, small shop fronts built from sheet metal and wood serviced masked customers. Strings of hanging bulbs and more gas lanterns competed with encroaching moonlight let in through the warehouse's massive sliding doors. Built up on the remaining three sides of the room were more shipping containers nests–more scaffolds.

There was a pounding on the door. Martin went to it–tried to guess the visitor through the frosted glass. He pulled it open, and saw Zakaria. Martin nodded a greeting.

"Sorry to wake you, boy."

"That's alright."

Zak pulled his leather face to re-center the mouth slits. "We've gotta errand to run tomorrow morning and it's best you join us. Can't have King Pig sneaking in while I'm gone to snatch you up under my nose."

A cough. "What errand?"

"I've brokered a deal with a sympathetic party. Mister Leland Dufresne–man used to run Leland's whorehouse 'fore the cult pricks started sending pigs in to anywhere like that to kill the workforce. Hear about that?"

"In one announcement, maybe. Yeah, I heard it."

"Whenever that happened, I helped Mister Dufresne slip out with his girls. Got 'em safe and squirrelled away. So he owes me a favor or three." A cigarillo appeared in his hand already sparked. He put it to his lips and sucked, then blew the smoke. "Now he sets up shop one night, packs it up in the morning, sets up somewhere else the next night. Pigs can't catch him that way. Anyways, one 'a his clientele got a little carried away one night and choked a girl to death. He gave Mister Dufresne a wack-ton 'a guns in this big case so he wouldn't cut his hands off. Now my band has guns but we don't have enough. Mister Dufresne is gonna pay me back for my prior kindness."

Martin blinked through nicotine smoke. Coughed again.

"You come with me and a couple men. We meet him where he is and collect. That work for you?" Another drag from the cigarillo. "And I won't tell you where. You'll just see when we get there. As per your… request."

"Alright. Fine."

"See ya in the morning, then." A smile, then Zakaria turned and headed across the wooden scaffolds.

Across from Martin's door was another shipping container–another door. He squinted, then had the door closed halfway before he stopped. He swung it back out and squinted harder. There was a silhouette behind the frosted glass door across, features muddled. But it looked like a woman. Dark hair. Dark outfit. She was small and thin. He wanted to recognize her face.

Then she opened the door.

She stepped out onto the scaffold and smiled at him.

His hand was trembling on the door handle. Warmth grew behind his eyes, and moisture. Droplets carved streams down his cheeks, into his beard. The darkness around her was made more dark in her wake, giving itself up.

He stepped back inside and shut the door, then went to his cot to lie down. When he drifted off now, he didn't wake, and had no nightmares.

She was dead, and he buried her.

22

"She won't let us see him."

"What?"

"She won't say what hospital he's in."

"Why?"

"She wants him to die before I can say goodbye to him."

The hospital corridors hummed and flickered. Nurses and doctors in blue smocks hurried between open doorways carrying clipboards. Martin and his mother dodged a stretcher bearing the suggestion of a limp body, wrapped tightly in ratty cloth. The reception counter was up ahead, manned by a petite woman with a world-weary expression and bags under her eyes. She looked up, didn't smile. "Hi, can I help you?"

Martin's mother grabbed the edge of the counter. "Yes, is there a Francisco Navarro on this floor?"

"What's your name?"

"Paloma Navarro… He's my father."

Keyboard click-clack. The nurse let out a long huff and scanned the monitor left to right. "Uh… sorry. There's no one by that name."

Paloma's brow furrowed deeply. "But I called this desk an hour ago and I was told he was here."

"No, that must have been a mistake."

Her mouth open and shut. She turned around to look at Martin, saying something with her eyes. Then she stepped away from the counter and plunged further into the wing, ignoring the shrieks from the nurse at the counter. Martin followed behind, scanning the place. Each breath he took smelled of decay and sour chemicals. There were posters taped to the walls every few feet. *EVERYTHING WILL BE ALRIGHT. Remember to breathe using these four steps.* If he caught a glance through an open room door, he would see gnarled, discolored feet hanging off the edge of a bed, or a nurse cleaning shit from a yellowed plastic chamber pot. His mother was ravenously scanning the paper name tags slid into the plaques on each door. Each dud summoned whispered profanity.

Eventually, they found one labeled: *NAVARRO.*

And they entered.

He lay in the second bed at the far back of the room, breathing frail beneath a thin blanket. Tubes and wires grew like roots out of his flesh and his flaring nostrils. A small box television hung from the ceiling, vomiting color-shifting light and static onto every darkened surface.

"Papa?" Paloma pulled a chair over from the wall. She grabbed a skeletal hand from beneath the blanket. "Papa? It's Paloma. I'm here."

Eyes closed. Steady breathing.

"Martin is here, too. *Estoy aquí, papá. Vine a verte.*"

There was shifting out in the hall. Martin glanced over his shoulder and saw nurses running across the open doorway. Then a man passed by clad in black, his hands looped through a belt that held a taser and handcuffs. He was bound for the reception counter.

"Papa, wake up… *Te amo.*"

Flashes of the basement stairway. Mousie had fallen down. Grandpa was there, beneath the severed head of a bull. He'd never been able to recall the details of the face he'd seen at the bottom of the stairs, but now it seemed he could. Something had broken. It could come through, after so long being locked behind a wall. Now the mortar between the bricks was beginning to crumble and unstick. The face was there, and it was staring at him. Pale… paper skin. Eyes that never closed. No mouth.

"Don't go down there when it's night. That's where the bad man lives."

Grandpa... where are you going?

"Miss Navarro?"

Martin turned to see three nurses–including the one from behind the counter. Leading them was the man in black, the cop–or security guard. It looked as though he wasn't going to move, but he suddenly grabbed Martin by the arm.

The nurse pulled away the hanging curtain. "We have a note from your sister, Malosa. You're not allowed to visit your father."

"What?" Paloma stood up fast, her mouth agape. "But he's my father."

"I'm sorry, but you're going to have to leave."

"Let go of my son, you fucking animal!" She was across to him in a flash, digging her nails into the security guard's hand. He flinched and released Martin's arm. "How can you kick me out of my own father's room? What the fuck is wrong with you people?"

"We have instruction from Ma-"

"-Instructions? Does she own the fucking hospital? Huh? Does she tell you what to do?"

"Miss Navarro, please cooperate."

"This is my father!"

And the guard grabbed her arm, as well as Martin's once more before leading them out into the hallway. "Both of you out, or you'll be charged."

"Charged for visiting my father in the hospital?"

The guard said nothing more. He walked them to the elevator and pressed the button. It blinked amber, and the cables behind the wall began to buzz and hum. Once the door opened, he pushed them through, and waited for it to close with his fingers looped through his belt.

—

Ding!

The elevator doors peeled apart like steel gift wrap. The gift inside was another rotting hallway, overgrown with plantlife. Zakaria was the first to step off–into a puddle of broken glass. "Man's got power through this shithole. Maybe there's still some morphine lying around, too."

Martin stepped out into the hallway where the security guard had seen him off many years ago. Some of the posters were still taped up, although flaking and soaked through.

EVERYTHING WILL BE... me... eat...u...hese... ur steps. Panels had been pulled off the ceiling to expose hanging wire entrails, picked over by scavengers. The shattered glass had come from a large window, which was now just a frame–letting in snow that floated through the shafts of sunlight like dust particles.

Dino the guitar player looked the walls up and down through his devil mask. His guitar hung behind him from a strap, swaying off his body like a tired lover. There were two other men with him: nameless masks who hadn't spoken once during their trip. They kicked at bits of debris, or checked the magazines on their rifles.

"Look now."Zak stood over a chunk of fallen wall. "Pixie dust." Where he pointed was a long trail of purple sand, glimmering wherever it was hit by sunlight. It fled off down the hallway towards the reception counter, then banked hard right into an adjacent hall. He let it guide the way, and his pack followed closely.

Once they came upon the reception, Martin tried to remember the face of the tired bag who'd been working that day–the click-clack of her keyboard as she brought up the patient data with its warning note. Now the counter was a mess of rubble and popped-open computer parts–all of it coated in a thick layer of dust. He wondered what happened to her.

A door. The sand trail led under it, so Zak pushed it open. Behind was the hallway of room doors, all open and likely looted. The stench of death and feces was strong out of one. Martin held his breath and turned away; he'd never smelled something so horrible. Eventually the sand turned left into one of the rooms. Before going forward, Zak stopped and spun in place. His voice was a whisper. "We're not here for fun. Mister Dufresne is a business man, now. His girls'll try and talk to y'all and rub up like a bunch 'a kittens, but you ignore 'em. We're not paying him 'nothing. He's paying us. That understood?"

Martin and the two nameless men nodded.

"Right. Plus, y'all don't want no Hep-*ee*–titus from those alley cats, do ya now?–*Ha!*" His chuckling leaked out like air from a tire. He led them to the door and peeked his head through, then he held out his arms as if to embrace someone. "You fuckin' rabbit! Got people pickin' their way through Chernobyl out here."

A man appeared from out of the darkness and received Zak's embrace. His features were dark and mottled–or so Martin thought, until he stepped a bit more into the sunlight. Whatever face he had was wrapped in gray bandages from neck to forehead–a mummy woken from a tomb. The bandages were designed in their placement to give the impression of a face, with one across the brow to cast shadows into the eye sockets. His voice was muffled, and Martin had to strain to hear it. "This is what it takes now, Zak. Ain't no easy way to do business."

"How's your profits?"

"Come in." The wrapped face took in those of the three stragglers, pausing a little longer on Martin. Then Mister Dufresne slipped back through the door to allow them entry.

Incense was burning in a holder shaped like a nude woman. It did a little to offset the rot of the hospital air–enough at least to help one ignore it. A sheet was hung over the window and medical junk had been pushed up against one wall: the two beds; the husk of the gutted heart monitor. Their feet were cushioned by a large purple shag rug. Mud came off them and matted the fibers.

"You redecorated nice."

Mister Dufresne was standing beside a stack of boxes, whispering into the ear of a girl sitting atop it. Her leopard eyes were on the pack of strangers, running up and down from their boots to their heads. Her bare legs were crossed under a short, white skirt; she leaned back on her outstretched arms, trying to accentuate herself beneath a matching crop top. Dufresne finished what he had to say and caressed her cheek–pushed a short, cobalt blue lock of hair out of her face. "Things to create a mood–but things we can take down easy. I have three of the rooms down the hall made up. Good thing 'bout a hospital is there's beds already." A purple blanket, golden fringes, was covering a chair. He planted himself in it, then motioned for his visitors to find a seat. "My girls can give you a tour."

A hard plastic seat took Zakaria. "We're here for business."

"And your boys?"

"Just the same." Zak hunched forward–put his forearms on his knees.

Martin felt heat on his neck, then a body pressed up against him. He tried to look, but was guided to a hefty beanbag chair and made to sit. There were two other girls in the room–one crouched on the counter beneath the covered window, chin on her knees. The other walked around from behind Martin's chair and brushed him with the long, braided ponytail she was wielding like a whip.

"This one's not wearing a mask." Dufresne used his open palm to smooth the snow leopard patterning running down each collar. Gold buttons sparkled from a three-piece suit beneath his coat. "He not jiving with your cause just yet? Pick him up off the street?"

The ponytail girl tried to rub Zakaria's shoulders and nearly pricked herself on his needle choker. She let off and transferred to the next man. "He's alright. Just tagging along."

"What's that mean?"

"Means it doesn't matter."

Dufresne pulled a cigarette out of his pocket. "Alright now, don't get catty." He used its butt to pull down the strap of cloth over his mouth, then he caught it between two wet, pink lips. A flicker and burst of flame. The tobacco rustled and shriveled as it burned.

"You have the guns?"

Smoke erupted from the glowing tip and wafted through the room, mingling with incense. "I do."

"Where?"

"So impatient, Zak. Talk for a little while–I haven't seen you in a long time. Since you smuggled me outta the pile 'a shit I was in."

"Take them bandages off your head and I'll understand you better."

"No, no. Your boys here don't know my face."

Somewhere outside, a car engine sputtered and screamed. Martin felt the beanbag's weight shift, and he turned to see the girl with the blue hair lowering herself down beside him. She put an arm around his shoulders and ran her fingers through his hair. "You're handsome. You won't put a bag over your head, will you?"

He turned away. "Not planning on it."

"Good. The world would be so much worse if it couldn't

see your face."

A delicate hand took hold of his chin and coaxed it up. He let her see him, and saw her in return. Light makeup was done over a tired smile. Sad eyes were drowning in pools of eyeshadow. She pursed her dry lips, whispered something. He didn't hear it. Staring at him seemed to transport her somewhere else.

"How's your profits?"

Dufresne snapped his fingers and the blue haired girl let go of Martin's chin. She got up, as if being dragged, and went back to her stack of crates. She never again looked up from the floor.

"How many clients do you get now?"

A puff of smoke. "Well, Zak… This town is a damn shithole. You know, before the cult of bullshit moved in here, I'd make sixty thousand a day. Ten girls workin' all day, in between their breaks–got a lot of clientele. But uh… cult keeps track of all the money they have circulating in town. It always filters back to them one way or another–minus the allowed losses. The more I take, the more I keep–you know me. I'm a big saver."

"Yeah."

"But then there's less money for everyone else, and I think people are startin' to figure that. I was the highest earner in town, Zak. I made fuckloads. I'm gonna skyrocket inflation if I ever dump all this out into the streets. So people don't come that used to, or they come and try to pay me a pallet a' beans or something shit like that. I don't know, I can make guesses all day."

"Or maybe your broads got some kinda bug between their legs."

The ponytail girl came over and kicked the back of his chair. He whirled his arms, as if the chair might fall back, but it didn't. It sent Dufresne into a fit of muffled, hyena-like laughter. "Don't you know not to talk about a woman like that, Zak? Makes 'em all heated. You want a drink?"

"No."

"Your boys?"

"They're fine."

Dufresne spun the threads of a gold tassel hung from his chair. "You're antsy."

A creak as Zakaria relaxed in his chair.

"You got a tail?"

"You think I got a metal ball in my skull?"

"Then what's with the tension? Relax, Zak." It didn't sound like a suggestion–the way he said it. "Take one 'a my girls and go next door. Unwind yourself–I won't even charge for it."

"How about we bring out the guns–see if that calms me down."

The cigarette shed a rod of ash. It hit the ground and let out its final glowing breaths before going cold. "Alright… Fine, then." He snapped his fingers a few times at the blue haired girl until she got down off the stack of crates. In the corner of the room, by the girl crouched on the back counter, a curtain lay over something. Both girls got down to grab it and haul it off, revealing a gun safe. Thin muscles bulged desperately beneath ghostly, tattooed skin in an effort to roll the steel monster on its casters. Out of the dark–up to Dufresne's makeshift throne. Once there, he sprung to his feet and twisted the code dial–right, left, right. *CLANG!* The door groaned like something woken from slumber, and its deadly innards were bared. "Sixteen *Baretta Cx4 Storm SMG*'s, sixteen *HK P30* pistols, twelve *Bushmaster M*4 assault rifles and one *CheyTac Intervention* sniper. Ammo included for all of 'em, of course." He sat back down and took another drag of his cigarette. "Calming enough for you, Zak?"

A smile formed beneath a leather mask. "Like a massage from a busty Russian."

Martin was eyeing the safe when he felt a presence beside him. He turned–saw the blue haired girl; she'd stopped on the way back to her stack of crates. Her expression was empty. Slowly, she ran her hand down along her thigh, to the end of her white skirt. It began to lift. Before he turned to look away in shame, he noticed black writing against the pale backdrop of skin. A sharp breath. Just beneath the line of her underwear: *He knows who you are. Get out.*

Wide eyes. His heart snapped once, hard against his breast.

She released the skirt before drifting back to her perch.

"You fired them all? Know they work?"

Dufresne coughed. "Now that's the thing. Not many places in town to test fire a crate 'a guns without drawing some attention. But I personally pulled 'em all apart and put 'em back together; the parts are all nice and clean. No broken shit."

"I can trust you?"

"Zak… What kinda question is that?"

Zakaria turned to look at his brother, who looked back beneath his devil horns. The guitar was laid out across his lap; he turned the gain knobs absently with his thumb. Then the devil said: "So we're done here."

Dufresne peered through his veil of smoke at the guitar player. "Dino… hardly even knew you were there. You're like a church mouse, kid. How's that guitar treating you?"

"Perfectly."

A chuckle. "I appreciate a man dedicated to an instrument. He does everything with it. Maybe you could set it aside for a while and one 'a my girls can let you play her strings instead."

Zakaria began to rise. "I think I'll inspect one 'a these myself. Check the metal–you'll understand." He sauntered towards the gun safe, but a hand clutching the butt of a cigarette tapped the door into a backward swing. A clanking lock, then a spin of the dial.

Silence.

The cigarette fell to the floor–was crushed beneath a polished spectator dress shoe.

Zakaria remained standing, the centerpiece of the room with all eyes on him. His fingers rubbed together on his right hand; he tapped his foot on the carpet. "Is that the elevator?"

Martin could hear it now. A low rumble coming from down the hall, then the *PING!* of the floor buzzer. He looked over at the blue haired girl, and found her staring at him with something desperate in her tired eyes.

"Probably more clients," said Dufresne.

A pause, then: "Is this what I think it is?"

"What do you think it is, Zak?"

"They would've killed you, Leland. I saved your fucking ass."

"That kid you've got with you is expensive. And like I said, business is tough."

There was a chorus of footsteps from the hallway,

stamping over debris and crushing dust.

"Motherfucker." There was a pistol in Zakaria's hand, and he'd already shot.

Dufresne's chair fell backward under his dead weight. A hole was punched through his mummy fabric face. Screaming. The girls fled to the corners of the room, faces scrunched up into fearful, wet masks. The gunshot had reached the ears of the intruders outside, and they started shouting and running.

"Police! Put the gun down now!"

Everyone was up on their feet. They found cover and aimed their weapons at the yawning doorway. With the first peeks of grey uniforms came gunfire. Bullets sparked and ricocheted off the walls. One or two hit the window behind the hanging sheet and glass shattered into sparkling daggers, tearing the cloth. Sunlight was released like water through a dam, blinding the officers who stormed the room. There were twenty, or close to it; they all entered at once, firing at whatever moved and hitting nothing. But the building was old, and it had been old before it was abandoned. The weight of the stampeding bodies was too much for it to bear.

The floor collapsed as the termite and moisture-eaten structure gave way beneath. The police were sucked into the orifice of the hospital, and fell four storeys down, cracking the floors of each as they went. Debris and flesh ragdolls bounced and broke against edges and beams on the way, and a monster cloud of dust erupted into the humid air.

Once the sound and motion had come to rest, Zakaria stepped away from the wall he'd pressed himself against. It was near impossible to see through the cloud. "Hey! Who's here?"

Three voices: Dino and the two masked men. A cry for help from a woman–he didn't know which.

"Martin?"

Silence.

They waited for the dust to settle–at least enough to see a few feet. The hole was massive, but the edges near the walls hadn't gone. Zak could see Dino, his two men, and two of the women, one of whom was limp against the wall with a bullet in her head. Ponytail girl.

But Martin was gone.

23

"Hey, mister… Please don't be dead."

He opened his eyes and saw his legs; he was lying upside down against a pile of rubble. A kink in his neck. A push with his arms. Dust ground into his hair as he slid his weight from his shoulders to his back. Then he lay and stared up at the jagged hole in the ceiling, through which snow was sprinkling. His backpack clung awkwardly around his shoulders, forced up under his head like a pillow. A hard pillow, filled with bullets. Flakes melted on the mangled corpse-flesh of a police officer, who'd become one with the stone–entangled in a web of rebar and concrete.

Martin started up his lungs, and they sputtered like an old engine. "Who… Where are you?" Then a warm hand cupped his cheek in response. He craned to see who it was attached to.

Blue hair. Heart-shaped face. She looked like an Elizabethan queen wearing white face powder, except the powder was in her hair as well, and on her clothes. Blood ran down her neck and into her top–turned the fabric red. She said: "We survived."

And he asked: "How? … Is anything broken? My… arms." But he could move his arms–full mobility. He looked around at the darkness lying beyond the soft cold sunlight–saw hints of walls and hallways plunging into shadow. Pipes ran along the ceiling; one was labeled in flaking text: *SEWAGE.* Cork-looking tiles from the drop ceiling lay on the ground–broken off chunks strewn in piles around them. In their absent places, wires were hanging down like long, tangled fingers. He got to his feet with a groan, then gave a hand to the blue-haired woman.

She'd suddenly forgotten the seduction and lurid movements from before; now she hugged herself, arms crossed over her chest. Every so often came a tremble or clattering of teeth. "Are they all dead?"

He looked down at the rubble pile. Near the top, a single arm was protruding, still clutching a pistol. Around the back, he found two officers who'd also escaped the crush, lying like ragdolls on the linoleum. A cursory glance could tell their chests were rising and falling, then one coughed up a wad of sputum and dirt.

"Shit… Kill them."

He looked at her.

"Or they'll kill *us*… They'll get up and follow us." Her throat bulged around swallowed saliva. "Fucking pigs deserve it anyway."

His hand searched for the metal bulge in his belt. The gun came out after catching on fabric. A loose string torn off his waistline clung onto the edge of the slide. He plucked it off with his free hand–saw the scar running from wrist to knuckles. "Looks like they're choking on their own blood. Not worth the bullets."

"How do you know that?"

"They're on the ground, woman." He turned to her. "Quit. It's like shooting a stray dog."

A scowl. "Yeah, cause it'll bite you and give your ass rabies. Shoot the sons-a-bitches!"

"*Drop the gun!*"

Martin turned quick–saw one of the cops had seemingly collected himself. He was showing Martin the nose of a barrel. The man hadn't gotten up from the floor–he was still flat on his back. Blood was trickling slowly down the edge of his mouth.

Silence.

"Put it down, kid." A violent cough, and more dirty phlegm. He pulled his campaign hat off and threw it away. "Get on the ground. 'Fore a blow your head off… And you, bitch–same thing."

Martin held his free hand up, open palm. “You’re bleeding, officer. Looks bad.”

“And I intend to make it outta this, so put the gun down.”

“How do I know you won’t shoot me?”

Another cough–spray of blood. “What’s that?”

“Do you know who I am?”

The officer squinted. “Mothe-”

A loud snap, and the cop fell back flat. What blood had been in his head was now a long spray across the floor. Martin shifted his aim–shot again. The second officer who hadn’t yet woken up would never have the chance. Then he walked a circle around the mound of concrete, checking every body for signs of life. But there weren’t any.

“I fucking told you.” She spat dust out from between her teeth.

The rubble had piled against a wall. Also against that wall, he found what remained of Leland Dufresne–his limbs were shattered and bent into wrong angles. Dirt and blood matted the snow leopard lining around his neck. Loosening in the bandages wrapped around his head allowed peeks at what kind of face they’d meant to hide. Martin grabbed them and pulled, eventually peeling them off. It was an unassuming face–unremarkable. He imagined he wouldn’t be able to pick it out of a group if he were asked to.

Light feet crunched from behind. “We always said he

looked like some guy you'd see in a dream–but not, like a good dream. Just a dream." She was still hugging herself. "Looks like nobody. Perfect kinda guy to pimp chicks." Her hand rubbed up and down her bicep. "You see… uh… You see the other two girls anywhere?"

"Nah." He dropped the bandages and stepped down off his shattered concrete perch. "We should get back up to the surface."

"What if they're buried?"

He paused–looked at her. "Then they're dead." He didn't wait to see if that answer was satisfactory. There was a scar on the wall where the paint was just a bit less yellowed. Screw holes. He looked around–spotted a metal plate lying face down. It scraped as he picked it up, like he'd disturbed its rest. Wing numbers and names were printed in white, alongside arrows. That could have been helpful, until he noticed the wall across was also missing a sign plate. Where that second plate was, he couldn't see. Maybe buried.

"What?"

He showed her the hunk of metal. "Which way is which?" No answer. He hadn't expected one. It occurred to him to hold the plate up flat against the spaces on the walls–see where it fit best. But they were identical. Perfect alignment both times. He looked one direction, then the other. Both ended in double doors half-hidden in darkness.

The plate wheeled in a lazy arc–snapped a spurt of dust off the concrete rubble. A dark speck shot out from a crack, woken by the vibration. It skittered up one rock and down another–fled down the hallway. Eight legs. Big like a dollar coin. Martin shivered. "Eenie-meenie." Stamps from his boot heels ricocheted back and forth off the walls. He went the opposite direction.

The woman followed.

—

STAFF KITCHEN.

The wood of the door was rough and swollen. He pushed it–it whined, then caught against something. His full weight got it to move further, and created a piercing metallic scream: bare metal on concrete–a knife grinding a plate and nails on a chalkboard. It made him cringe. On the other side was a decently sized room stocked with the corpse of a basic kitchen: empty cupboards with their doors hanging on one hinge; a sink pulled out of its housing and tossed onto the floor; broken cutlery spread over the countertops–a handful of knives rammed blade-down into the laminate.

And scrawled in paint in the center of the room was a pentagram.

"Jesus. What were they doing in here?" She cautiously

found footing around the piles of scrap and used needles. It was an endurance exercise for stiletto heels.

Martin bent down at the center of the pentagram–picked up the book lying open there. The covers were black snakeskin and bare. It didn't look like it came off a bookstore shelf. He scanned the pages it was open to, around the stains and dust:

Occultist Rudolph Steiner decreed: Sorath is the Sun-demon of Revelation, more powerful than Lucifer or Ahriman, who are Lords of Darkness. His negative workings include war, crime, hatred and sexual deviance, yet he who forms a pact with him shall gain knowledge of black magic, and powers that are God-like. Sorath shall work, as all demons do, with your Id–that which is basest in human nature. Neither the Ego, nor the Superego may overpower the Id whilst a demon possesses it. You must ask yourself, then, if you are prepared to commune with Sorath, lest you lose control and submit to his will.

He flipped through the pages and encountered more of the same. He put it back down on the ground.

"Look." She was standing by the door–pulled it closed a little to bring the pasted printer paper on the back into view. Laminated, stained. A map of the whole building floor by floor. "We turn left up ahead. There's the stairs."

As they were leaving the room, Martin saw the dark speck shoot like a rocket from under the door. It peeled away–turned left, towards the stairs.

"What?"

"Nothing."

She smiled. "You scared of spiders?"

Hand on the door–he pulled it open all the way, so he could slip past her. "Let's go."

A short walk brought them to the base of a concrete stairwell. At the top of the first stretch was a landing, which switched back into the second stretch and a presumable doorway hidden from view. Sunlight came from that hidden exit–shone frosted in the ancient plastic of another motivational poster. *When things look hopeless; and everything goes wrong; remember to thank God; and he'll help you carry on.* Jesus held his arms outspread. His plastic smile beckoned.

The woman stepped up onto the stairs and placed her feet like a child engaged in a game of hopscotch. Plywood boards and fallen bricks littered the way. Plants grew through cracks between the steps and the wall. Martin followed after her, paying attention to where she placed her steps. She got to the landing and turned around–maybe to check on him. Then her eyes popped open the size of teacups. “Oh my *God*!”

Before he could fully register her snap in demeanor, he felt something grab his leg and pull hard and fast. He went down–was dragged down the steps he’d just climbed, banging his limbs on the bricks and dislodging the plywood. It skated down with him like a sled on a snowy hill. The ground met him painfully. He flailed his body around to get a view of what was still locked around his leg. It was a hand, and that hand was attached to a figure dressed in black.

Her face was twisted in glee–a smile too stiff and wide to be natural. Teeth snapping, like a shark. “Your *tia* wants a word, child.” The eyes were skin. Those same eyes that had been watching him his whole life. They bulged and rolled around; he thought of bones moving beneath skin, of infected meat crawling and writhing. “I had them throw you out of here, Martin! Why’d you come back?” Malosa Navarro opened her mouth to expel ink-black vomit in violent pulses, the way a cat coughs up a hairball–full body racking and squeezing.

A crack and flash, then the scent of gunpowder. The hand released him, and he crawled back a little. He looked up the stairs for the blue-haired girl, and caught a flash of her tail, fleeing up the second section into the sunlight. Gone.

“*DO NOT SHOOT ME, BOY.*”

He leaned on the wall–pulled himself up to his feet. The

dark figure spasmed. Now he saw the rusty hooks pulling on the edges of her mouth–forcing that unyielding grin. Insectoid limbs controlled them by chain–a puppet master. Some mass of infected flesh on her back sprouted those limbs; and now it sprouted some more. They unfurled–pushed out into the humid, stinking air through a bruised pustule slit. In total were eight–hair covered and near nine feet tall. When they extended, Malosa was lifted into the air, still smiling, tar slinking in thick strands from between her teeth.

Martin ran. And she followed him.

Each time one of the eight legs came down, the hall would tremble. The noise was oppressive and always just behind him. He turned occasionally to fire a volley of shots; each time it intensified the tightness in his chest–the panic screaming in his head. His skin was crawling. Visions of being consumed by arachnid fangs. He worried his heart would explode.

Malosa hung beneath the legs like a limp sack. "*C O M E B A C K C H I L D . G I V E M E T H E D O L L . T H E D O L L . T H E D O L L . T H E D O L L .*"

His backpack beat at him as he ran, flailing back and forth to counter each step. Its straps yanked on his shoulders; he wanted to throw it off, but he could never bring himself to. Boxes of bullets jingle-jangled; his hair flew across his eyes and got caught in his rapid, heaving breaths–sucked into his mouth.

"*GIVE IT TO ME NOW*."

The hallway was ending up ahead. Bare wall–another poster. This one had a beaming sun-yellow smiley face and *Pray for a sunny day* in bold text beneath. He nearly tripped on the web-like roots of the encroaching plantlife. The only place left to go was through a half-open door. He slammed it shut behind and felt his whole frame rattle with the force coming in blasts from the other side. His gun spit smoke and ejected casings. Wood splintered–forced out of the way of red-hot bullets. The creature screamed each time it was pierced–in between thrashes at the door.

Now he pulled off his backpack and furiously unzipped. Out came a preloaded magazine. *Click, pop*–sliding metal. The empty mag fell out of the pistol and clattered on the tiles. Then he racked the slide once the new one had snapped home. He emptied it just as fast as he'd loaded it. Sunlight poked through like shafts of fire, let in by the now swiss-cheesed door.

One final strike from outside turned it to sawdust.

Into the room barreled the monster, legs stretched long to squeeze through the frame. When that didn't service it, it broke apart the obstacle and kicked bits of plaster and wood in an explosive shower. Dust was up in thick clouds when the whole wall toppled–broken off at the studs.

Martin heard the shattering of glass. He looked over one shoulder–saw he'd entered a room packed full of shelving units. Piled high on every one were jars of multicolored pills: hundreds and hundreds–thousands of pills. The shelves were tipping, knocking their neighbors like a domino chain. When a jar struck the ground, it evacuated its contents in wide and random patterns. He fled further into the room, but lost footing on the pills. He was on his ass. Scrambling arms and kicking feet. All the while, he fired shots intermittently. Each time, Malosa shrieked high enough to shatter glass. Her face had become a Hell faucet, spewing black mire from the mouth–crying it from her eyes. But the rusty hooks kept her smiling. "*Y O U I N G R A T I O U S L I T T L E F U C K. I G A V E Y O U G U I D A N C E, A N D Y O U S P I T I N M Y F A C E. Y O U R A U N T I S D E A D. Y O U R M O T H E R I S D E A D. S O S O O N S H A L L Y O U B E D E A D.*"

He was swimming through pills and broken glass. It cut him and bled him all over the sparkling sea.

The beast did not advance. It watched him struggle. "*D R O W N I N Y O U R A D D I C T I O N.*"

A gasp of air. He managed to push his head up, but before a steady hold could be found, one of the eight gargantuan legs lunged–grabbed his back and forced him down.

"*YOU WILL ALWAYS SLIP*."

In between gaps in the overflow of pills, he caught glimpses of the beast. The body hanging down beneath the legs was never the same twice: it was Malosa, crying black tar; then it was the skin man–the bad man in the basement.

—

"Martin. Come here."

He could see her through the tinted car window. The top of his head only just reached it. Dashboard air freshener was leaking out through the gap between the glass and the doorframe–she'd rolled it down a little. He gripped the handle and pulled. A click, and the smell came wafting–with warmth, and her expensive perfume. The seat was leather. It scorched his hand when he placed it to pull himself up. He planted himself–reached to his limit to get a hold of the open door. A slam, and the outside was cut off. Now a delicate silence.

"Hi, buddy."

"Hi, *Tia*."

Empty coffee cup in the cup holder. Lipstick on the rim. A jingling chain of plastic and metal stuck into the ignition. Trash was strewn around the back seat: more coffee cups; lip balm tubes; plastic bags.

"What did your mother say?"

Blank confusion. "About what?"

"About me. Did she say anything?"

"No. She just said '*have fun.*'"

Silence.

He picked at a loose string on his sleeve. "Where are we going?"

"We've gotta stop by my church to drop something off. Then we can go to the mall. That sound okay?"

A smile. "Okay! Can we look at the *Gameboy* games?"

She turned in her seat to reach into the back. "Sure, buddy. Yeah, we can do that." A shifting of garbage, until she excavated her black leather purse. It came back with her to the front. The zipper made a sound like a drowning cry for help. "I have something for you."

Martin looked down at the purse. It writhed and squirmed as she dug around. Soon, it relinquished a small plastic bag filled with little white tablets. Her acrylic nails chittered with the movements of her fingers. The plastic parted, and she tapped one of the little tablets into his open palm. "I opened a pack of candy yesterday and didn't like it. It tastes really sour, so you're not supposed to chew them. Just swallow it. You wanna try and see if you like it?"

"What is it?"

"Candy. Hard candy."

He had his eyes on it like he expected it to grow legs. "But why can't you chew it?"

"Just swallow it." The smile was gone.

Hesitation.

"Do you trust your *Tia*? It's candy, buddy."

"Okay." When it touched his tongue, his mouth filled with bitter saliva. But he did as she'd said, and swallowed it without chewing.

—

BANG!

A shriek, but the leg didn't let off. He shot again, and again. The next time, he waited–lined up the sights with trembling arms. He held his breath, and pulled the trigger. A bullseye, right through the forehead. Breath flowed back into his lungs as the weight on his back was lifted. And he rolled, fighting the ever increasing flow of pills. They were no longer just coming from the jars on the shelves–those had all broken. It seemed as if they were multiplying on their own. "Fuck you!" He dug around his bag, which clung to him by one strap. Boxes of bullets splattered their contents–shells rolled out to get lost amongst the pills. The rest of them were lodged beneath Mousie. The doll. He pulled it out–or tried to. His plastic face got caught on the zipper teeth. "Fuck!" Frantic pulling, then a sudden release.

Mousie's face popped off–fell back into the bag.

And the pills… were gone. All of them. As if they'd never been there.

But Martin's eyes were locked on the doll in his hands. The cacophony of sound was also gone, like he was sitting in a vacuum–in space. In the place of Mousie's face was now a mirror, in which he saw himself staring back.

He, himself.

Though he could see in his own face that which he'd never seen. It was the face he'd hidden from himself–scratched away in his bathroom mirror. He didn't recognize the finer details; he'd never seen them before. Time had aged him–started to turn his hair gray at the ends. His eyes were hollow and wracked, bloodshot. His lips, hanging open, were cracked and dry. His stubble had overgrown–made him ragged. And he was gaunt as living death.

He looked up over Mousie as he remembered the beast, but it was no longer there. In its place was *Her*. Cloaked in blackness–midnight Cleopatra. Those horrid growths formed on her back had vanished, as had the rusty hooks pushed through her cheeks. She looked emotionless.

"Why did you do it?"

She answered: "Because you were my sister's son."

Martin furrowed his brow. “What did she do to you… to deserve torture?”

There was a long pause, before: “She was happy.”

Snow fell through a hole in the ceiling, just behind the dark apparition. Martin looked around–saw his spilled boxes of bullets, but no shelves and no jars of pills. Wind hammered the exterior walls over his head.

When he looked back, Malosa was gone.

And he never saw her again.

24

He could hear them above–on the next floor up. Hauling, crashing and cursing. He drifted through the halls, Mousie clutched loosely at his side. Mirrors–everywhere. In the rooms, in the hall–the reflection in the interior windows. Each time he spotted one, he would check to make sure the man staring back hadn't changed. Not once. He was clear as crystal–ragged and disheveled. Unmasked.

Rubble ground into the linoleum under his boots. It felt as if he'd surfaced from out of a black pool. He could hear better, smell better, see better. No longer did his head stab and hum. His oft-returning migraine had fled totally.

A slow ascent. Each stair clapped reverb up and down the echoing stairwell. He swung his backpack around and fit Mousie back inside–zipped up. Another set of steps, cracked tiles. The walls were sprouting vines and webs of root. The crashing and dragging was louder now.

They were kneeling over her body when he got to the

main floor. The blue haired girl, and the one who'd been sitting on the counter. He stood at the top of the stairwell and watched them until they noticed.

"They shot her in the head." Blue hair had her hands in her lap, rubbing her palms. "Pigshit fucking…"

He approached and looked down at the corpse. The long ponytail was matted red. He could see through into the gooey wetness behind her forehead. It was drooling down her nose and into the nostrils.

"Did you… kill that coyote in the basement?"

A blink. "What?"

Blue hair continued: "Or… I don't know what it was–looked like a coyote or some kinda dog."

"Yeah… I killed it."

No response.

"Are you gonna bury her outside?"

The women nodded, and said nothing more to him. So he left them in pursuit of the noise. He found it around the corner, by the front reception desk. Masked men, dragging–using a thick blanket under the gun safe to slide it.

"Holy Lord…" Zak let go and rounded the safe. He grabbed Martin by the shoulders and looked hard into his face. "How… I thought you were dead, son–no two ways about it."

Martin could only shrug helplessly.

"Must have a guardian angel on your ass. There were, uh… we heard gunshots in the basement somewhere–thought the pigs must'a finished you off. Or whatever was left of ya."

"No," he said. "No, uh… I made it."

"That hussy there with the blue hair came runnin' up outta the basement then–said you were dragged down by a dog or some shit. We were gonna come lookin' for ya, I swear, son. Just as soon as we got this safe loaded up on our truck. You understand, don't ya?"

He itched his beard.

"Come on."

He shrugged his slipping backpack strap.

Zak cupped his cheek–smacked it lightly. "You don't think I'd leave you, now."

"I think me being dead doesn't inconvenience you terribly enough."

A sigh was the answer to that.

"I don't care, Zak. Whatever. What's the plan now?"

The leather mask pivoted one-eighty, met the gaze of a denim devil. Dino was leaning on his guitar. Back around to Martin. "Well, as long as we're still chumps."

"As long as we know what we both want."

Ting! Fingernail off a choker needle. "What do you want, son?"

"I wanna leave town when this is done."

"Tired of the scenery?"

"I guess you could say that, yeah."

A smile. "That's fine with me. Long as you stick it out 'til the end… but I don't think we'll have to worry about that."

"No. No, we won't."

A pause. "Then we'll make like rabbits and get fucking at it. Keep that safe movin' boys, we don't have all week, now." He took Martin by the shoulder and led him out the front door into the sunlight. Burning sunlight. "Like as not, Roman Ward now knows we're arming ourselves. Our element of surprise is fucked-off now. Best chance we have is to hit 'em today, before they get their eggs in order and lock everything down."

Martin held his hand up to shield his eyes. The sun backlit the Red Abbey on its hill–spire of white and rust. "Are your people ready today?"

"We've been ready for three years, son."

The men were lifting the safe on a rolling jack. Cranking metal teeth sounded like popcorn in the wind. The back suspension of the band's truck bowed and yelped, but bore the weight.

Zak said: "Ah, I forgot. Your uh…" He tapped the side of his head.

A gust of wind smelled of frost. It whipped Martin's hair. "No, it's alright. He can't hear me anymore."

"How's that?"

"He's gone… I can't feel him–now I know… what it felt like, now that it's gone."

Then came a snicker. "Fuckin' Hell. Whatever you say, son. So I can tell you what the plan is now? Good. We go back home and round everyone up, get 'em armed. Then we head to the church and send someone in disguise. Some of our former cultists ran with their robes still on. We'll use one of 'em." He led Martin to the truck and checked over the straps holding the safe down. "Right, good. We'll, uh- we'll have him try to make it up to the roof and destroy the signal jammer they've got up there, remember?"

"Yeah."

"If we don't hear from him in an hour, we… well, storm the fucking church and fill every one 'a them sons-'a-bitches with lead. That's what these puppies are for." He flat-palm smacked the safe. It thumped like a drum. "That good enough for ya?"

Martin sniffled against the cold. "I don't have anything better."

"Right. Good. Now let's move, ladies. Let's free this fucking town! Three years too late!"

The truck was loaded up and started. A sputtering

rumble, and black smoke from the exhaust. Tires plowed through slush and sheets of wet snow melting on the asphalt parking lot.

Martin sat in the flatbed, watching the trees and derelict buildings fly past. For the first time in as long as he could remember, his mind was quiet.

—

Their road took them close to the police station. The pavement broke off on one side and shot through the trees; at the end of that side road it stood. A squat building–slanted roof, chimney smoking opaque gray clouds. Dino stepped on the gas to pass as quick as he could. But someone said: "Look at all the cars. You see that?"

"Yeah. A whole fleet. And *ATV*'s too, I think. Fuck."

Whatever they'd seen was now behind the treeline. But one of the unnamed masked men pulled on the sliding piece in the back windshield, then stuck his hand through to grab Zak's shoulder. "Hey, you see that?"

The answer was: "Yeah, I saw it. Keep your eyes on the road behind us."

Martin watched the roadway snaking back and forth. It didn't take long before the first patrol car came into view. Black and white, sirens off. Another followed close behind it, then another, and another. Ten now. And the *ATVs* came next. A long snake, slithering its way closer and closer.

"Zak!"

He spun in his seat. "Shit."

Dino put his foot down. Wind buffeted the faces in the truck bed. Martin pulled his pistol–the others followed his example.

"Are they coming to the train yard?"

"Don't know what else they'd be doing. Take a few shots at 'em."

Snapping gunpowder. A crisp, biting sound dampened by the forest on either side. Their breath was turned to clouds in the chill, mimicking the clouds from their pistols. Shots began to land, and police windshields thrummed and cracked. One car skated off the road, went sideways and rolled over into the ditch, spraying blood and motor oil.

"Good! That's o-"

A sudden spray of bullets hit the flatbed door–staccato. Martin dropped to his stomach behind the safe. Someone was bleeding–one of the unnamed men. His arm was draining into his shirt fiber.

"Watch your heads!"

Martin aimed down his sights, pulled. Blood erupted behind a distant windshield. Passenger seat. But it was enough to distract the driver. He whipped his wheel and crashed head-on into an embankment.

A fizzle of static came from inside the cabin. "Danny, we've got pigs on our tail. We're coming home. Get people ready–put 'em on the roof."

The answer came, inaudibly, through the plastic walkie speaker.

Martin glimpsed a car in the middle of the metallic snake–different than the other cruisers. A *Ford Skyranger* wrapped in a skirt of metal. Black, twisted bull bars were bolted over a snarling front grill. He could just barely see the phantom of a beige campaign hat at the wheel.

They drove on, snapping shots at the cops, until they rounded a corner into view of the railyard. The truck rattled over gravel, then came to a stop. It evacuated its human contents, which ran towards the warehouse, armed and yelling. But the roar of pursuing engines was quick to emerge from out of the trees–along with a hail of bullets.

Martin dove behind a boxcar, breathing hard. He was starting to feel dizzy–get tunnel vision. He lay flat to get a view under the car and saw black boots emerging from the cruisers. They spread, all running in different directions to find their own cover.

CRACK!

It echoed. Martin turned to see a glint from the roof of the warehouse–no, multiple glints. Maybe five. Rifles spit death down onto the running cops. He looked under again, just in time to see a mist of crimson and a lifeless corpse falling. The black campaign hat fell off, landed separate with a hole punched clean through the felt.

"*Police! Drop your weapons!*"

Some of the cops had automatics. They rattled and smoked, ejecting casings in whirling streams. One of the glints from the roof was snuffed. The rest vanished like blinking eyes–reappeared in different positions to get new angles. Then the deafening cracks resumed their cacophony.

Martin snuck his pistol under the box car, aimed it. Pulled. A head was punctured across the yard–it drew attention. Bullets kicked up dust from the gravel, just barely missing his own head. He needed to move, so he snuck along the length of the car, careful of any openings. His new angle offered a shot at the band's truck, where a bold cop was venturing onto the flatbed. He began to cut at the straps holding the safe with a pocketknife. One of them snapped and sprung, elastic. Then he grabbed the next one. Martin aimed, pulled. He hit the cop in the neck, and he stumbled backwards off the flatbed. The thud his body made on the ground was masked by gunfire.

A masked man not far from him was hit through the jaw. It severed flesh, made it hang by the muscle and ripping skin. He screamed, unformed and inhuman. Then a second shot blew out his brain.

"Martin!"

He turned. Zak was pointing frantically.

Engine roaring. Martin was struck in the side and thrown across the yard. Spinning flashes of the truck he'd seen. Then he landed, groaning. Tires spun on the gravel–gasoline pumped through pistons. The truck reversed, lined up, then snorted and coughed a burst of black smoke. It sped towards him where he lay, and he rolled out of the path of its bull bars. He got to his feet, as quick as his screaming body would allow.

The truck was turning while being peppered by gunfire. Its windows looked to be bullet-proof. Another line up, then a step on the gas. But Martin was up this time, and he leapt clear–fired a volley of shots at the tires. They popped and started to whistle, but the truck wasn't done yet. It wheeled around, struggling with the gravel. One final bout. It huffed black clouds and went at him faster than before. He froze. Just before it struck, he jumped up and hit the windshield–rolled over the roof. Then he hit the ground and yelped loudly. A stabbing pain shot up his arm from deep inside.

Tires flapped like broken bird wings–rubber on rock. The engine cut off and the driver side door popped open. A pair of black boots stepped out onto the gravel, then came around the front. "You're a tough one, boss. Full 'a spunk."

Martin rolled over. The gunfire in the air had lessened now. Gray-clad corpses littered the yard. He tried to lift himself to a seated position, but a boot came down on his chest, crushing the air out of his lungs.

"Said I'd come back here. But as it happens, I got a call from Roman Ward not an hour ago–said you'd managed to pull Golgotha outta your head. And y'all were meaning to arm yourselves. It's funny, ain't it? You got Golgotha out, but Roman still wants you dead for another reason altogether. Can't catch a break, can you, boss?"

A box car shielded the sergeant from the snipers on the warehouse roof. Martin looked around, saw his pistol lying some feet away; the truck had knocked it out of his hand.

"Y'all are pickin' off my men like flies–fuckin' useless sacks 'a shit they were. Before I die here today, I'm takin' you with me, boss. So we can head wherever we're heading together. That sound nice?"

He beat at Toledo's legs, trying to remove the leg. The sergeant grabbed at his arms, gun in his free hand–ready to fire.

"Come on, now. Don't fight it. Just let it happen."

He tried to throw his weight with his legs, but it did nothing. The pistol came down against his forehead–cold metal. Any second, it would empty into his skull.

A punch, to the sergeant's groin.

That made him yelp, and he folded. A grunt–he tried to re-center his pistol, but Martin punched again. "Fuck!" He took his leg off, clutching himself. The gun was knocked out of his grip and hit the gravel. A lunge at it, trying to reclaim it. But Martin kicked his legs out. A plume of smoke as Toledo fell.

And Martin got to his feet. He kicked the gun out of reach, then waited for the sergeant to get up.

"Wanna beat on me, boss?"

Silence. He raised his fists.

Toledo threw a punch. It missed. A return. It struck the sergeant in the nose. Blood ran down into his mustache. They both jabbed and missed, over and over, wheeling around in circles.

Footsteps.

Martin took a moment to look. Zakaria walked into view around the box car, rifle in his hands. At his back was a group of men. They didn't intervene.

Another punch. Toledo was grinning now, perhaps with realization. Blood filled the grooves around his gums. "This is it, boss. Finish me off, will ya? Or your daddy will."

He punched the sergeant in the nose again, then lifted his boot and brought it down on his knee. The crack was audible, and Toledo was down instantly, crumpled like a doll. He lay on his back, laughing madly, one hand up in a weak attempt to shield his face. Martin put down his fists and walked over to where his gun was lying in the dust. He collected it, brushed it off.

"Gonna shoot me like a fucking pussy?"

"You aren't worth busting my knuckles." Slowly, he hobbled back over to the lying cop, took aim down the ironsights. "You're hardly worth this bullet." And the gun snapped–spit smoke and a burst of fire. The hole carved through Toledo's eye socket–right out the back into the rocks.

The sound of the shot traveled far, over the trees through the winter air.

He looked up at Zak, who said nothing.

25

The streets were near empty. Any who remained looked homeless or angry. Wind rushed through empty alleyways and rustled the trees on an empty main street. A heavy quiet hung in the air–only nature's ambience remained. The motorcade rumbled through in a solemn line, sprouting masked bodies from open car windows, rifles clutched in their grip.

They found the black iron gates of the Abbey open wide, but they didn't drive through. A turn, down a side road. Around the skirt of the hill. Martin looked out the passenger window of the police cruiser; flickering images of the Abbey between the bars of the iron fence–a zoetrope display from some old Hollywood horror. Dracula's gothic castle shrouded in mist. The car began to slow, then came to a stop. His driver unbuckled–stepped out. He followed suit.

"Alright, are we all here? Good." Zak stood on the hood of a cruiser. "Colin, are you ready?"

"Yeah."

"Alright. So here's the idea–listen up all 'a ya'll."

Near fifty bodies packed in around the leatherfaced speaker. Fifty masks–sagging human skin and leather and denim and burlap. All wielded something that spit lead. They'd commandeered all the police cruisers, which had just recently been abandoned by their owners.

And Zak had a new belt accessory. Skin. Sagging like a handkerchief. There was still a mustache above the lip. "Colin, you head down inside and try to make it up to the roof. We'll be watching. If you don't show in an hour, it's time for fireworks. Simple."

So they used one of the cruisers parked up close to the fence, jumped up and helped each other over. Then they ascended the grassy incline on their stomachs, or crouched.

Martin slipped a few times on the dew. The grass was cold on his palms. Dirt and snow worked up under his fingernails. He looked up and saw the crimson eye glowing in its rusted obelisk. Searchlight, scanning the rooftops of the town behind them. Once they reached the crest of the hill, he surveyed the scene. There were people entering through the Abbey's tall doors–gray ants, all walking into an open mouth. Flanking the doors were Roman's two sentinels: the pigfaces. Their Sten guns hung from over-shoulder straps.

"He's got security." Switchblade. It was hacking at clumps of beard hair escaped through his leather mouth hole. "Big fuckers, they are. Lookie. Seven feet tall, must be–if they aren't eight."

"But they'll go down with a bullet, doesn't matter how tall." Dino lay beside his brother, prone.

"Colin. Slip down that-a-ways, back behind there. Make sure they don't see you." Zak retracted his blade–wriggled awkwardly to shove it in a pocket.

At that order, the man named Colin rose from the field of shifting bodies and crouch-walked along the ridgeline. Red cloak–blood red. One of the ones from the ex-cultists. The trails got tangled up in his legs, he fought the cloth, all the way down the hill.

"Don't fuck it up, now." A mumble, then he flicked a needle on his choker.

Martin could smell smoke. The winter wind was growing stronger–colder. He shivered. Now the decoy was in view again; he watched as the red cloak approached the front doors and was halted by the sentinels. Talking, too distant to be heard. A particularly strong gust blew Martin's hair into his eyes. More talking. Then the red robes were swallowed by the doorway.

"Alright… That's fine."

One of the pigfaces pulled a walkie to his helmet–said

something into it. The other stepped over to grab the handle to the doors–shut them with a reverberating sound like a drum beat. Then there was stillness–and the wind.

"Time him, Dino."

A beep. Digital. Dino was crushing a plastic button on his analog watch. The little green light digits started to spin, counting seconds.

And they waited.

—

He didn't know how long they had left. Every second felt like sixty. He lay on his side, propped up on his shoulder. A glance behind–the sea of humanity: someone rocking back and forth, hugging themselves; skinned face-masks already gray, but now grayer under winter light, staring down at the ground with thoughts somewhere other than here. All were silent.

"We've been waiting for this day for a long time, son."

Martin sniffled.

"It feels like a dream." Zak's pupils were shrunk. "Where'll you go when you leave?"

A pause. "Roanoke. Find my mother."

Nodding. "That's good."

Silence.

"I don't have anyone in the world, except my brothers." He looked up at the sour milk sky. "The four of us'll head out somewhere. Someplace warm, and we'll take these masks off… Know what's funny, is I don't even know what I look like under here. How much I've aged, or whether I look like a ghoul. I just see our old band posters." He scratched his nose. "But at this point, it's like looking at someone else–or it will be, I guess. 'Cause that man isn't the one under this leather anymore."

"I think I know what you mean."

Zak smiled and grabbed Martin's shoulder–shook it. "It's almost over, son."

Chimes from the carillon, deep within the Abbey. A light dusting began to drift to earth from heaven–sparkling ice.

Beep... beep... beep...

Dino smothered the sound. "He'd dead, Zak. I fucking told you."

Zak looked behind himself at his anxious legion, then to his brother. "I haven't seen no movement on the roof. Fuck me…" He chambered a round in his rifle. "We do it the hard way, then." Fingers in his mouth and a sharp breath. Then a whistle to call attention. A motion of his hand lifted the horde to their feet.

And Martin had to move or be trampled. They crested the hill like a wave, quiet and quick. It wouldn't be long before the sentinels noticed. Down onto flatter ground, over the flowerbeds bordered in stone.

Then the first shots.

Bullets *plinked* off the pigface helmets. The two colossi raised their Sten guns and sprayed. Crackling, snapping metal. Whizzing lead, finding targets amongst the crowd. Wood splintered off the abbey's goliath doors–sparks exploded off the great steel sigil bolted to them.

Martin snapped shots at the sentinels, hitting one in the chest. A blood mural was thrown up on the masonwork behind him. Then a bullet whistled close to Martin's ear–found a target. He turned and saw Zak reeling with his hand clutching his breast. A few more shots and both sentinels were down, bleeding from a smattering of holes. Martin grabbed at Zak's shoulder and was pushed off.

"Inside! Everyone inside!" The leather mask led the way–pushed on the doors and screamed with pain.

More hands joined in, until both doors were swinging. They flowed into the nave like water, but stopped dead in their tracks.

"What the… fuck…"

Each of the pews was filled to capacity, and the bodies in them were engaged in worship. But it was worship unnatural. They bowed, all of them, in the direction of the chancel–all of them perfectly in sync. Their movements were smooth and perfect, like a tape being played and rewound over and over and over again. No variation, no individual movement. And it was fast, like clockwork–ticking with the passing seconds. This spastic movement did not shake the pews. It was as if the hundreds of bodies were being driven like puppets, or dolls.

Standing upon the chancel, the object of their worship, was Roman. He stood beneath a massive crucifixion, arms outstretched, just as the arms of the man bolted to it were outstretched.

"Fucking Hell… Colin." Zak cut himself off.

The man on the cross was naked, and the space between his legs was raw and leaking blood down his thighs. What had once been there had been cut off–messily, with a jagged, ripping knife. Scrawled across his chest, words cut into flesh, was the word *IMPOSTER*.

Roman's booming voice carried across the chamber. "Welcome to our holy ceremony. Martin… It's been so long." A burgundy glove reached out to him. "Come here, son."

But he did not.

Then gunfire rattled, echoing into the high ceilings. It came from Zakaria. The bullets plinked off the podium and the grid wall behind the chancel, throwing sparks and splitting lacquered wood to smitherines. One seemed to catch Roman in the side, but before any more had a chance at him, he'd fallen through a trapdoor in the stage.

Screaming. Howling, painful screaming.

The people in the pews had regained consciousness, and now seemed aware of their pain. Around the room, they began to drop like ragdolls. Heads cracking off the pews, blood erupting from their mouths. Men, women and children–the citizenry of Snowy Oaks. All succumbed and collapsed, lifeless, to the ground.

"Jesus… Jesus Christ."

Martin proceeded further into the nave, spinning slow circles. He bent down at the nearest body–checked it for a pulse. Nothing. Blood was running out of the child's mouth, down the ridges of his face and into his widened eyes.

Zakaria's band dispersed into the room, every man picking a direction. Occasional bursts of gunfire cracked like thunder up into the high ceilings whenever a red-robed cultist was found. Unarmed, red robed cultists–but they were filled with lead nonetheless. Occasional cries of anguish intermingled.

"*Julia! Fucking Hell... No... No...*"

"*Oh my God... Steven... Steven, oh my God...*"

The room stank of blood. Martin turned to see Zak propping himself against a pew. "He killed them. All of them."

A groan. A red stain was growing on Zak's vest. "Find him, son. Go after him... Go! Now!"

So Martin ran down the center aisle. At the front, beneath the chancel, he found a wide pot nearly empty of clear liquid. A plastic bag was turned over on the table: paper cups. More were strewn around on the floor, some crushed, others leaking dregs. *Blood of Christ... or Golgotha.* But it was no wine.

The building hummed. Wind played the sculpted channels up near the ceiling. A haunting, whistling melody. A victory song.

Martin crashed through the door beside the chancel and plunged into the abbey's arterial hallways. Sconces flickered–turned the brick walls to burnished bronze. Red robed figures would sometimes emerge from doorways to stand in his way. He would lift his pistol and a pop of smoke would flood the narrow corridor. As he rushed ahead, he pushed over the bodies. There was only one place he could think Roman would go, and he remembered the way from the time he'd been brought here to get his hand stitched. He ran, as fast as he could, until he was heaving. When he reached the door, he burst through–the garage, empty, save for Roman's *Daimler Double-Six.*

"Get out."

The robes bunched and fluttered. He moved slow,

placing one foot at a time. He'd been pushing something into the passenger seat, but Martin could only see the very edge of it. It looked like a box, with golden trim. "Mister Navarro."

"Turn around."

He did as he was told, with his hands up by his head. Crystal blue eyes, still unwavering–even now. "You've become so strong."

"Pity for you." Something tickled the back of his mind, asking why he would point a gun at this man. It was an insect still alive beneath a boot. He pressed that boot down harder. "Golgotha is gone now. He's out of my head."

"No. No, you're not a dead man, Mister Navarro. He's still within you."

A blink. "What do you mean?"

"You trapped him within yourself–pushed him down into some deep place where he has no control. Yet he is there still, and will forever be there. While you sleep, you may be reminded of his presence. When you are reminded of your degenerate addiction by passing a pharmacy, or seeing a filthy addict huddled in an alleyway, he will whisper to you. Forever trying to be set free. When you see a picture of your beloved aunt, or your Bonnie dear, he will whisper. Yes, Mister Navarro, you've hardly done much to set yourself free."

He sucked in air, still breathless. “Maybe… Maybe that’s true, maybe it’s not. But I’m stronger than him now… I don’t need him anymore.”

Silence. The priest’s face was unreadable.

“What’s that you put in the car?”

No answer.

“Answer me.”

The priest took a deep breath. “That, son, is something very important.”

He took slow steps towards the car, found a viewing angle past Roman and into the open door. The box was made of glass, and trimmed in ornaments. Sitting inside was a human head–preserved somehow, though still deteriorated. It was an old man, balding. “Who is that?” “He is the man who broke the seal between our mortal world, and that of Heaven–allowed Golgotha to cross over. A talented doctor, for whom I worked before you were born.”

Martin shifted his grip on the gun. “Why… how?”

“A simple matter of grave robbery. He was never given a respectful burial. The world did not understand.”

All at once, the garage was alive with sound and energy. There was a small radio on a workbench; it sputtered to life and began to sing. The same happened with the radio in the car, playing a different channel. Martin pointed his gun downward. "Looks like they destroyed your signal jammer."

Silence.

"I want you to tell me something." He lowered his finger, onto the trigger. "Was this… all in my head? Did you poison me? Or… drug me or hypnotise me? With Mr. Crooked and the dog and… Bonnie…"

The priest smiled. A grim smile, carved out between wrinkles. "There is no greater drug than faith."

Two snaps of the pistol sounded over the radio chatter. Roman fell to the floor, his legs having given up their strength. His ankles bled through his boots. He did not groan or scream out in pain. He looked as if he were about to fall asleep against the back tire of his car.

Martin went to search the garage for something tieable. He found a garden hose and brought it back around. The priest was heavy, and he went limp in Martin's arms, mouthing quietly towards the sky. Before long, he had him tied to a table leg, unable to move–though he wasn't trying. Then Martin crossed to the passenger side door and pulled it open. The box was heavier than he expected. He held it up–looked into the mummified face of a man he didn't know. He tossed it aside, and the glass shattered loudly.

"NO!" The protest was feeble.

He shut the door. "No more." He crossed over to where the head had rolled, lifted his leg up high…

"*DO NOT!*"

...and brought his heel down. It caved in the withered skull, spilled coagulated blood and brain across the floor of the garage. An important brain–expensive brain–that had accomplished so much. Now spread over concrete.

26

They'd laid Zak down on the grass outside.

Now they stood around him–fifty heads, masked and quiet. Snow gathered on their shoulders.

Martin knelt beside him, grabbed his shoulder.

A cough. "Did you… get him, son?"

"I did."

"Good." A long breath. He rested his hands on his chest, looked up at the sky. "I think they… hit- hit… my organs or some… shit." Another cough. It racked his whole body. "But I'm bleedin' out anyway. Dino! Di- Dino! Come here."

The denim devil mask lowered into view from out of the crowd.

"Will ya bury me… somewhere that isn't *here*?"

"Wherever you want."

"Up in the Appalachians, maybe… In a ni- in a nice clearing… So I can see the sun. Will ya?"

"Whatever you want." The guitarist's eyes were glassy,

filled with tears.

Zak grabbed his arm. "Remember we used to… play up there as runts."

"I remember."

The next cough was violent. "Thank you, Dino. I love you."

"I… love you."

Then he turned to Martin and said: "Thank you, son. We're free."

They lifted his body into the back of the pickup and shut the door. The crowd of masks began to embrace and cheer. They began to rip the helmets and valuables off of the pigface sentinels, who still lay by the doors. But there were others who sat on the ground with their heads in their hands and wept.

"Thank you, Martin."

He stood, shook the guitarist's hand. "I wish you luck. I'll… visit his grave, wherever you put him."

"That's good. Thank you." And then he entered the pickup and drove down the road. Some of the band followed in the stolen police cruisers–others stayed behind to pick over the dead.

Martin stood in the yard, looking down over the town. He could hear the thundering hum of helicopters. Distant black specks, summoned by a mysterious call from a signal they'd never seen, in a place thought to be dead. He made his way back to the garage as the sound of their blades grew louder.

—

The streets were gray and damp with snow. He drove past the underpass and the small door leading to darkness, past his destroyed apartment. The town was near empty now. A memory. Before too long he was at the border fence–in the place where he'd spoken to the cop. Rotting animal heads were still skewered to the chainlink, though some had fallen, or been snatched off by hungry things.

He parked and got out. The *Daimler* crinkled and whispered–cooling engine.

The gate was open.

He looked around, searching the dark treeline. Lifeless. No sound, save for the ambience of nature. Rustling leaves, animals calling into the cold. Someone must have opened the gate from the abbey. If that's where the controls were. Or were they? He didn't know.

So he got back in and started the car. It spouted and roared. Gas pedal. It lumbered forward, through the open gate and onto the forest road. Passing the threshold felt like breaking the surface of a pool. A contraction, then release.

He looked into the rear view mirror. Frowned.

The door popped open and he stepped out. His breath caught in his throat.

The fence was gone.

"What the… fuck?"

No chainlink, no rotting animal heads. No barbed wire, and no speaker on a tall wooden post. Just a road, heading into town. A sign stood off the side in the grass. *SNOWY OAKS VIRGINIA. POP. 207.* The cartoon cardinal, Cardel, was stuck waving in print. *Goodbye.*

He got back in the car, shut the door, and continued down the road, into the nighted forest.

Epilogue

She lived in a small, white house in a quiet suburb. He'd discovered that with the phonebook. It was early morning when he drove up to the house in the *Daimler* and shut it down against the sidewalk. He'd been driving all through the night and into the morning, and hadn't changed or showered. The man he saw in the rear view was a ghastly, disheveled mess… but it was *him.*

Mousie was sitting on the dashboard, soaking up the sunlight through the windshield. He felt his heart thrumming as he picked it up and turned it over in his hands. A click of the magnets coming apart. He looked into the doll's hidden mirror. It was the same face he saw in the rearview–in the side mirrors. Nothing different.

He opened the door and got out.

Her lawn was manicured and vibrant green. Little ornaments and sculptures were stuck into the flowerbeds. Hung over the doorbell was a little wooden sign. Welcome

Home. Another breath, then he pushed the yellowed plastic. It lit up orange, then made the house ring.

A shadow through the frosted glass of the door.

A lock snapping open.

A swinging door.

She stared into the face of her son, who she'd never buried–who'd never told her goodbye. "*Oh my God...*"

"Hi, Mama," he said.

And she embraced him.

ABOUT THE AUTHOR

Tony Del Degan was born on January 4, 2003 in the city of Calgary, Alberta. He is a Canadian author and visual artist who commonly writes in horror and science fiction genres. He is the lead editor and creator of Dug Up Magazine-a digital horror art publication, in which he seeks to platform upcoming artistic talent.

Visit tony.deldegan.ca to explore the Red Runnel universe.

www.ingramcontent.com/pod-product-compliance
Lightning Source LLC
Chambersburg PA
CBHW010339170726
48283CB00009B/2871

9781778233111